"We're not d[...]

"We don't take cha[...]

"No one plans acci[...]
"That's why they'[...]

Scott closed the distance between them. Hesitantly he reached his hand toward her, gently touching her cheek with his fingertips until he was cupping her face in a gesture of comfort and tenderness. "Kristi, you can't worry about tomorrow. None of us has any guarantees, whether we're in the air or walking along the beach. You've got to relax and not be afraid to live."

Tears pooled in her soft blue eyes. "It never occurred to me that each day might be my last. And when the reality hit me, it hit hard."

"You and I have both gone through almost the same experience. We were both kissed by the angel of death, but survived to live another day," Scott said. "Except we're accepting that gift of life in different ways."

"Yes," she agreed. "I'm cherishing mine and you're risking yours, daring that angel to catch you again."

ABOUT THE AUTHOR

The idea for *Kissed by an Angel* came to Kathy Clark while she was a spectator at a Blue Angels air show in Denver. She researched the book through the staff of the Blue Angels and appreciates their help.

Kathy was voted the Colorado Romance Writer of the Year for 1987-1988. She has written a total of eleven romance novels and lives in Colorado with her husband and three sons.

Books by Kathy Clark

HARLEQUIN AMERICAN ROMANCE
224—SWEET ANTICIPATION

Kissed by an Angel
Kathy Clark

Harlequin Books

TORONTO • NEW YORK • LONDON
AMSTERDAM • PARIS • SYDNEY • HAMBURG
STOCKHOLM • ATHENS • TOKYO • MILAN

Published February 1989

First printing December 1988

ISBN 0-373-16282-0

Chapter One

"My God! We're going to crash!"

The exclamation began as a nervous whisper when a violent shudder shook the large plane. As if joking about it would make it less frightening, the passengers tried to pretend the instability of the aircraft was perfectly normal. But when the plane hesitated, seeming to almost stop in midair, then suddenly plunged several hundred feet, it became a terrifying reality that they were definitely in grave trouble. This kind of turbulence could not be blamed on an air pocket.

"Ladies and gentlemen," the first officer announced through the loudspeaker, interrupting the hysteria with a voice that was both calm and authoritative. "We are experiencing minor difficulties and must make an emergency landing. Please remain in your seats, observe the No Smoking sign and fasten your seat belts immediately. Secure all your carry-on items either in the overhead storage areas or under the seat in front of you, remove your shoes and eyeglasses and store them in the pocket on the back of that seat. Your flight attendants will be demonstrating the recommended position you should assume for the landing."

Kristi Harrison hurried down the aisle, checking that the tables had been fastened back in place and the seat belts were tightened snugly around each passenger's lower abdomen. She had been picking up the dinner trays and drink glasses, but the abrupt descent of the plane had sent the food remaining on the plates and liquid in the glasses splashing all over the walls, floor and ceiling as well as onto the cloth seats and passengers' clothing. Pausing only to remove the worst of the mess and the dishes that were cluttering the aisle, Kristi tried to appear poised and unafraid, in the hope that her attitude would be contagious and avert a dangerous frenzy. Behind her, she could hear the soft Southern voice of her best friend Diane answering questions and trying to keep everyone calm. And all the while Kristi's senses were alert to any unusual noise or smell of smoke that would indicate the source of the problem.

"Above all," the first officer continued, "don't panic. We want to get this plane on the ground safely, as much as you want us to."

Don't panic, Kristi echoed to herself. Her training with Worldwide Airlines and the twelve years she had worked as a flight attendant had prepared her for just such an eventuality. However, as she faced the probability of a crash landing now, she knew that mentally, a person could never be totally prepared. Rick's reassuring voice seemed to be calming down the passengers, but it wasn't helping Kristi at all. She knew he must be as frightened as she was, while also aware his job included not only trying to regain control of the plane, but exercising a positive influence on the passengers, as well. She knew she had to pull herself together. The passengers were her responsibility, and they were depending on her for reassurance and guidance.

Again the plane plummeted like a stone through the heavy cloud bank, then bucked and quivered like a nervous mustang, wild and uncontrollable. The violence of the movement wrenched open the doors of many of the overhead compartments, allowing briefcases and overnight bags to tumble down and bounce around the cabin. People were crying openly now, terror glazing their widened eyes as they waited for the inevitable. Sounds of prayers and promises mingled with screams and the strident peal of the emergency bells ringing in the galley.

Kristi struggled to pull herself up from the floor where she had been thrown. With one hand she gripped the back of a seat to steady herself, while she pushed her pale blond hair away from her face with her free hand. Something heavy had hit her head with a glancing blow, momentarily stunning her, so it took her several seconds to gather what was left of her strained composure. Her legs were unsteady beneath her, and a wave of nausea rushed into her throat. The floor rose and fell beneath her feet, making it even more difficult to keep her balance as she tried to carry on.

From all sides, people were grabbing her, pleading with her to tell them that everything would be all right . . . but she couldn't open her mouth for fear she would be physically ill. Instead, she forced her lips into a tight smile, shook off their hands and tossed aside the plastic bag she had been filling with garbage. With things thrown all over the cabin, it was too late to worry about the trash now, so Kristi continued making her way down the aisle toward the back of the plane, trying to comfort the children and stopping every five or six rows to demonstrate the brace position so everyone could see it clearly. Sitting on the arm of a seat, she would bend over, put her hands on her ankles and put her head between her knees, then urge everyone to practice it before they actually had to use it. She also paused to point out once again the emergency exits, and to explain how to open them and leave the plane as quickly, but calmly, as possible. And as she went on her way she pushed back the items still remaining in the overhead storage areas and relatched the doors, although she knew the impact of the landing would probably pop them open again.

"Keep your head down and grab your ankles," she repeated again and again, wondering if those would be the last words she would ever speak. The passengers, desperate for hope, obeyed readily.

Automatically she went through the motions of preparing for the emergency landing, but her mind wasn't on it. What she really wanted to do was run to the cockpit and throw herself into Rick's arms. It hurt so much to hear his beloved voice and know that she might not ever see him again. Even though she knew he would be entirely too busy to take care of her right now, Kristi wanted more than anything to be with him.

"I think we should sit down." Diane had to shout to be heard above the scream of the engines and cries of the passengers. "There's nothing left for us to do . . . except pray."

Kristi shook her head, suddenly deciding that it was now or never. "You go ahead. I've got to see Rick."

Her friend started to argue the sense of that, but stopped. What possible difference could it make whether Kristi died in the back of the plane or in her lover's arms? If this was her time to go, Diane couldn't help but wish that she too might have someone she loved to hold her until the end.

"Yes, go to Rick. I'm sure he wants to see you as badly as you want to see him," Diane urged as she stumbled over the pile of baggage on the floor before practically falling onto the fold-down jump seat at the back of the plane and fastening her seat belt.

"Diane, you know you're my best friend. If anything should happen..." Kristi said, then stopped, unable to go on. At a moment such as this, she supposed the urge to reaffirm affection was a natural response. But if she actually spoke what was on her mind, she was somehow afraid it would make it come true.

"Sure, I know." Diane smiled and shooed her away. "Friends forever. Now hurry to Rick...before it's too late."

The plane was shaking so badly, Kristi was amazed that the wings were still attached. As it struggled through the darkened sky, the aircraft was groaning as if it were a living creature, aware of its fate and protesting. Kristi staggered up the aisle, clinging to each seat and not releasing it until she had a firm grip on the next one. But it seemed that every time she was able to take one step forward, the plane dipped or swerved, knocking her two steps backward. She didn't appear to be making any headway at all. But she knew she must hurry. Instinctively she sensed they must be almost on the ground, even though the plane was still shrouded in thick heavy clouds, and she couldn't see past the wing tips.

"Kristi..." a voice called, and she looked up to see Rick standing in the doorway of the cockpit. Dressed in his dark blue uniform, the gold braid sparkling on his shoulders and around the wrists of his jacket, he was the perfect picture of a competent, unquestionably trustworthy pilot. Outwardly he appeared to be calm and totally in control. The passengers closest to him automatically began to relax. Kristi, too, felt comforted as she looked at him, but she wouldn't feel completely safe until his arms were wrapped tightly around her.

"Rick," Kristi answered, kicking aside a cosmetic case and stepping over a suitcase that had burst open. She tried to move faster. "I'm coming, Rick."

The plane's belly bounced once on the ground, the force of the impact causing several seats toward the rear to be ripped from their moorings. Kristi swung forward, slamming her hip painfully into the armrest, but she braced herself between the aisle seats and miraculously stayed on her feet.

"Kristi..." Rick repeated loudly, but his voice was barely audible over the racket.

"Rick...!" Kristi screamed, the sound of his name tearing from her throat as she struggled desperately to reach him.

Again the plane hit the ground, but this time it stayed down, sliding roughly across the concrete runway. Over the hysterical cries and pained moans of the passengers, Kristi heard the roar of the engines as the pilot threw them into reverse, then the piercing screech of metal as the plane's belly was ripped open. Apparently the landing gear hadn't engaged, so the brakes were useless. Kristi could see the colorful stream of lights flowing past the windows as the helpless aircraft careered toward the hangars.

As Kristi continued her effort to get around the piles of luggage so she could reach Rick, the plane was beginning to slow down. She was making progress at last, moving closer and closer until they were only a few feet apart. She stretched out her hands toward Rick's extended arms until mere inches separated them. He was so close she could feel the heat of his body.

But before her fingers could touch his, the plane skidded off the runway, its momentum propelling it across a grassy field. A fuel storage tank loomed directly in their path, drawing them toward it as if it were a gigantic magnet. Despite the pilot's best efforts to turn them away, the plane's right wing plowed into the tank's round side, piercing the heavy metal before being ripped off with an earsplitting scream of steel. Almost instantly, a huge ball of fire enveloped the plane with an explosion so powerful that the windows in the terminal and the control tower were shattered. Pieces of metal flew in all directions as flames shot several hundred feet into the air.

There were no survivors.

THE SCREAMS WOKE HER. It wasn't until she was sitting up in bed that she realized those hoarse shrieks were her own. Her heart was thundering wildly in her chest and her breath was coming in short, ragged gasps. Kristi groped for the lamp, her shaking fingers having difficulty locating the switch. Even after light flooded the dark room, it took her several minutes to get her bearings. As her panic-stricken gaze swept from the heavily lined, floral-patterned draperies to the vaulted ceiling and the four-poster bed of bleached wood in which she sat, there wasn't a single item in the large room that was familiar.

Where was she? What was she doing here?

Rubbing a hand over her eyes, then across her forehead, pushing back the thick, silky strands of her silvery-blond hair, Kristi's brain started sorting through the dreams and the realities. She began to remember... and wish that she could forget.

She fell back against the pillows, throwing her arm across her tear-flooded eyes to block out the light and the rush of unwelcome thoughts that plagued her every waking hour and persisted in haunting her dreams.

It hadn't been a dream. Every second of it had been real . . . except that Kristi hadn't been on that plane when it crashed. Rick had been, however, and so had Diane. And now they, along with Captain Mathison, the navigator, two more flight attendants and one hundred thirty-four passengers were dead, while Kristi was alive . . . and alone.

The six months that had passed since the accident hadn't dulled the pain or relieved any of Kristi's feelings of loss or guilt. Her grief counselor had assured her that each new day would bring her closer to accepting the terrible tragedy, but Kristi hadn't noticed any improvement. Not a moment went by that she didn't think of Rick or Diane, and not a single night's sleep had gone unmarred by that hideous nightmare.

If only the dream didn't seem so real. Kristi knew the routine so well, she could imagine exactly what Diane had been doing when the plane developed trouble and how the crew would have responded. And because Kristi truly felt she had experienced the tragedy, it hadn't been difficult to inject herself into the situation in her dream. Of course, as the subconscious is likely to do, the succession of events in the dream hadn't been completely probable. Kristi knew Rick would never have left the cockpit at so critical a moment. He would have had his hands full, trying to help the pilot save everyone's lives. And she would never have been able to see the cockpit all the way from the rear of the plane, much less navigate up the cluttered aisle, nor would she have ignored the distraught people needing her help. As a flight attendant it had been drilled into her that the passengers were her first and foremost responsibility.

But even more disturbing than these discrepancies was one very real fact that she couldn't forget, no matter how hard she tried.

Diane shouldn't have died in the crash. It should have been Kristi.

Abruptly she threw back the sheet and swung her legs over the edge of the bed. As soon as the cool air in the room touched her, her body shook with a sudden chill. For the first time, Kristi realized she was drenched in the perspiration of terror that had been brought on by that dream. Shivering slightly, she walked to the dresser, took a clean gown from one of the drawers and went into the bathroom. Quickly, hoping to get rid of the cold that had enveloped her for the last few weeks, she turned on the shower and set it as hot as she dared, then stripped off the thin cotton gown that clung wetly to her chilled skin. She pinned up her hair, then stepped into the shower and stood for long moments in the pulsating stream before rubbing down and dressing in the fresh gown.

But it didn't help. Nothing helped. *Sure,* she was warmer and drier on the outside, but inside she was frozen solid. Brushing that close to death had taken away all her emotions and left nothing but a hollow shell. There was nothing of importance left in her life. Her fiancé, her best friend and her career had all gone down together. And, odd as it might seem, Kristi had cared for them all equally. She truly loved to fly, and it would be a great loss to her if she had to give it up forever.

But so far she hadn't been able to force herself to get back onto a plane. Even when she had gone to the funerals and then to Denver where she and Diane had been based, she hadn't been able to fly there. Instead she had spent long, dreadful days and restless nights on a train.

And the worst of it was, Kristi had no idea when or even *if* she would ever get over this debilitating phobia.

Fortunately, Worldwide understood her problem and had allowed her to take a leave of absence. They had provided her with free counseling and given her their assurance that as soon as she was ready, they would gladly welcome her back. If she couldn't overcome her fear of flying, they offered to give her an office or ground job if one became available. They had been more than generous with their sympathy and their workers' compensation. What they hadn't given her was answers.

The National Transportation Safety Board investigation was still going on, so no public announcement had been made about the probable cause of the plane's emergency landing. They had no idea if it had been caused by mechanical failure, a structural flaw or human error, which left Kristi with mixed feelings. She sincerely hoped that pilot negligence hadn't been the problem, so Rick would not be blamed.

On the other hand, she was furious and resentful that someone somewhere hadn't done his or her job properly. A faulty or weakened part hadn't been noticed and replaced. Some step had been missed in the routine maintenance. Or a design error had cost those many lives and might be endangering even more. And although knowing the true reason wouldn't help bring any of the crash victims back, Kristi sensed she couldn't let it go until she knew the whole truth.

Meanwhile her life must go on. She quickly recognized the need to get away from the familiar locale long enough to let the wounds heal. It was too painful to return to the apartment she and Diane had shared or to eat in any of the restaurants where she and Rick had enjoyed many pleasant evenings. She had spent some time with her family in Seattle, and her mother had stayed with her in Denver while Kristi was undergoing therapy.

She had considered taking an extended vacation in Europe or Hawaii, but her heart wasn't in it; flying was out of the question, and she wasn't in the kind of mood that would make her feel comfortable on a cruise. What she needed was someplace she could drive to, somewhere she could disappear for a while.

When one of the pilots with whom she had flown at Worldwide offered her the use of his beach house in Florida near Pensacola, Kristi accepted it gratefully. The change of scenery would do her good. Perhaps a quiet month or two near the Gulf would be exactly what she needed to overcome her grief and her fears.

Restlessly she paced around the small bedroom. Insomnia had never been one of her problems. Diane had always teased that Kristi could fall asleep in the middle of a sentence. But since the crash she hadn't had even one good night's sleep. Four or five hours seemed to be the maximum, and they were always interrupted by that nightmare.

She didn't have to look into the mirror to know there was a smudge of dark shadows beneath her cerulean-blue eyes. If only she could go back to bed right now and sleep until noon! But she knew it was hopeless.

Kristi stopped next to the draperies and found the cord to pull them back. It had been dark when she arrived at the house this evening, and she hadn't had a chance to give the place a thorough inspection. So it came as a pleasant surprise when the curtains parted to reveal a wide patio door that led to a huge deck.

She had been told the houses on this section of the beach were positioned for privacy as well as for the terrific view, so Kristi felt perfectly comfortable walking out onto the deck while wearing nothing more than her nightgown. It was after midnight, and she had been assured by the pilot that this was a relatively private area even during the peak tourist hours. And even if there had been anyone on the deserted strip of sand that stretched on both sides of the house as far as Kristi could see, her apparel was much more modest than most of the brightly colored bikinis that were usually worn there. The crinkled cotton of her gown was lightweight, but not transparent. Its soft white folds curled around her ankles as she stepped out into the brisk, salty breeze.

It was a picture-perfect night, the kind chambers of commerce pray for. A full moon hovered just above the horizon, sending a wide, glistening streak of light shimmering toward her on top of the water. Thousands of stars twinkled against the black velvet of the night sky. And all the while, the waves rushed onto the sand with a muted roar, then slipped back into the shadowy sea, waiting to regroup and form a new charge.

Kristi had spent most of the last few years in the air. Because she loved her job so much, she had volunteered for the maximum number of flights that was allowed, accumulating many more hours per week than were required. Her seniority had given her the freedom to choose where she wanted to go and how often. But even though she had traveled to some very exotic, exciting places, she hadn't taken the time for an honest-to-goodness, do-nothing vacation for as far back as she could remember. She had forgotten how nice it was to sit back, smell the salty air, and listen to the sound of the waves. The desire to feel the soothing caress of the water against her legs and the silky tickle of the sand beneath her feet proved irresistible, so Kristi walked along the deck that stretched across the entire width of the back of the house, until she found a flight of wooden steps that led down to the beach.

It was every bit as wonderful as she had imagined. Not wanting to wander too far from the house, since her surroundings were still unfamiliar, Kristi confined her walk to the water's edge. Holding up the hem of her gown to keep it from getting wet, she stood for several minutes letting the waves foam and fizzle around her ankles. As layer after layer of sand was sucked out from beneath her feet, she wiggled her toes, digging them deeper and deeper into the hungry sand.

Even when her feet began to get chilled, she didn't want to leave. Out here there were no reminders of things she'd rather forget. The beauty of the night surrounded her, and she felt closer to the sky than she ever had except when she had been in a plane. Now, however, her feet were planted firmly. . . safely on solid ground.

Chapter Two

He looked down at the boomerang-shaped coastline as he passed over it. The sparkling white sands and inviting blue waves looked deceptively tranquil. It reminded him of long, lazy days he and his teenage buddies had spent sprawled on sandy towels, checking out the bikini-clad girls or floating on surfboards, waiting for that elusive perfect wave. They hadn't known how sweet and easy their lives had been back then.

The sight of the beach slipped behind him as his F-4 Phantom jet streaked inland. The shadow of the sleek Navy plane passed over bright green rice paddies that had been carved out of thick, lush jungles and over small thatched cottages that dotted the countryside. But the poor villages below were not his targets, so he continued on his mission, his eyes searching for the narrow, ladderlike tracks snaking through the mangrove forests that would lead him to his goal.

"Hey Kahuna. Do you see it on the radar screen yet?" He spoke into the microphone attached to his headset. "What are you doing back there? Watching *Casablanca*?"

"Nah," his buddy, the RIO officer, who was sitting in the seat directly behind the pilot, answered with a chuckle. "The reception's lousy on this thing. Actually, I'm just sitting back and taking a little nap. I've flown with you long enough to know those eagle eyes of yours will see the target before it shows up on my screen, anyway. You make this job too easy for me. I don't have anything to do but think about all those groovy wahines waiting for me back home.

"That is, unless you need some help flying this rhino," the man called Kahuna continued. "I'm a great back-seat driver, you know, but I wouldn't mind trying my hand at the controls. Of course, we would have to keep flying until we found a nice long, wide runway in a friendly country, because I sure couldn't land this baby on the deck of our ship. Have I ever confessed that I close my eyes every time you take us down?" Kahuna chuckled but in spite of their light banter, he never took his gaze off the small radar screen in front of him. He was well aware of the gravity of their situation.

"No thanks," the pilot answered back. "You just keep your eyes peeled for a MiG, and I'll find that little ol' choo-choo we've been sent to get rid of." Behind mirrored goggles, his piercing gaze continued to search the tangle of wildly overgrown vegetation for any sign of the train tracks. This was taking them much longer than he had expected . . . much longer than was safe, considering they were deep inside the danger zone. Any time a pilot crossed the border between North and South Vietnam, he knew it was in his best interest to get the job done quickly and precisely, then get the hell out over the demilitarized zone. "I'm feeling sort of nervous this far north without any backup," he admitted aloud. "I just want to make our deliveries and head for the ship. How much farther is it to Vinh?"

"It should be due north of us." The navigator rechecked their bearings with a chart and confirmed, "Yes, it can't be much farther."

"There they are," the pilot announced with obvious relief, as he spotted the narrow strip of tracks that was almost completely concealed by the trees and bushes growing densely up to the edges of the roadbed. Now he had to make the decision whether to follow the tracks north or south, in order to catch the train before it could deliver any more of its deadly supplies to the Vietcong troops near the border. According to the intelligence reports, the train should have left Vinh about an hour ago, which would place it several miles south of the city. That is, if they'd left on time. The only thing that was predictable about the Vietcong was their unpredictability. Acting more on intuition than hard information, the pilot turned the plane north.

"I suppose you know what you're doing," Kahuna remarked with the merest hint of a query. "I don't know about you, but I'd prefer we didn't get any closer to the Hanoi Hilton than necessary. I'd rather spend a week in hell."

"I didn't realize there was a difference," the pilot muttered. After flying several dozen missions, he didn't know why this one should feel any different. But it did. For some reason the short black hairs on the back of his neck were standing up and icy fingers were tickling up and down his spine. He glanced at his watch and decided to allow just half a minute more to spot the target, or he would turn around and head south.

But something told him the train was close. And something else, which he was trying to ignore, was telling him that he had better move fast, because danger was also very near. Only a few more seconds. He was sure of it. He knew how important this mission was, how thousands of lives, many of them American, would be saved once this transport line was put permanently out of commission. Since the war had begun years ago, this route, no longer used by civilians, had become strictly a military artery on which tons of Communist-provided supplies were brought in weekly to increase the power of the Vietcong. As long as it was operational, the South Vietnamese didn't have a chance of survival.

The F-4 skimmed the treetops, high enough for safety, but low enough to escape some of the Vietcong radar scanners. The pilot was just about to give up and switch courses when he saw *it*. The train, heavily loaded with crates of guns and ammunition as well as four large Soviet tanks chained securely on the tops of flatcars, was moving slowly but steadily toward the border, just as he had suspected.

"Hang on, Kahuna. We're going to drop our goodies into those tanks' turrets, then make it back to the carrier in no time."

"Sounds good to me. Sock it to 'em, Saint. I hear the cook's frying up some chicken for lunch and I'm starving."

As they flew over the train, the Saint sighted on the target and pushed the Release button with his thumb, sending down a shower of bombs in his wake. Circling back, he smiled with satisfaction as he watched the train and its cargo blow into millions of harmless pieces. So pleased that this mission was almost over, he momentarily let his guard drop and didn't notice the sleek green-and-brown-camouflaged MiGs sneak up behind him.

Kahuna shouted a curse. "We've got three MiGs on our tail! Let's get out of here, man!"

But it was too late to run away from the lighter, faster Russian-built fighter jets. Drawing on the power he knew his own jet contained, the Saint pulled the controls backward, causing the Phantom's nose to shoot almost straight up. After making a few swoops and turns to confuse the enemy, he looped around and quickly maneuvered for position, as one of the MiGs reacted an instant too slowly and found itself on the receiving end of one of the Phantom's powerful heat-seeking missiles. Centering it in his cross hairs, the Saint flipped the detonator switch and pushed the Launch button, sending a Sidewinder blasting toward the enemy plane. He barely took time to note that the missile had hit its mark, then banked his F-4 to the left in an effort to escape from the two MiGs that were jockeying for position behind him, and hopefully to figure out some way to get a shot at one of them before they locked in on him.

"I hope you like roller coasters, because we're in for one hell of a ride," he muttered, warning his navigator as the remaining MiGs followed them zig for zag.

For what seemed like hours, but was, in reality, only a few minutes, the three planes continued playing cat and mouse, each trying to outguess the other and bring a quick end to the dangerous game. Most air fights took less than two minutes, which was much too short a time when making love, but forever when trying to avoid an enemy missile. Besides, this was not a normal battle. The smoke from the burning train billowed into the sky, marring what had been a beautiful blue backdrop. Rivulets of sweat trickled down the Phantom pilot's forehead and along the curve of his prominent cheekbones, following the strong, square line of his jaw, dripping out of his helmet and on down his corded neck into the collar of his olive drab flight suit.

Damn, these guys are good, he thought with grudging respect. The first plane had gone down so easily, causing him to have false expectations about quickly getting rid of the other two. As a rule Vietnamese pilots were not properly trained and if seriously challenged, they would usually flee. But not these two. Every time he tried to get into an aggressive position, one of them would threaten, making his F-4 vulnerable so that he had to back off. However, he had been able to avoid the few shots the MiGs had taken at him, so the fight continued without a victor.

Like flies swarming over a picnic, the three planes dipped and darted, striking when they dared. In a tight battle like this, a good pilot shouldn't react to what had just happened, but to what was going to happen next. He must rely on his primal instinct, because if he has to take the time to think ... he's dead.

The Saint knew all these things and his adrenaline was really pumping. Air-to-air combat was the ultimate challenge to a fighter pilot: *do it right and stay alive, do it wrong and die.* And the Saint was determined to do it right. He wasn't ready to die today.

He couldn't resist a shout of victory when another of his missiles connected...at last...with one of the MiGs, evening the odds. But before he could roll out and change directions, the last MiG, in sudden desperation, headed straight for him, firing a salvo of bullets from its guns.

"We've been hit! We've been hit!" Kahuna shouted in alarm as he watched the fuel gauge drop from half full to empty in a matter of seconds.

Still the two planes flew directly toward each other. The F-4 wasn't equipped with guns, so the Saint had to wait for an opportunity to get a shot at the Russian plane.

"Just one more second and I've got the S.O.B.," the Saint growled huskily as he caught the Vietcong MiG in the cross hairs of his sights. With deadly accuracy, his thumb flipped the switch, then pressed down, sending his last Sidewinder missile on an unerring path. At the last possible second, he drew from the final drops of fuel in the tanks and pulled up in time to miss the debris from the exploding enemy craft.

But the price of their success was high. Before the Saint and Kahuna had time to savor the moment, the engines sputtered and died, leaving them momentarily suspended in midair. Then the age-old law of gravity took over, plucking the large, silver bird from the sky. The plane began spinning dizzily, and the F-4's black nose pointed toward the rapidly approaching earth.

"Eject! Eject!" the pilot commanded, reaching for the ejection handle. The pressure and disorientation of the spin, combined with the positive and negative G forces against his body made it difficult for him to control his own movements. He knew he had only seconds before he would pass out from the stress. But his hand finally closed around the metal loop and he pulled. There was an explosion as the canopy was blown off, sounding even louder than usual because of the silence from the dead engines, and suddenly the Saint and Kahuna were blasted from their seats. Their parachutes opened almost simultaneously and, as they dangled from their drifting perches, they watched the Phantom jet with their names stenciled neatly on the sides of the cockpit continue its spiraling drop until it plummeted into the jungle.

The Saint looked up, catching his buddy's attention. They were both in deep trouble and they knew it. Their air battle could not have gone unnoticed, and they had been forced to bail out almost two hundred miles north

of the DMZ. If only they didn't have to return to earth.
The reception that was sure to be given them was not one
that either man wished to experience.

They drifted apart in the stiff wind, but were still
within sight of each other as their booted feet neared the
tops of the trees. In a final show of false bravado, the
Saint saluted and flashed his friend an optimistic thumbs-
up gesture. Actually it was more of a good-luck
wish . . . because God knew they would need all the good
luck they could get to survive in the enemy's heartless
bosom.

HIS HEAD TOSSED WILDLY on the damp pillowcase, and
his long, bare legs kicked off the sheet as he tried to stop
his fall. All the breath whooshed out of his lungs as he
caught himself, abruptly waking up. Leaping out of bed
without taking the time to turn on the lamp, he banged
his shin on the nightstand drawer, stumbled over the dog
who had been sleeping on the floor, then sat back down
on the edge of the bed.

"What idiot left that drawer open?" the man muttered, interspersing his question with a string of choice
oaths, even though he knew the question was hypotheti-
cal. He was the only person, idiot or otherwise, residing
in the house. The dog offered a whimpered apology in an
attempt to appease his master and rested his black head
on the man's knee.

"Sorry, fella," the man said, his voice softening as he
stroked the velvet-soft hair of the big Labrador re-
triever. "It wasn't your fault. It was Humphrey Bo-
gart's."

The dog's tail thumped a staccato beat on the thick
navy-blue carpeting.

"It was that damned nightmare again," the man explained, raking his fingers through his own ebony-colored hair. "If *Casablanca* hadn't been on the late show tonight, I wouldn't have been reminded of. . ." His voice trailed away as he remembered the dream. Actually it was an exact replay of the worst day of his life . . . the day he and his buddy had been shot out of the sky and straight into a wide-awake nightmare.

It was odd that after all these years he could still recall his and Kahuna's conversation word for word, but then those few moments had been burned forever into his memory. At first the dream had come often. Gradually, though, the days, the miles and the long talks with friends and doctors had pushed it and the memories into a dark, quiet corner of his past. *Oh sure,* he still thought of his stint in Vietnam and the horror of it all. Anyone who had gone through that war could never forget it . . . no matter how hard they tried.

But having the dream was worse, because it took him back physically to that day. It was so real, he could still smell the acrid odor of smoke and gunpowder and taste the bitter bile of fear in his mouth.

Gently pushing the dog's head off his knee, the man stood up and walked to the patio door. The incandescent glow of the full moon poured through the open draperies, making the bedroom so bright that he could see clearly without help of artificial light. The man slid the glass door open to let in the salty night breeze, then leaned against the doorjamb as he gazed sightlessly out to sea.

The Saint. That had been his nickname back then. They had somehow been christened with a nickname in college or flight school that had carried over to their active duty with the Navy. At the time, he hadn't felt he deserved such a pious sobriquet. But the very fact he was still alive today was proof he had a divine protector of some sort.

His dog brushed past and walked out onto the redwood deck. After a slow-motion stretch and wide-mouthed yawn, the Lab cocked his head and looked questioningly up at his master.

"So you think it's time for a walk, eh, Maverick? That's not a bad idea. I won't be able to sleep anytime soon, so we might as well go down to the beach and get rid of some of this energy."

As if he understood every word, the dog wagged his tail enthusiastically and bounded across the deck toward the stairs.

"Hey, wait a minute, fella," the man called. "I know the beach is deserted at this time of night, but I think it would be wise if I put on some pants before we go."

Maverick's body stopped, but his feet danced in place as he waited impatiently while his master pulled on a pair of nylon jogging shorts and a T-shirt. They walked together down the stairs and across the loose sand until they reached the edge of the water, then Maverick set out alone on an exploratory trek. Because it didn't really matter which way they went and because his mind wasn't concentrating on his surroundings, the man followed, at a much more leisurely pace.

Even though it was mid-November, the days had been warm enough to heat the sand during the day, so it still held the warmth of the sun for several hours after dark. The man stayed just above the waterline, where the sand was dry and soft beneath his bare feet. The clean, fresh air usually helped clear his mind, but tonight's recurrence of the dream had disturbed him more than usual.

Sixteen years was a long time. A lot of things had
happened in his life since then, some even worse, but the
vast majority much, much better. He couldn't completely put the past behind him, but he had become more
comfortable with the memories.

A baby hammerhead shark had been washed up onto
the beach and the man paused to look at it. Mildly as-
tonished that Maverick had not been attracted to the
smelly "treasure," the man shifted his gaze farther down
the beach in search of his dog.

Maverick, like all Labrador retrievers, loved water. So
it came as no surprise to see the dog standing belly deep
in the foamy surf. What was surprising was that he was
not alone.

The man rubbed his hand over his eyes as if he didn't
trust what they were seeing. However, when he looked
again, the figure was still there. Obviously female, it appeared to hover on the surface of the water. Her slender
body was covered by a long, white gossamer robe. Long
silver-blond hair seemed to float like a silken veil around
her shoulders, while the wind whipped strands across her
face, obscuring it from view. In a splash of moonlight,
her hair appeared to be glowing around her head, almost like a halo.

For the briefest of moments, he wondered if he was
imagining the scene. He knew his mind wasn't as lucid as
usual and the stress of rehashing that nightmare was
making him a little crazy. But it was obvious that Maverick saw the woman, too, and there was no reason for
the dog to share his master's temporary insanity.

The woman was bending over, talking to the dog while
she held out her hand for him to sniff. Maverick's tail was
wagging wildly, his limp pink tongue hanging out the side

of his open mouth. Even from this distance, the man could see him listening intently and loving what he heard.

So she was real. He didn't know whether to step forward and introduce himself...and probably frighten her out of her wits at being accosted by a total stranger, or leave quietly...and chance never having the opportunity to actually meet this vision. As he continued in his usual analytical process to weigh his options, the matter was taken out of his hands.

Maverick, dragging his attention away from the woman long enough to notice his master standing on the shore, barked a greeting and bounded through the waves, sending sheets of water splashing in all directions. The woman tried without much success to dodge the impromptu shower. Automatically she lifted her hands to protect her face, which meant she had to let go of the hem of her gown. She retreated to the sand as quickly as she could, but not before she was thoroughly wet from the knees down and doused with liberal sprinkles over the rest of her body from the dog's splashing.

"I'm awfully sorry," the man apologized quickly as he reached down and took a firm hold on Maverick's collar. "I can't keep him dry."

"I seem to have the same problem," she responded, lifting her damp skirt and holding it away from her legs. "I take it he's your dog."

"He probably thinks it's the other way around, but yes, we belong to each other," the man answered with an indulgent chuckle.

"And I suppose he likes to take late-night walks on the beach?"

"Actually, the walk was my idea tonight. I was having a little trouble sleeping and thought I could use the exercise."

"I know what you mean," she admitted with a sympathetic nod. "I couldn't sleep, either. It was a combination of a strange bed and bad dreams."

"I had a rip-roaring nightmare, myself. Must be the full moon or something." He glanced up at the gleaming alabaster ball that was bathing the beach in an ethereal, almost dreamlike flow. For all he knew, this might still be a part of his dream and this woman a figment of his imagination. He hadn't been able to get a good look at her face yet, but if she turned out to be Ingrid Bergman, he'd know he was still asleep. "You didn't by any chance fall asleep while watching *Casablanca*, did you?"

"What?" she asked, completely confused by the seemingly off-the-wall question.

The man shook his head and flashed her a crooked grin. "Never mind. By the way, my name is Scott Sanders and I live about a quarter of a mile down the beach." He gestured in the direction from which he had come.

"Hello. I'm Kristine Harrison...Kristi." She shifted slightly, turning so that she faced him fully.

Maverick had stood still long enough and began to twist and wiggle beneath his master's tight grip, finally making the man aware he still held the dog's collar. Now that Scott could see Kristi clearly, he still wasn't certain he hadn't dreamed her. He couldn't have made up a face more beautiful than the one he was looking at right now. She was watching him with wide intelligent eyes that were a light, clear color, although the moon was not providing enough illumination for him to see their exact shade. Her cheekbones were high and elegant with model-like perfection, her nose was small and straight, and her mouth was full and friendly.

But her most striking feature was her hair. A glorious mixture of the palest gold and sparkling silver, it was long and straight, with the tiniest hint of curl where the ends touched her shoulders. Even though the breeze was tossing it around, the shining strands would fall obediently back into place as soon as they could slip away.

Scott's fingers twitched with desire to touch the spun gold beauty of it to see if it was even half as soft as it looked. He relaxed his hold and the dog, immediately sensing his master's distraction, escaped in a burst of hyperactive speed, to continue his inquisitive gambol down the beach.

It broke the spell and brought Scott to the realization that he was staring openly and probably not making the best of first impressions. He didn't want to leave yet, but for the first time in a long time, he didn't know how to carry the conversation.

"I guess I'd better get going before he has too much of a head start on me," he said, trying to keep his reluctance from being too obvious.

"And I should go back and try to get a few hours sleep," she replied, noting how high the moon had risen in the sky since she had first walked out to the beach.

They lingered for a moment longer, each deep in thought, neither eager to return to bed and bad dreams.

"Did you buy one of these houses, or are you just visiting?" He knew he was stalling, but hated to let this moment slip away without some hope of meeting her again.

"Just visiting."

"Short- or long-term?" he couldn't resist asking.

"I'm not sure," she answered honestly. "Probably a month or two."

"Well then, I guess I'll be seeing you around."

Maverick's bark echoed from far down the sandy shore. He had apparently made a discovery he felt was important enough to call his master to join him. Knowing that the dog's loud, deep voice was sure to make more enemies than friends, Scott decided he had better move on so he could silence him as quickly as possible. He shrugged and flashed Kristi one last smile as he began jogging toward his pet.

Scott hadn't gone more than a few dozen yards when he could no longer resist the urge to look back. Once more he wanted to see the moonlight shimmering in her hair and the wind pressing the lightweight gown against her feminine curves.

But as he turned and stared back at the spot where she had stood, he saw only the water lapping at deserted sand. She had vanished...if she had ever truly been there at all.

Chapter Three

New England was suffering through a bitterly cold snowstorm. It was raining cats and dogs in Kansas, and California was slipping into the Pacific Ocean on the crest of its latest plague of mud slides. Florida, however, was still enjoying unseasonably warm temperatures. The weathermen were promising a cold front before Thanksgiving, but no one who lived along the Gulf Coast of Florida was wasting time unpacking sweaters.

Kristi listened to the weather reports on the radio and was extremely glad she had decided at the last minute to include a few summer clothes in her suitcase. Her years of experience traveling the globe had taught her to pack a little of everything, regardless of her plans. As the sun rose high enough to direct its rays onto the deck of the beach house, Kristi almost felt overdressed in her one-piece cherry-red sunsuit. A strip of elastic held the strapless top firmly above her bust, while a wide band of smocking wrapped snugly around her slim waist. Lazily she leaned back in a canvas lawn chair and stretched out her long, bare legs in front of her, propping her feet on the lower rail of the balcony fence.

There must be something to the rumors that fresh air and sunshine had medicinal powers. Already she felt just the tiniest bit better. She had even been able to get four hours of uninterrupted sleep this morning, after she returned from the beach and the unexpected encounter with Maverick and Scott Sanders.

Now that she had time to reflect on the moonlit meeting, she was surprised by her complete lack of fear at being approached by a strange man on a deserted beach in the wee hours of the morning. Perhaps she had still been slightly disoriented by her dream, or maybe her subconscious had recognized a kindred spirit. But whatever the reason, she had felt not the least bit intimidated by Scott or his huge black dog.

The dog had seemed to be more friendly than threatening, and so had the man. Right away she had noticed Scott was quick to smile and easy to talk with. And the fact that he too suffered from nightmares that were bad enough to send him out of his bed in an attempt to escape, had created an immediate bond between them. But that had been last night under surrealistic circumstances. Kristi had no way of knowing how she would react to him should she meet him again, or even if she would recognize him.

She was staring at the waves that hypnotically pushed and pulled at the shoreline, when the subjects of her thoughts came into sight. Actually she recognized the dog first.

Of course, there were probably hundreds of black Labs in the Pensacola area, several even living near the beach. There was, however, something familiar about the energetic way the dog bounced around in the surf, jumping waves like a child. Whenever a gull ventured too close, the dog would spring straight up, his jaws snapping, but always narrowly missing, as if it were all a game to him. Apparently he was proving to himself and to those birds unwise enough to venture too close that he could catch one of them if he really wanted.

Several seconds later, her attention turned to the man as he jogged along. As she watched his tall, lithe body, she realized that last night her subconscious had registered more about his appearance than she had thought. He was tall, probably a couple of inches over six feet and muscular. But they were not the brawny, hulk-type muscles of a Mr. America. Rather, his physique was lean and taut without the slightest hint of excess fat anywhere. In fact, except for athletic shoes and socks that stretched over well-developed calves, he was wearing nothing but tiny black shorts, so there was little left of his exceptional form that wasn't visible for her inspection.

She sipped from her second cup of morning coffee while letting her analytical gaze follow his steady progress. Only a thin sheen of perspiration that covered every inch of his sun-bronzed skin hinted he was putting forth any physical effort. Layers of muscles bunched and flexed in his thighs with each footfall on the packed sand. The sinews of his broad shoulders and arms bulged as they worked in fluid unison with his legs.

Perched ten feet above the sand and several yards from the waterline, Kristi felt strangely invisible. Even as he neared her section of the beachfront, he didn't appear to notice her behind the flimsy barrier of wooden porch rails.

But as he drew even with the house, he glanced in her direction. Across the expanse of heated air that separated them, their eyes met and locked. His left foot, mere inches above the sand, hesitated before continuing its downward stroke, throwing him off stride. He lifted his hand in a congenial wave and veered away from the surf, not stopping until he was standing in front of the deck.

"Hi," he called up to her, his breathing barely labored. "How'd it go last night? Did you get any sleep?"

Kristi stood up and leaned her elbows on the top rail of the balcony as she looked down at him and answered, "You mean this morning. Yes, I got a few hours. How about you? Any more nightmares?"

"After I finally caught up with Maverick and got him back to the house, we both were so exhausted we slept like babies."

"So whose idea was this morning's jog?"

"Mine. I'm on vacation now, but my regular schedule makes me get up very early. I've found if I jog a few miles first thing, I wake up faster and feel better for the rest of the day."

"That sounds too energetic for me," she protested, lifting a hand to hide a pretended yawn. "I can't seem to talk myself into anything more strenuous than watching the waves roll in."

"And watch them roll away again," Scott promptly finished the line from the old Otis Redding tune.

"I remember that song, except I think it was 'watching the *ships* roll in,'" she pointed out. "The band used to play it at pep rallies in junior high."

"Nineteen sixty-eight," he added. "That was a very good year. I was a senior in high school with the world at my feet. God, if I'd known then what I know now..." He left the thought dangling.

"You'd do what?" she prompted. "What would you do differently?"

He was silent for a moment, considering the question. Then a charmingly crooked grin lifted the corners of his mouth and he answered, "Not a damn thing."

Kristi couldn't resist a disbelieving tease. "It must be nice to be perfectly satisfied with your life."

"Oh sure, there are a few things I would change," he admitted. "The United States would have won the Vietnam war, or better yet, never have got involved in it. My dad would still be alive, and I would probably be happily married and have a couple of kids by now. But all in all, I personally wouldn't do anything differently."

Happily married? A couple of kids? For some reason those two things caught Kristi's attention. He had thrown them in so casually, she couldn't help but wonder what had gone wrong in his life to keep him from having the very things most men took for granted. The way he had included them with the impossible requests about the war and his father's death made it sound as if a family was totally out of the question for him. Had he lost a child? Or had a woman hurt him so badly that he had never recovered?

Kristi could sympathize with the loss of a loved one. In spite of his smile, she sensed an unhealed wound beneath his brave exterior. A part of her own numbed heart warmed slightly in silent empathy.

"I've got an almost full pot of coffee and a couple of extra croissants, if you'd like to take a break," she suggested in an unexpected burst of generosity. She had come to Florida to spend some time alone, yet here she was offering to share her breakfast with a man who was almost a total stranger. In all fairness, he didn't seem to be intentionally intruding on her privacy. He wasn't coming on to her or forcing her to talk to him. He just happened to be one of those people whom it was impossible not to like.

Scott had been watching the play of emotions flicker across her expressive face. He sensed she had surprised herself with the suggestion he join her. She hadn't said it in so many words, but he surmised from her actions and attitude that she was here alone and that she was running away from something or someone. *A broken marriage? A hopeless love affair?* His imagination ran wild as he speculated what could have caused her unhappiness and the bad dream that apparently recurred much too frequently.

He suspected she wasn't the type to share her secrets with just anyone. And it was obvious there were many secrets hiding behind that lovely face. There was a sadness about her he couldn't quite describe. Even though he had never seen her before early this morning, he would be willing to bet a month's salary that she didn't normally look so pale and fragile. Maybe that was her problem. Perhaps she was recovering from a serious illness.

However, although she could stand to gain a couple of pounds, he could find no fault with her figure. The curves were in all the right places, and her legs...Brigitte Nielsen would be green with envy. Even the slight hollows beneath her cheekbones only added elegance to her natural beauty. And, he had to admit, he was totally bewitched by the large eyes that dominated her face. Today he could see they were of such a clear, light blue that they were almost transparent.

Probably she was already sorry she had invited him to stay for a while longer, but he wasn't strong enough or stupid enough to turn down what might be a one-time offer.

"Sure, I'd like something to drink. But I'd rather have a glass of water," he said, casually accepting. He whistled for Maverick, then walked over to the stairs and climbed up to her level.

Kristi returned from the kitchen with a tall glass filled with ice and water and a shallow bowl half full of cool water for Maverick. She handed the glass to Scott, then knelt down and set the bowl in front of the dog, who promptly rewarded her thoughtfulness with a wet canine kiss on her cheek.

"He's a nice dog," she remarked, her smile telling Scott that she was not the least bit displeased by the animal's show of affection. "I've missed having a pet for the last few years. I've always wanted a puppy. But when a person travels as much as I do, it wouldn't be fair to the animal."

She stood up and returned to the lawn chair where she had been sitting earlier. Gesturing toward the chair on the other side of the round, glass-topped table, she picked up the plate of croissants and offered them to Scott. After he took one, she took the other and covered it liberally with butter and honey.

"Why do you travel so much?" Scott asked between bites of the flaky pastry.

"I've been working as a flight attendant for Worldwide Airlines for the past twelve years."

"Worldwide Airlines? Didn't one of their planes crash a few months ago?"

Kristi abruptly lost her appetite. She tossed the rest of the croissant to Maverick, then wiped her hands on a napkin, taking much more time and care with each finger than was necessary. She had to wait until the lump in her throat dissolved before she could answer. "Yes," she said, almost inaudibly.

Scott started to ask another question about the accident, but was alarmed by the sudden stricken look on her face. What little color had been in her cheeks drained away entirely and the screen of her thick, dark lashes dropped to hide whatever expression might be revealed in the endless depths of her remarkable eyes. He had obviously stumbled onto a touchy subject.

"Don't you love this weather?" he commented in a flustered attempt to change the subject. *Good Lord, couldn't I have come up with something a little more original?* he asked himself with a mental groan. "I've lived near a beach all my life and I think it makes a person much more aware of the weather. Everything seems to be magnified—as if the sun is brighter and hotter, the winds stronger, the rain wetter. Where did you grow up?"

Kristi kept her attention focused on Maverick, who was stretched out on the deck, sleeping peacefully in a pool of sunshine. She knew Scott was trying to help her out by taking her mind off Worldwide, and she was grateful for his perceptiveness. But she couldn't chance looking at him yet for fear he would see the tears in her eyes and the pain in her heart. Instead, she forced her mind to focus on the more distant past.

"I was born in San Antonio—" she began.

"No kidding? I was born in Texas, too," Scott interrupted. "You don't have a Texas accent."

"That's because I didn't stay there long enough to learn to talk. My father was in the Air Force and, at the time I decided to come along, he was assigned to Randolph Air Force Base. But I was only a few weeks old when he was transferred to Andrews in Maryland. From there we bounced around from state to state and even spent several years in Europe."

"So you were an Air Force brat. How did you like the vagabond life?"

"I loved it. I guess that's one of the reasons I enjoy being a flight attendant so much. I must have gotten used to not staying in one place long enough to let the grass grow under my feet. And that's probably where I learned to love flying. The planes, the noise, the excitement . . . I loved it all. I loved it until . . ."

There it was again. Scott wished he knew what was bothering her. It obviously had something to do with her job at Worldwide. He had been through a lot of hell in Vietnam, losing his F-4, watching his friends die, killing other human beings because they were supposed to be the enemy. Maybe he would be able to help Kristi get through her problem. But until she was ready to talk about it, there was nothing he could do. Possibly if he told her a little about his own past, she would feel more comfortable and open up about hers.

"My dad was an aircraft mechanic at the naval air base in Corpus Christi, so I sort of grew up in a military atmosphere, too," he said, settling back in his chair and forcing his gaze away from Kristi and onto a tanker far out at sea. "My best friend, Kahuna and I used to hang around the base, soaking up everything we heard about the planes and the pilots."

"Kahuna?" Kristi couldn't resist interrupting. "It sounds like someone from a Gidget movie."

"His real name was Billy Dayton, but like I said before, we lived so close to the beach that we both thought we were surfing dudes. And we saw our share of beach party movies. I can't remember how old we were when everyone started calling him Kahuna, but it was probably the summer we learned to fly. We had worked and saved for more than a year. Heck, I had my pilot's license before I got my driver's license."

A casual glance toward Kristi reassured him she was interested in hearing more, so he continued. "Kahuna and I couldn't wait to graduate from high school so we could enlist. The Vietnam War had started to heat up and with us being around the naval base every day, we were naively gung ho. My dad was the level head in the midst of our burst of patriotism, and he reminded us that unless we had at least two years of college under our belts, we'd be spending more time on the decks of ships than flying jets, which is what we really wanted to do.

"So Kahuna and I chose a college that had a good N.R.O.T.C. program and counted the days until we could be behind the controls of an F-4 Phantom jet. In flight school, where it's a prestige thing to have a cool nickname, it was natural for Billy to keep his old one." Scott frowned and combed his fingers through his black hair. Somehow this wasn't turning out as he'd expected. Instead of exorcising Kristi's ghosts, he was stirring up his own. First the nightmare had returned, now this. But strangely, it felt sort of good to talk about Kahuna with someone other than a chaplain or a shrink. He hadn't planned to spill his guts to this pretty lady. And yet, now that he had begun, he couldn't seem to stop.

"Kahuna would have loved it here," Scott mused, his attention centering on a lone gull as it swooped and soared with the wind. "He was crazy about the waves, the sand, the smell . . . everything about the beach."

"Where is he now?" Kristi inquired softly, afraid of the answer, but so involved in the story that she had to know.

For several minutes Scott was silent. Just when she began to think he hadn't heard her question, he spoke, his voice a pitch lower and curiously husky.

"You know, it's ironic that Billy should have chosen the nickname Kahuna. I think it's a Hawaiian word for witch doctor, which didn't really suit Billy at all. He was the nicest, gentlest guy you'd ever hope to meet. Under normal circumstances, he never would have hurt a bug. But like me, he wanted to fly, and back then we viewed the war as a big game."

He rubbed his hand over his eyes and sighed. "I was the pilot and he was my RIO, which, as you probably know, means I handled the plane and he sat in the seat behind me, taking care of the navigational systems and communications equipment. We'd been over there for a little less than a year and had flown dozens of missions together. We were a great team. Together we had shot down four MiGs and we were making quite a reputation for ourselves. It only takes five to classify a pilot as an ace, so we were getting close."

Scott clenched his hands into fists, he pushed himself out of the chair and strode over to the railing. Kristi sat silently, her gaze taking in the tenseness of the muscles at the base of his neck and across the back of his shoulders. His story had taken on the dimension of a confession, and she could tell it was hurting him to go on. She felt an almost overwhelming urge to go to him, to wrap her arms around him and comfort him. But the gesture might be misunderstood, and she didn't want to do anything to damage this fragile friendship they were developing. So she waited . . . and listened.

"We were out on a mission that was supposed to be a piece of cake. Because it should have been quick and easy and to decrease our chances of detection, our wingman stayed behind on the carrier. We located our target, destroyed it and were heading back, when three MiGs sneaked up on us and engaged us in an air fight. To make a long story short, we got them, but they also got us. Our plane went down, and we had to eject over the jungles in North Vietnam." Again the silence stretched into minutes.

"And?"

"I made it out. It took me twenty days of hiding and crawling on my belly through rice paddies and forests, trying to avoid being eaten alive by mosquitoes, bitten by poisonous snakes or butchered by the Vietcong, but I made it. The enemy was all around me, and I knew if I got caught they'd throw me into the Hanoi Hilton and I would disappear like hundreds of other POWs and MIAs. Since war had never officially been declared, all the Americans that were captured were considered criminals instead of war prisoners, so the Vietcong didn't have to account for their treatment of them. I was determined that I would get out or I would die trying.

"I survived by eating berries, fruit, and whatever I dared steal out of Vietnamese gardens. I drained water out of banana trees and drank it. I hiked for miles at night and tried to become invisible during the day. I finally found my way back to the beach and signaled my ship with my pocket radio. The sight of that rescue helicopter and the fighter jets that were chaperoning it was the most beautiful sight I had ever seen.

"I had lost more than twenty pounds and hadn't had more than a few hours' sleep the whole time I was out there. Not having spoken to another human being for almost a month, I can't tell you how good it was to hear voices I could understand and see faces I could trust. But Kahuna wasn't with them. As soon as I was safely in that chopper, I asked about him. For some reason, I was sure he had beat me out of that damned jungle.

"But he didn't get out. I know he was okay when we were coming down in our parachutes. I'm certain he survived. The last time I saw him, we were floating into the treetops. But he never made it out of there. I had to fly the rest of my missions with a new RIO, then come home alone. And the worst of it is, I don't know if he's dead or if those savages still have him."

Chapter Four

As the moon, only slightly less full than the night before, floated high in the midnight sky, once again its silvery glow bathed a solitary figure on the lonely beach. Kristi sat on the sand, several feet away from the foaming curl of the waterline. Tonight she had taken the precaution of exchanging her perspiration-soaked nightgown for a bulky knit sweater and a pair of jeans before seeking the calming rhythm of the surf. There was something about the steadiness, the never ending cycle of ebb and flow of the tumbling water that cleansed her mind of unwelcome thoughts.

She had been physically exhausted when she went to bed several hours ago. Scott had given her directions to several of the local stores and after he left this—or rather yesterday—morning, for it was already the wee hours of a new day, she had showered and dressed, then ventured into Pensacola. Kristi hadn't planned to stay all day, but it had taken longer than she expected to stock up on some of the supplies she would need for the next few weeks. Because of their erratic and opposing airline schedules, she and Diane had rarely eaten at their apartment and had even more rarely shopped for groceries. So even though Kristi had made a list, she had wandered up and down the aisles of the unfamiliar supermarket, searching for each item until her basket was full.

Though it was still weeks until Thanksgiving, the stores were already dressed for Christmas. It seemed doubly strange to see life-size Santas and twinkling Christmas trees when the temperatures outside were in the eighties. Each store had signs proclaiming pre-Christmas sales, but Kristi wasn't in the mood to shop. She doubted she would feel very festive this holiday season and was even glad she was far from family and friends, hoping they wouldn't feel obligated to try to cheer her up. She didn't want to be a wet blanket at anyone's celebration, but she couldn't imagine going through the motions of decorating a tree and wrapping presents.

Back at the beach house, she had unpacked the groceries and explored her temporary home. The pilot had told her he had bought the place as a tax write-off and didn't have time to spend there very often. His lack of attention was obvious, Kristi thought as she spent most of the evening dusting off the layers of grit on the surface of the furniture and vacuuming up the sand that had sifted in around the doors and windows.

Kristi discovered that cleaning a strange house was the best way to get to know it. She found a broken necklace under one of the beds and a cuff link with the Worldwide insignia embossed on it beneath a couch cushion. As she moved from room to room, she became so involved in her task that she even took the liberty of rearranging the furniture in the living room. By the time she had finished, it was after eleven.

After a relaxing bubble bath she had barely been able to keep her eyes open long enough to stretch out on the king-size bed before falling asleep. Surely tonight, after the mental stress of shopping and all her physical labor, she would sleep like a baby.

But the dream had returned, just as it had every night since the crash. Sometimes it began at a point earlier in the flight; at others it jumped right into the middle of the hysteria as the plane began to drop from the sky. Always the ending was the same. Kristi would have done anything to be able to change those final moments. If only she could relive that day and . . .

What would she have done? She couldn't have helped the pilot fly the plane any better than he had. She couldn't have warned the passengers that the flight was doomed. She couldn't have changed one single thing without being able to see into the future. The only life she had been able to save had been her own . . . but at how great a cost? Would she never be free from her guilt, and the pain she felt about that flight?

Kristi circled her bent legs with her arms and pulled her knees up to her chest. As she sat, staring out at the moonlight dancing on top of the waves, her chin resting on her knees, she tried to focus on more pleasant thoughts. Nothing could have been more different from the busy schedule she had kept than sitting quietly for hours. Even without the troubling persistence of the dream, she would have had a difficult time adjusting from the variety and excitement of flitting from city to city, sleeping in a different hotel every night and looking out at scenery that changed daily—to doing nothing. Her time had been planned down to the last minute. She had enjoyed her job so much that she hadn't needed to take a vacation to relax.

Now the hours stretched endlessly in front of her. Her only plans were to get past this crisis and try to decide what to do with the rest of her life. For the first time in years, she would be sleeping, or at least trying to, in the same bed every night for weeks on end, and the view from the deck would change only with the weather or the time of day.

Small, spindly-legged birds scurried along the water's edge, talking to each other in shrill whistles as they moved along. The gulls and other birds had already settled for the night, making Kristi wonder why these little guys were still up and about. Surely they had no bad dreams to haunt them?

She lifted her gaze to the Gulf of Mexico and thought how different the beach appeared at night. The sea looked dark and moody, its moon-frosted waves thundering onto the shore, sounding louder in the stillness. During the day, with the sun shining brightly on the pale sand and blue-green water, there was an openness... an unbounded expanse to the beach that somehow disappeared after the sun had set and the night crept in. Kristi shivered and hugged her legs tighter. There was an almost claustrophobic feeling about the beach at night. It was as if she were all alone, cut off from the rest of civilization by the black cloak of darkness that surrounded her.

The birds, who had ventured quite close, apparently unaware of her presence, suddenly shrieked a panicky cry and lifted in flight, scattering in every direction. Their abrupt and noisy departure startled Kristi and she glanced behind her to see what had frightened them so.

She heard him before she saw him, his galloping paws thudding on the packed sand. Finally her eyes were able to separate the outline of the dog's black body from the night just seconds before he reached her. He greeted her with the enthusiasm of someone who has been reunited with a long-lost friend, nudging her neck with his cold, wet nose and following that with an affectionate lick on her cheek. His tail was wagging wildly and he pressed against her with such vigor that his weight almost pushed her over.

"Wait a minute, fella," Kristi pleaded, wrapping one arm around his neck to balance herself. She glanced over her shoulder, but saw no sign of the dog's master. "What are you doing out here all by yourself?" she asked, almost as if she expected the friendly animal to answer.

Maverick made no attempt to move away, but sat down on the sand next to her. The mouth that appeared to be stretched into a perpetual smile was open, and his tongue dangled out one side as he panted. Obviously he had been on another of his exploratory jaunts and was willing to stay with her for a few moments and rest.

His large body was warm and oddly comforting against hers. Even though she had thought herself happy to be alone, she was glad to have his companionship. "You shouldn't be this far from home so late at night," she murmured as he tilted his head against her hand, encouraging her to scratch his floppy ears. "Someone might try to steal a handsome fella like you. Someone who needs a friend on a dark, lonely night. Someone who needs—" She paused, a sob catching in her throat and leaned her forehead against the dog's square, bony head. "—someone to help them forget . . . someone who'll listen...and care," she whispered. Tears welled in her eyes until they overflowed and dripped onto Maverick's velvety-black fur.

As if sensing her distress, Maverick gave a sympathetic whimper and twisted his head until he could reach her cheek with a generous portion of his long, very wet tongue. For some inexplicable reason, his show of affection only caused her to cry harder. All control left her and the tears poured down her cheeks. The breakdown was unexpected, but now that the floodgates had been opened, she couldn't seem to stop.

Even though her emotional condition was none too stable right now, she couldn't help but find her reactions odd. She had shed few tears since the accident. Not even when she had been informed that Flight 2302 had gone down and everyone aboard had perished had she cried. Throughout the harrowing experience of Diane's funeral, followed closely by Rick's, Kristi had felt almost suffocated by the deep sadness, but her eyes had remained painfully dry. Not even the hours of grief therapy had given her the cleansing release of tears.

So what was it about being on this stretch of beach at midnight, all alone except for a big, friendly dog who had given up his exploration time to sit with her, that made her fall apart? Was it because the dog didn't understand her problem, but unconditionally gave her all the moral support he could?

Wrapped in the caring cocoon of her family and her friends and co-workers at Worldwide, she hadn't had to face the reality of her loss. Mentally she knew Rick and Diane were dead, but emotionally she had shut off her feelings, never accepting that they were gone from her life forever. As long as she had been surrounded by people who were determined to keep her so busy that she wouldn't have time to think about the crash, she could avoid the truth. So inadvertently, instead of helping, all their activity had only served to help her tuck her pain deeper inside.

Except for Scott's brief visit, today had been the first day she had been entirely alone with her thoughts. Even while she had been searching the grocery aisles for cinnamon or looking through the shop windows at toy

Santas and red velvet dresses for holiday parties, always in the back of her mind were the nagging thoughts that she and Rick wouldn't be exchanging gifts this year and Diane wouldn't be going home for Christmas...ever again.

But that still didn't explain why tonight, of all nights, she had no longer been able to swallow back the tears. Here, surrounded by darkness with the only visible signs of human life coming from the small squares of light in those few beach houses that were occupied year-round, she was perhaps experiencing a sensation of solitude such as she had never felt before. *This is how it feels to be truly alone,* she reflected.

Or maybe by getting away from all that was familiar and letting her thoughts dwell on the loss of her friend and fiancé, it was finally all soaking in. That part of her life was over and she had to accept it...which was easier said than done, especially since the future with all its changes and absences was extremely frightening.

Maverick squirmed beneath her, obviously growing tired of being drenched in tears. Kristi was vaguely aware of her arms being moved from around the dog and transferred to a man's neck. She felt herself being lifted from the hard, packed sand onto the man's lap. He wrapped his own arms around her and held her close to his broad chest, while one of his large hands stroked her hair. She couldn't see his face, but Kristi knew it was Scott. The fact that Maverick hadn't barked was enough of an identification, but even beyond that, she had somehow known it was him by the strong, yet tender way he had taken over.

For a split second Kristi started to pull away, but her need for comforting and the totally nonsexual, almost paternal way he was holding her caused her to relax against him, bury her face in his shoulder and continue with her crying jag. Not that she could stop the flow of tears. Apparently this was something that had been building inside her and wouldn't quit until the tears were all gone.

Neither of them moved for several minutes. They remained in the same position until Kristi's sobs at last began to fade away, gradually dissolving into hiccupy sniffles. Still Scott continued to soothe her. He brushed her golden hair back from her face as he held her securely, but not tightly enough to be constrictive.

As the wind dried the rivers of tears on her cheeks, Kristi's distress was heightened as she began to fully realize the intimacy and awkwardness of the situation. His shirt was sopping wet beneath her cheek. She could hear his heartbeat pulsing beneath her ear, slow and steady, obviously unaffected by the fact that she was sitting on his lap and their bodies were about as close as two bodies could be. His lack of response to her as a woman helped to relieve her embarrassment. Apparently the friendship that had sparked yesterday morning was stronger than any male-female type of attraction.

Because there was nothing else available except his shirt, which she felt she had already abused enough, Kristi wiped her nose on the sleeve of her sweater and dabbed at the remnants of tears in the corners of her swollen eyes with the edge of her cuff. With a final sniff, she pushed herself away from the haven of his chest and murmured apologetically, "I don't know what happened to me. I don't normally act that."

Scott studied her intently. Her head was still bowed, so he couldn't get a good look at her face. "Was it something he said?"

Her head snapped up and she met his gaze. "Something who said?" she asked in bewilderment.

"Maverick," Scott answered, a hint of a smile playing around the corners of his mouth. "I saw the way the two of you were carrying on such a deep conversation. And I want to apologize for him. He's man's best friend and a wonderful listener, but you know how dogs are. Sometimes they don't take the time to beat around the bush."

Kristi felt all the tension flow out of her body. At that moment she knew he was aware of her discomfort; he had touched on a simple way to put her at ease, and she appreciated his addition of humor.

"No, Maverick was a perfect gentleman. He gave me his shoulder to cry on when I needed it most."

"Bad dreams again?"

"That was part of it. But I guess I was overdue for a good cry and it just hit me tonight."

"Do you want to talk about it?" he offered gently. "Maybe I could pick up where Maverick left off?"

Kristi shrugged and ducked her head again. "I'm not sure if I could. We barely know each other...." Her voice trailed off as she realized how ridiculous that observation was. Surely if they knew each other well enough for her to be sitting on his lap in the middle of the night on a Florida beach, she should feel comfortable sharing her pain with him!

As if sensing her dilemma, Scott eased her off his lap and waited while she settled down on the sand.

And it did help. Somehow it wasn't so daunting to talk to him about her innermost thoughts while she wasn't looking into his eyes or studying the spray of dark hair on his chest that was visible in the V of his T-shirt. Sitting so close that their shoulders and arms were touching, both focused their gaze on the tumbling waves as she spoke.

"I was thinking of some good friends of mine," she began. "They were killed in an accident, and I guess I'm having trouble accepting it."

"Worldwide Flight 2302?"

"Yes," she confirmed, pausing to cast him a puzzled glance. "How did you know?"

"I didn't. I just guessed from your reaction yesterday, when I mentioned it while we were talking on your deck."

Kristi leaned forward, picked up a small stick and began drawing circles in the coarse sand.

"I suppose a person can't spend her life in the air without accepting the fact that sooner or later she or someone she knows will be involved in a crash," she said thoughtfully. "I've been lucky...so lucky. I guess I've always taken it for granted, but until six months ago the airline I worked for had never suffered a major accident.

"Oh sure, there was an occasional mechanical difficulty that either delayed a flight, grounded a plane, or forced one to make an emergency landing. But no one I knew had ever been hurt or killed." She hesitated, taking a moment to swallow back the lump in her throat.

"I remember how Diane and I used to joke about how the odds were getting worse and worse and our time was coming. But of course, neither of us *really* thought it would ever happen or we would have quit. Even when there seemed to be a rash of airplane crashes in the last couple of years, we didn't think it could happen to us. I suppose that it must be human nature to assume bad things always happen to the other guy."

"Diane was your friend?" Scott interjected the question.

"Yes, my *best* friend. We had gone through flight attendant school together and were roommates, although we rarely flew on the same flights and we were hardly ever home at the same time. Both of us loved to zip around the world, seeing new places and meeting new people. It was a real kick and I didn't think we would ever have to come back to earth.''

She pushed her wind-tousled hair back from her forehead and watched the blinking lights of a jet twinkle across the blackened sky. "I truly love to fly. I love the freedom...the speed...the power of defying gravity to lift into the air. There's something incredibly exciting about eating breakfast in New York City, lunch in Acapulco, and dinner in Honolulu. But then, you used to be a pilot, so you know what I mean.''

"Yes, I do,'' he agreed, but let her continue rather than add further information about his own life. Now that she seemed to be willing to talk, he didn't want to do anything to shut her up. It was obvious she needed a friendly ear, and he was glad to offer his. Perhaps by getting involved with someone else's problems, he would be able to forget his own. Ever since Kahuna had popped back into his thoughts, Scott hadn't had a moment's peace. It was almost as if Kahuna was trying to reach him across the barriers of time and space.

Scott didn't want to dwell on that; getting over his own trauma from his escape from the Vietnam jungles had been difficult enough. And not knowing whether his best friend was dead or alive was something he couldn't handle. It was easier to try not to think of it, because if he even considered the possibility that Kahuna was still locked away in a rat hole of a prison somewhere, the guilt and sadness were unbearable.

His own experience made him understand and sympathize with Kristi more than the average person would. He knew the agony she was going through, but unfortunately had no solution. Nothing but time had helped him, and even now he couldn't entirely put the memories of his last flight with Kahuna to rest. Since she hadn't actually been piloting the plane as he had been, maybe her grief would be shorter-lived and she would be able to expel it by talking about it. Scott was willing to listen.

"And then there was Rick." Kristi spoke so softly that the wind almost snatched the words away before Scott could hear them.

"Rick?"

"He was the first officer on the flight...and my fiancé. We had intended to get married last spring, but for one reason or another kept putting it off. We usually could arrange our schedules so we were on the same flight, which worked out well for both of us. It was nice having someone to go out to dinner and see the sights with while we were in strange cities. And it provided a buffer for me, because not only was I not alone, but all the other pilots and officers knew of our relationship and respected Rick and me enough not to make any unwelcome advances. Not that most of the pilots fool around, but just like all other work situations, there will be a certain percentage who do.

"And even though stewardesses have progressed beyond the 'coffee, tea or me' stigma, there are still those passengers who think that since we are spending the night away from home, we might as well spend it with them. So I always had a good excuse...and so did he. I suppose it's as difficult for attractive men as it is for women. You wouldn't believe the type and number of propositions he used to get."

Scott didn't comment. But he knew she was not exaggerating.

"Rick was an excellent pilot. I would have trusted him with my life. In fact, I did almost every day. I just know it wasn't his fault or Captain Mathison's. They were both too efficient and experienced. It just had to be a mechanical failure. It just had to be," she repeated desperately, then fell silent.

"Has the N.T.S.B. released its findings yet?" Scott asked.

"No, but they've said they will make an announcement about probable cause in early December."

"And you think they might rule pilot error?"

"I think it's very likely. When you consider that the airlines don't want to be held responsible because of a maintenance lapse, and that the manufacturer of the aircraft—who probably has hundreds of planes in commercial use and hundreds more under contract—would do anything to keep it from looking like it was a design problem or mechanical failure. So of course they're going to pin it onto the pilots. After all, they're dead. They can't defend themselves. They're the obvious scapegoats."

"But you don't believe they contributed to the crash at all."

"Lord, I hope not," she answered with a worried sigh. "It's bad enough for Rick and Diane to be gone, but if I thought he had somehow caused the accident, I'd..."

"Is that what your dream is about?"

Kristi hugged her knees, pulling herself back into the protective ball she had been curled up in earlier. "It's about the whole flight, and what's really weird is that I'm always in it, going through those final moments of terror with everyone else. It's so real. I live it as if I had been there... but it always ends just as it actually did. Everyone on board, including myself dies."

Scott looked at her curiously. He sensed there was more to the story than she was telling. As much from what she hadn't said as from what she had, he suspected that something had happened that made her feel responsible for the deaths of her friends. He was no psychologist, but he guessed that Kristi was almost sorry she had *not* been on that plane, because her subconscious kept putting her through the trauma over and over. The fact that she was still alive, while her friends were gone, was causing her an overload of self-condemnation. For some reason she blamed herself, and in that warped frame of mind, she needed to have someone keep an eye on her and help her work through her problem and eventually exorcise her ghosts.

Which was ironic, Scott thought to himself. How could he begin to assume he could help her, when he had ghosts still haunting his own life?

Chapter Five

In the stark light of day, Kristi was embarrassed by what had happened the night before. She wasn't sure what was more humiliating, practically drowning Scott and his dog with her tears or letting herself be cuddled on his lap like a child. If she kept acting like that, he would think she was some sort of lunatic. But whether it was their talk, or a combination of her crying spell and exhaustion, she had felt so much better that after he left her outside the door around 2:00 a.m., she had gone straight to bed and slept peacefully until midmorning.

As she sat on the deck, soaking up the mild November sun, she caught herself watching for Scott and Maverick to jog by as they had yesterday. When they didn't put in an appearance, she figured they must have passed by while she was still asleep. The realization brought a feeling that she couldn't quite define—relief, or disappointment?

One part of her suspected she wouldn't be able to face him in the daylight, while another wanted to see him and listen to his stories...and talk to him. He seemed to understand as no one else she had talked to about the accident had. Maybe it was his own experiences as a fighter pilot or his grief when he lost his best friend, but she sensed she had met a kindred spirit, at least as far as sharing a tragedy went.

In spite of the comradery that had begun to build between them, she felt a freedom with him at night on the beach that wasn't there in broad daylight. She realized this was a little silly, and her counselor would probably have a twenty-syllable name for her phobia, but she couldn't help it.

Kristi reached for the novel she had been trying to get interested in for the last two days. She mused that for a woman who had thought she had her life together and knew just where she was going next, she sure did have a lot of adjustment problems. She could talk until she was blue in the face, but in the end, she would have to be the one who worked through all the things that were bothering her.

All the same, that night she found herself back on the beach, wondering if Scott would show up and asking herself why it mattered so much. She excused her lack of logic, reasoning that she must be lonelier than she'd imagined if she cared one way or the other. Would she feel awkward with him after her behavior last night? Would he find her single-minded focus on the crash so boring that he would avoid her from now on?

It took her several minutes to realize her mind was so distracted because of Scott that her reaction to *the* dream had been much milder tonight. *Oh sure,* it had still pushed its way into her subconscious, thoroughly disrupting her sleep. But tonight she had jerked herself awake just seconds before the crash, and was greatly encouraged by the simple fact that she had not had to suffer through to the bitter end. Perhaps she was at last making headway. It would be a slow process, but she now had hope that she would one day be completely free from the nightmare.

As she walked along the foam line, letting the cool water curl over and around her feet, her thoughts were tumbling through her head as wildly as the waves out at sea. Why was she spending so much time thinking about Scott? She had seen him only once in the light of day, and yet she could call a mental picture of him quickly to mind. That was disturbing, because as each day passed she seemed to be having more and more difficulty remembering exactly what Rick had looked like.

She frowned, trying to recall the shape of his mouth and the set of his eyes. But instead of visualizing Rick's handsome, perfectly formed features, a much clearer image of Scott's crooked grin and laughing eyes—such a dark shade of blue that they were almost black—superimposed itself on the increasingly fuzzy picture of Rick. Both men had been approximately the same height, with Scott possibly having an inch or two advantage, and both men had been pilots, but that was where the resemblance ended.

Rick's body had been lean and trim and when not dressed in the Worldwide uniform, he had worn well-tailored, expensive garments, as if he had just stepped out of *Gentlemen's Quarterly*. Since Kristi had never seen Scott in anything other than jogging shorts or jeans, it was difficult to compare how well he wore street clothes. But his lack of covering had certainly shown his body off to its best advantage. He, too, wasn't carrying any extra weight, but his shoulders were broader and his muscles better toned than Rick's.

Whether or not a man was breathtakingly handsome didn't matter to Kristi. But the men she was most attracted to were always neatly dressed and well-groomed.

Those were two of the things she'd liked most about Rick. Regardless of the weather or activity, his slightly curly blond hair had always been perfectly styled and his fingernails clean. This was another point about Scott that she couldn't judge clearly. Every time she had seen Scott they had been outdoors. Even though his hair was relatively short, the wind had tossed it across his forehead in a charmingly tousled way.

Kristi shook her head, trying to rechannel her thoughts. It was disturbing enough to sit here and moon over Rick, but she was thinking far too much about Scott. Of all the things she needed in her life right now, a new man was not one of them, especially this man. For all she knew, he could be a beach bum, working only when he had to to put food onto his table and dog chow into Maverick's dish. However, Kristi couldn't truly believe that scenario. For one thing, the houses on this beach were definitely not cheap. And what was more important, she didn't feel Scott was the type of man to be satisfied with such a life-style.

But now that she considered it, what did she really know about him? He had told her bits and pieces of his past, but she knew precious little about his present. When she thought about how much she had told him about herself, it multiplied her embarrassment. He either thought she was a blithering idiot, spilling her guts to anyone who would listen, or that she was terribly self-centered, so concerned about her own problems that she didn't care about anyone else's.

She had come to Florida to sort things out, and the first person she had met was causing her more turmoil, turmoil of a different kind. Kristi didn't know what his motives were for continuing their association. He didn't seem to be interested in her romantically. Other than last night when he had gathered her into his arms in a totally platonic, almost brotherly gesture, he had never so much as held her hand. That suited her just fine, because she wasn't interested in getting sexually involved with anyone for a long time.

Perhaps he was as lonely as she. But she dismissed this theory as quickly as the first. A man as attractive and personable as Scott was wouldn't be suffering from lack of female companionship. If he spent his evenings alone, Kristi had no doubt it was because he chose to.

Regardless of his reasons, Kristi wanted to keep to herself, spending all her time and energy recovering and thinking about her future. It would probably be wise for her to make every effort to avoid him for the rest of her visit. Admittedly, she would miss their therapeutic meetings, but there was too much about Scott that was disturbing her peace of mind.

Kristi stopped, intending to turn around and hurry back to the house before she bumped into him. But as she lifted her gaze from the water's edge where she had been keeping an eye out for stingrays, jellyfish, and sharp shells that would cut her bare feet, she saw that it was too late.

The moon was at his back, throwing his face into deep shadow, but Kristi recognized Scott by the outline of his body and his long, athletic stride as he approached her, not to mention by the big dog who was trotting along beside him. It was too dark and he was too far away, but somehow she knew Scott's mouth would be stretched in that adorably crooked grin.

Pull yourself together, girl, Kristi admonished herself. *If I didn't know better, I would think I was beginning to be attracted to this man . . . which would, of course, be a bad mistake.* The timing couldn't be worse, and she was absolutely ashamed of being so shallow and fickle, considering her fiancé had been gone but a little over six months.

Maverick reached her first, his thick, heavy tail beating a cheerful greeting against her leg while he nudged her hand with his head, reminding her how much he liked to have his ears scratched. Kristi absently complied with the dog's wishes, bending over slightly so her fingers could reach him. But even though she wasn't looking in his direction, she was aware of every step Scott made as he quickly closed the distance between them.

"I've never seen him take to someone new like he has to you," Scott commented as he drew close. "He's always friendly, but he doesn't let just anyone sidetrack him from his explorations."

An uncharacteristic shyness swept over Kristi as she straightened, turning her attention from the dog to the man in front of her. *Yes,* just as she'd suspected, he was smiling, and even in the dimness of the moonlight she could see the friendly twinkle in his eyes.

"The feeling's mutual," she responded, shaking herself back to normal. "He knows I like him."

"It's just not fair. All a dog has to do is look cute and lick your hand for you to like him," Scott pretended to complain, "while I, a mere human, have to resort to bribery." As he spoke, he lifted an unopened bottle of wine and rested it on the crook of his arm, offering it for her inspection just as a waiter in an elegant restaurant would.

Kristi chuckled, amazed at how quickly he could put her at ease, and couldn't resist asking, "Have you ever tried licking a woman's hand? Maybe it would work for you with the same level of success as it does for Maverick."

"I can't say that I have," he answered, one dark eyebrow arching drolly. "If you'll give me your hand, I'll give it a try."

A tiny shiver streaked up her spine. Even though he had spoken jokingly, there had been a subtle change of tone in his deep voice that had reached across the small space that separated them and touched her. Her hands curled into balls at her sides, as if responding to his suggested caress. Slightly flustered at her unexpected reaction, she finally managed to say, "I'd better not. We wouldn't want Maverick to get jealous."

"Oh well, I guess it's back to the old 'ply her with wine' routine," he teased, seeming to take her rejection in good humor.

Maybe she had read too much in it, after all.

"The only problem is that I forgot the glasses. I could run back and get some, but it's a little too windy tonight for a toast on the beach, unless you're particularly partial to gritty wine. Personally, I prefer mine to have a little less body."

Kristi nodded in agreement as he continued. "So maybe we could go to your place, or mine. It's a nice night for sitting on the deck and enjoying the moonlight."

Although she wasn't sure how comfortable she would feel at either house with him, she didn't refuse his offer. She certainly didn't want to go back to bed and chance being visited by the dream again tonight.

"My place would be fine," she answered quickly.

Scott whistled for Maverick, who had continued his romp down the beach, and they turned and headed toward the house where Kristi was staying. As they sloughed through the granular sand, she was compelled to ask, "So how did you know I'd be out here tonight?

Or had you planned on drinking that entire bottle by yourself?''

"I wasn't sure you'd be here," he replied, casting her a sideways glance as if to gauge her reaction. "But I was hoping.''

Kristi's breath caught in her throat. How was she supposed to interpret that? Was he serious? Did she want him to be serious? She looked over at him and met his steady gaze. So intent was she in trying to read his expression that she didn't see the piece of driftwood until it was too late to avoid it. Her foot slid under one of the twisted branches and she stumbled, falling forward.

Scott reacted with catlike swiftness, leaping over the log and pivoting so that he faced her. Her forward progress was halted as she stumbled into his arms.

Her body was pressed against his as she struggled to regain her footing and stand up. The texture of his T-shirt against her cheek was soft, but the muscles beneath it were as hard as steel. She could hear the beat of his heart pounding in double time—from the exertion? Or something else? Whatever, it was definitely not the slow, steady rhythm of last night.

Kristi straightened, but the grip of his arms still held her close, preventing her from stepping away. Slowly she lifted her head until she could see his face staring down at her, his expression mirroring his concern...and more. Her own heart was matching his, beat for beat, and she couldn't seem to catch her breath. He was holding her much as he had when he had comforted her, but now there was a subtle, but very real difference. There was nothing paternal or brotherly about the way he was looking at her, the way his hands were splayed across her back, or the response he was stirring within her.

She felt her cheeks flush hotly, partly because of her clumsiness and partly because of the rush of emotions that were pulsing through her. It was obvious she needed to put some distance between them before she could hope to think clearly. Weakly, because her body didn't want to cooperate, she placed her hands against his chest and simultaneously took a step backward as she gently pushed away from him.

"Did I tell you my middle name is Grace?" She gave a shaky laugh as she tried to turn the whole incident into a joke.

"Did I tell you my middle name is Lucky?" he asked, his grin hiding whatever disappointment he might have been feeling that the moment had come to an abrupt and unsatisfying end. "Number one, because I caught you before you fell," he went on to explain, "and number two, because we're not standing on concrete." At her perplexed look, he walked back toward the driftwood and bent over, picking up the unbroken wine bottle from where it had landed, cushioned by the sand.

She returned his smile, relieved that he was treating it lightly, but she felt strangely let down. A tingle of pain in one foot brought her thoughts back to safer territory and she glanced down at it, pulling up the leg of her slacks so she could see the wound.

"You've cut your foot!" Scott exclaimed, immediately bending down to examine it. "I can't tell how bad it is in this light. Here, you hold the wine and I'll carry you to your house."

But Kristi turned down his chivalrous offer. "Oh no, you won't. I can walk. It's probably only a scratch."

He still looked doubtful, but her firm refusal left him no choice but to let her cross the final few yards by herself. But as soon as they reached the deck and he could examine it in a bright light, he took charge.

"Let's go in and wash off the blood and sand so I can see what sort of cut we are dealing with. Are there antiseptic and bandages in the medicine cabinet?"

"I don't know," she admitted. "I haven't looked in there. Medicine cabinets in someone else's house seem so personal."

"Well, let's hope your pilot friend was prepared for any emergency and kept his cabinet stocked."

Kristi led the way to the bathroom, being careful to walk on her heel so she wouldn't get any blood on the carpet. Straddling the side of the bathtub, she rolled up her pants leg and adjusted the water until it was warm, then put her foot gingerly under the faucet.

Scott completed his search of the medicine cabinet and, apparently satisfied with what he had found there, knelt down on the floor and reached for the soap. Rubbing the bar until his hands were covered in foam, he reached for her foot and with a gentleness that was surprising for a man of such strength and masculinity, he cleansed it thoroughly.

It was a new experience to have her foot washed...and unexpectedly sensual. Cradling her heel in one hand, he let the tips of the fingers of his other hand stroke over the top, then slide down the curve of her arch, along the bottom, and around her toes, pausing at each one. Kristi was reminded of the "This Little Piggy" game her mother used to play with her when she was a child, but there was nothing childlike about the sensations his fingers were arousing. Usually her most ticklish area, somehow his touch had been more of a caress than a tease.

This is ridiculous, she told herself. Here she was, sitting on the tub in a bathroom, with her hair tangled by the wind and her slacks rolled up to her knee, looking totally unattractive. Obviously her imagination was running wild if she could think he was doing anything other than simply washing her foot, gently and thoroughly, just as a doctor would.

Kristi was beginning to become worried about herself. She seemed to be losing all touch with reality, especially where Scott was concerned. The poor man was merely trying to be nice, and here she was, assuming he was trying to seduce her by massaging her foot. The simple solution would be to pull her foot away and finish the job herself. But that might hurt his feelings...and he did make it feel better.

He rinsed off the soap, dried her foot, then took a good look at the wound. "It's a nasty cut," he declared finally, "but it's not bad enough to need stitches. Actually, it looks like you peeled off several layers of skin on the bark of that tree." He reached for the antiseptic, then, holding her foot over the tub, he warned, "This might sting a little."

"Famous last words," she muttered, trying not to wince as he poured the cold liquid over the wound. Again he dried off the area around it, dabbed a little cream on the cut for good measure, then covered it with a gauze bandage and taped the edges.

"I really don't think all of this is necessary," she protested, but he waved it off.

"Just humor me. My mother wanted me to be a doctor, so whenever I have a patient to practice on, I feel like I'm fulfilling my destiny."

"That sounds like a crock if I've ever heard one."

"Well, the part about my mother was true," he said with a chuckle. "But taking care of the sick and dying didn't appeal to me. Being in the medical profession takes a special call, and I'm afraid I never heard it."

"Speaking of professions," Kristi began, taking advantage of the opening to satisfy her curiosity. "I've told you so much about myself, but I don't remember hearing what your occupation is. Since now I know you're not a doctor, I suppose that narrows it down somewhat."

Leaving her foot propped up on his leg, he answered, "I suppose you could say I'm career Navy."

"Which would explain why you have so much free time," she stated dryly.

"Actually I'm on a sort of vacation right now. Usually I work an odd schedule and my time off comes in lumps. You know how it is in the military. I imagine your father used to be away for months at a time and accumulate weeks off."

"Yes, he did. But the odd thing about military men is that even when they're not at the base or off fighting in a battle somewhere, they still can't let it go. Just as it takes a certain type of mentality and dedication to be a doctor, it's the same with the military."

Scott covered his heart with his hand and pretended to be wounded. "I think I've just been insulted."

"Not really. To a certain extent, working for a commercial airline is very similar. It requires the same gypsy life-style and ability to adapt to any situation or, as you said earlier, to handle any emergency."

"All of which I suspect you're very good at."

"I used to be. But my whole outlook has been changed by the crash. Now I'm beginning to think that it's time I took life more seriously and cautiously. I'm thirty-two years old and have absolutely nothing to show for it. I don't own a house or any furniture. I even borrowed my dishes from my mom. Most of the women I went to school with have been married at least once and have a couple of kids running around. I don't have a dog or even a goldfish.''

She sighed. It all sounded so depressing when she said it out loud. Only when she'd lost her future had she realized how empty her present was.

"At least it will be easy enough to give up the apartment, if I should decide to move. Diane's parents will already have picked up her things and it wouldn't take me but a couple of hours to pack. Actually, I'm not sure why I even kept it. My mother wanted me to move in with her, but I didn't want to do anything so drastic just yet.''

"Where do your parents live?''

"My mother lives in Seattle. My father was killed in a plane crash several years ago. This was really ironic. Here was a man who flew fighter planes in Korea and transports into Vietnam, literally risking his life dozens of times. And how did he die? Not gloriously for his country, as he probably would have preferred, but in a little Cessna while flying some friends to Canada for a hunting trip. I suppose that should have warned me, but I blamed it on the size of the plane and reasoned that the huge jets I flew in almost daily were much safer.''

"I'm sorry to hear about your father," Scott said, truly sympathetic about her loss. "No wonder you're feeling a little fragile after the latest crash.''

"It's unfortunate that the two most important men in my life have died at the controls of an airplane. I guess you could say I don't have much luck with pilots.''

Scott eased her foot from his lap and stood up somewhat abruptly, holding out his hand to help her up. "What are we doing sitting in here letting ourselves get morbid, when we could be out on the deck, sipping wine and talking about more cheerful things? Like my party tomorrow, to which I am now extending a personal invitation. Will you come?"

"I don't think so," was her automatic response. "I wouldn't know anyone else, and I'm not sure that I'd be very good company for a party."

"It's just the guys I work with and their families or girlfriends. They're all a little crazy, but very friendly and likable. I think it would be good for you."

"Oh you do, do you, *doctor*?" By now they had returned to the deck and she was seated on a lounge chair with her foot propped up while Scott opened the bottle and poured some wine into the two glasses he had picked up in the kitchen. Kristi cast him an amused look. "You're taking this doctor-patient thing a little too seriously, aren't you?"

"Absolutely not," he protested laughingly. "You'll be doing us a favor. If you don't come, it'll be the same old faces we see every day."

Kristi glanced down at her glass and appeared to study its ruby-red contents with great interest. "But you said the others will be with their families and girlfriends. What about you?"

"I haven't been dating anyone special lately, so I didn't have anyone I wanted to invite. See, that's another reason why you should come. It would help me to save face. If they think you're my date, maybe they won't give me such a hard time."

"Why would they give you a hard time about not having a date?"

"Because I'm sort of the old man of the group and the only one who isn't seriously involved with someone. I've been the target of dedicated matchmaking for the last few years. I'm not sure who's worse, the guys or their wives.''

"You're joking, aren't you?"

"Not at all. In fact, I'm willing to bet you a dinner at the restaurant of your choice that at least one of them will show up with a sister, a neighbor or a friend of the family.''

"And if I were there, I would be your buffer.''

He nodded and looked so pathetic that Kristi couldn't refuse, even though she was not in the mood for a party. Scott had been very sweet and solicitous this evening. It wouldn't hurt her to give up an afternoon to help him. It wasn't as if she had any other plans.

SCOTT DIDN'T THINK she would come. She had said she would, but he believed she would change her mind when it was actually time to walk the quarter mile down the beach to his house.

He had offered to pick her up, but she had refused, reasoning logically that since he was the host, he shouldn't leave in case his guests began arriving early. Which, as it turned out, they did. Already a half dozen people were setting up the volleyball net on the beach in front of his house, while Scott started a fire in the barbecue grill.

But even as he tore off sheets of aluminum foil and wrapped the potatoes, he was keeping a close watch on the section of sand that stretched toward her house. There were several other houses in between, so he couldn't get a clear view, but he would be able to see her if she walked in the harder-packed sand near the water.

"Hey, man. Need any help with those steaks? I'm starving.'' A short, blond-haired man who held more than a passing resemblance to an older Michael J. Fox came up to Scott and clapped him on the back.

"No, everything's under control here, Chuck. But it looks like they need some help with the volleyball net. They're stringing it so low we'll be able to drop the ball over."

"That's the way I like it, but if you insist, I'll go tell them it's not regulation height." The man named Chuck started to walk away, then paused. "Don't tell me you're flying solo again today. If you had let me know, I could have asked my secretary if that friend of hers is still interested in meeting you and . . ."

"No thanks," Scott quickly interrupted. "You'll be pleased to know I have a beautiful blonde lined up for today. She should be here any minute."

"Sure, sure," Chuck replied, obviously unconvinced. "That's what you told us last time, and she never did show."

Scott started to defend himself, but decided it would be wiser to remain silent. For all he knew Kristi wouldn't put in an appearance today and it would look as though he once again hadn't been able to come up with a decent date. It was ridiculous that a thirty-seven-, going on thirty-eight-year-old man had to make excuses for his dating habits. In spite of his job, his personality, and what he considered passably good looks, he never had been a Romeo. And it seemed that the older he grew, the pickier he became, no longer willing to settle for a cute face or a knockout figure if there wasn't some substance to go along with it. So far, he just hadn't been lucky enough to find a woman who had it all. Or had he?

From the first moment he laid eyes on her when she had been bathed in moonlight, looking for all the world like a water nymph rising out of the waves or an angel tiptoeing along the crests, Kristi Harrison had intrigued, fascinated and attracted him. More so than any woman he had met in a long time.

Her beauty was obvious, but she had intelligence and compassion to go along with it. And he was amazed at how much they had in common, from their military backgrounds to their love of flying. Besides, Maverick liked her and he was the best judge of character Scott knew.

"Hi, Scott. How's it going?"

"Just fine, Randy. I have high hopes that the potatoes and steak will be done at the same time, give or take thirty minutes," Scott called back, unable to resist the urge to tease his good friend.

"That would be a real breakthrough. The only time I ever eat a potato as dessert is at one of your barbecues. You'd think that sooner or later you'd get that timing down."

"Give me a break. I'm improving."

"If you were that much off when we were in the air, we'd all be in a heap of trouble."

"I've never led you wrong so far. And if I hear any more complaints from you, I'll recommend a transfer to maintenance," Scott warned jokingly.

Randy clicked his heels together as smartly as he could in rubber flip-flop sandals and snapped Scott a sharp salute. "Aye, aye, sir."

"Are you throwing your weight or rank around again, Scott?" another man inquired as he joined them.

"Just trying to get a little respect, Greg. You know how these young pups can be when they become celebrities," Scott replied in mock seriousness, but the twinkle in his eyes betrayed him. "And don't you start harassing me about the meal or my date, or I'll see what can be done about your transfer, too.''

"What date? I don't see any date,'' Randy stated and nudged Greg. "Do you suppose he's trying to con us again? Or is the man suffering from delusions?''

"Here I am,'' a female voice interrupted the banter, causing three pairs of eyes to turn and stare. "I'm sorry I'm late,'' Kristi apologized, but when the silence stretched uncomfortably, she went on to explain a little nervously, "I'm Scott's date.''

Scott breathed a deep sigh of relief and hurried toward her. Draping his arm casually around her shoulders, he murmured in a low voice so that only she could hear, "Boy, am I glad to see you.''

"You looked at me so strangely, I thought for a minute you didn't recognize me in broad daylight,'' she said. "Or that you wished you hadn't invited me.''

"I'm sorry but that wasn't it at all. It was just turning around and seeing you standing there that took me by surprise.''

"I told you I would come.''

"I know, but I was afraid you'd change your mind.'' At that moment he realized how very disappointed he would have been. It was more than having her here to quieten the jokers. Scott enjoyed being with her and wouldn't have been able to enjoy his own party if she hadn't shown up. He had wanted to ask her to come two days ago, but considering her frame of mind, he had been certain she would turn him down. He wasn't quite sure why the invitation had just popped out last night, but once it was spoken and she had accepted, he had hoped against hope that she would come.

"I've been watching the beach for you. Which way did you come?''

"Since this was a party, I decided to go the whole hog and wear shoes. I didn't want to get sand in them, so I walked along the road. When no one answered the front door but I could hear the noise, I found my way around to here."

Greg and Randy were still standing where he had left them and Scott couldn't resist giving them a little of their own medicine. "Close your mouths, guys, or a mosquito might fly in. And while you're at it, push your eyes back into your head while I introduce you to Kristi Harrison . . . my date for this afternoon."

Their mouths snapped shut and each gave her a sheepish grin as they held out their hands.

"The one on the left is Coyote," Scott continued, motioning toward each man in turn, "and the other one is Vampire."

"Pleased to meet you, ma'am," Greg, also known as Vampire, said.

"And please excuse our lack of manners," Randy, the Coyote, added. "It's just that we both thought we were seeing things, considering that ol' Scott is always putting us on. When he told us he was waiting for someone, we didn't think you were real."

"I've had that feeling, too," Scott admitted, his face relaxing into a genuine grin for the first time today. "But she's very real . . . and today, she's all mine. So you guys better head on back to your wives and kiddies before they get jealous."

"Vampire? Coyote?" Kristi asked as soon as they were alone.

"Those are their nicknames," he explained with wide-eyed innocence. "That one over there is Buckeye, and the other one is Dude. Zipper isn't here yet."

"I'm almost afraid to ask, but I assume you, too, have a nickname. As your *date*, don't you think you should let me in on it?"

He wiggled his black eyebrows mischievously up and down. "They call me the Saint," he announced in a dramatic voice.

"And I'll just bet I can guess how you earned that one!" she exclaimed with a laugh.

"You probably wouldn't believe it was because I was so chaste and angelic?"

Her skeptical look gave him her answer.

"Well it doesn't really matter, because we've all sort of outgrown our nicknames, anyway. What seemed so incredibly clever in flight school now sounds a little silly, especially now that Greg the Vampire is a father of four, Alan 'Buckeye' and his wife have twins, and Randy the Coyote's wife is expecting their second child. Zipper, otherwise known as Zack, and Chuck the Dude are the only two who still hang onto their nicknames, but since they're both bachelors I suppose they have images to keep up."

"But I thought you said everyone was on your case. Why don't they play their matchmaking games with Zipper and Dude?" Kristi reasoned.

"Because both Zipper and Dude have been married before, and are recycling into the dating game with great zeal. They are rarely seen with the same woman twice, but at least they always have a date for all the functions we attend."

"I still find it hard to believe that you don't. You seem to be a pretty nice guy. What happens to you when you go on a date? Do you turn from Dr. Jekyll into Mr. Hyde?"

"No, but my dates usually do."

"Well, *Saint,* we're getting some very strange looks. Do you suppose they're just hungry, or is it really so shocking that you're not at this party alone?"

"A little of both, I'd guess."

"Then let me help you with the food, so they can get their minds on something else."

Scott turned the potatoes on the coals while Kristi unwrapped the freezer paper from the steaks. For several minutes they worked smoothly side by side. When they finally had all the food arranged on the grill or in the coals, Scott shut the lid and adjusted the air intake, then turned to Kristi.

"I haven't had time to ask, but how's your foot? You don't seem to be limping."

"My *doctor* did a fine job, and except for a little stiffness I don't even notice it."

"We've got a few minutes before it's time to turn the steaks. Some of the others brought a salad or dessert, and I could use some help in the kitchen."

"Sure. As long as I don't have to actually cook something. I'm great at warming up little plastic trays of food and peeling off the foil, but I'm afraid I was away from a real kitchen too much to master any culinary skills."

"I'll remember that," he promised with a chuckle as he slid open the patio door that led to the breakfast room and stood aside for Kristi to enter, then followed her into the kitchen.

She took the bowls of salad and bottles of dressing out of the refrigerator, unwrapped them and set them on the rectangular glass-topped table, while Scott collected the plates and eating utensils from the cabinets. While she carried them to the breakfast room, he buttered several long loaves of French bread and put them into the oven.

"This is a beautiful house," Kristi commented as her gaze traveled around.

"I like it. A friend helped me design it, and I spent all my time off for months working with the builder. I wasn't sure if I would use this as my full-time home or a place to retreat from the real world. I moved in two years ago while I tried to make up my mind, and fell in love with the beauty and peace of living here. I decided the real world wasn't for me and I've stayed here ever since. Now I can't imagine living anywhere else."

Proud of the realization of his vision, Scott looked around as if trying to see it through her eyes. The house was built in a crescent shape so that it was longer than it was wide. Scott had tried to take advantage of the terrific view of the rolling surf and snowy sand by making the entire back of the house glass with patio doors leading from every room on that side. A curving deck filled in the open area between the kitchen and bedroom wings.

Designed with a minimum of walls and high soaring ceilings to bring the openness of outdoors indoors, there was a sense of vastness that surpassed the actual two thousand square feet. Scott leaned against the butcher block island that separated the kitchen from the breakfast room while he watched Kristi wander around the huge den, stopping often to examine a picture on the wall or a knickknack on the shelves. He realized he was holding his breath, waiting for her reaction to the memorabilia he had collected during the last sixteen years.

She studied the pictures from his Vietnam war days and the display case with his medals. Would she think he was showing off? Or would she realize this was his home and he had surrounded himself with those things that were most important to him? It mattered very much to him that she should understand.

She paused to look at a model of an F/A-18 Hornet jet painted with the distinctive Blue Angels design. Then she lifted her gaze to an enlarged photograph of four of the dark blue planes flying in their famous vertical diamond, in which their noses were pointed straight up and their wingtips almost touching, as trails of white smoke streaked behind him.

"It looks like you're a big Blue Angels fan," she commented. "I've been around aircraft fanatics all my life, but you win the prize hands down. I don't think I've ever seen such an extensive collection."

Scott started to make a comment, but before he had a chance, she leaned closer to a photograph of the Blue Angels' crew, then whirled around to face him.

"Why didn't you tell me?" she demanded in an accusatory tone. "You're an Angel! Of all the people in the world I don't want to get involved with, another pilot tops the list—especially one who is crazy enough to risk his life flying stunts with the Blue Angels!"

Chapter Six

"I wasn't trying to hide it from you. It simply never came up," he explained in his defense.

"Came up! Of course it came up. All we've talked about the last two nights was pilots and planes and danger. The Blue Angels fit into all three of those categories. In fact, they *lead* those categories."

"You have to understand that it's not something I talk about right away. I don't walk up to people and blurt out, 'Hi, my name is Scott Sanders and I'm the commanding officer and flight leader of the Blue Angels.' People would either think I was on the biggest ego trip in the world, or they would be unreasonably impressed, and I would never know if they were interested in knowing me, Scott, or me, the commander."

Kristi grudgingly admitted there was some logic to that. She was aware of the exalted status of the naval flight squadron. They were unquestionably the superstars of aviation. To people who were fans, to meet any member of the team would be the equivalent of a movie buff meeting Robert Redford or Tom Cruise.

Still, that didn't excuse his sin of omission.

"The commander?" she repeated incredulously. "So *you* fly the number one plane at all the air shows and lead the others through their hair-raising maneuvers at one thousand miles an hour only a few feet above the ground?''

"You've got the facts right, but you make them sound much worse than they really are. We practice our formations and maneuvers every day for months. We have an excellent safety record and if a maneuver doesn't seem safe, we don't do it. Everything is planned down to the nth degree. We're not daredevils. We don't take chances. We're professionals, doing our job the best we can.''

"No one plans accidents," she countered. "That's why they're called *accidents*.''

Scott studied her thoughtfully. "What did you mean by your statement that you don't want to get *involved* with another pilot?'' he asked, as if her first response had suddenly sunk in.

It was Kristi's turn to go on the defensive. What *had* she meant by that? It had just slipped out. His question left her totally flustered. "I didn't mean actually *involved*, except as a friend. At this point in my life, I don't even want to *like* someone who may die tomorrow. I've been through that and I don't want to go through it again. It's too painful.''

Scott had crossed the breakfast room at the beginning of their conversation and now he closed the distance between Kristi and himself, walking toward her until they were mere inches apart. Hesitantly, as if afraid of her reaction, he reached out a hand, gently touching her cheek with his fingertips until he was cupping her face in a gesture of comfort and tenderness. "Kristi, you can't worry about tomorrow. None of us have any guarantees, whether we're in the air or walking along the beach. You've got to relax and not be afraid to live.''

Tears pooled in her soft blue eyes. "I can't," she cried. "I used not to think about such serious things. It never occurred to me that each day might be my last. And when the reality hit me, it hit hard."

"That's one of the few things I can thank the war for giving me," Scott told her. "The first thing I learned was how precious life is and how quickly it can all be over. Making each day count *was* the reality. You and I have gone through almost the same experience. We were both kissed by an angel of death, but survived to live another day. Except we are accepting that gift of life in different ways."

"Yes," she agreed. "I'm cherishing mine and you're risking yours, daring that angel to catch you again."

"It won't."

"It could."

"Does it matter to you that much?"

His hand felt cool against the sudden flush of heat in her cheeks. He was looking at her with such intensity that it made her heart jump in her chest. As much as she hated to admit it, her attraction to this man was more than an interest in friendship. But he was a pilot...a man with what she felt was a death wish. She didn't agree with his reasoning that his survival in Vietnam gave him an excuse for taking such risks. She absolutely could not let herself care for someone who held life in so little esteem.

"It matters just as it would if any of my friends flouted danger," she finally replied cautiously.

"Am I forever to be stuck in the *friends* category?" he persisted, his voice low and excitingly husky.

Kristi opened her mouth to respond, but no words came out as she felt his hand slide into the silken strands of her hair and he bent his head toward her. She could feel the warmth of his breath on her face and her lips tingled in anticipation of the kiss she knew was to come.

"Whoops!" A masculine voice interrupted from across the room.

Kristi gulped in a mouthful of air, trying to fill her burning lungs; she realized she hadn't breathed since Scott had begun leaning toward her. She glanced over Scott's shoulder at the three people who were standing just inside the front door. Even though she didn't have a clue who they were, she was too shaken to be embarrassed by the compromising position in which these people had seen her.

Scott's hand fell away from her hair as he wheeled around to face the intruders. "Did anyone ever tell you what rotten timing you have, Zipper?"

"My, my. I can't believe my eyes," the man declared, totally nonplussed by Scott's reprimand. "And who is this lovely creature? Why don't you introduce us?" He crossed the room and held out his hand.

"Kristi, this turkey is Zack Jackson, also known as Zipper. And I haven't a clue who he brought with him," Scott stated flatly, obviously not happy with Zack's unexpected entrance and not making any attempt to be polite.

Zip held her hand for a second longer, punctuating his greeting with a flirtatious wink before stepping away and drawing the two women still standing near the doorway into their group. "This is my date Andrea, and this is her cousin LouAnn." He leaned closer so that only Kristi and Scott could hear as he added, "LouAnn is dying to meet you, Commander, and since you usually don't have someone as gorgeous as Kristi to neck with between courses, I invited her to tag along with Andrea and me. Sorry."

Scott shrugged, his good humor gradually returning. "That's okay. We have plenty of food and we can always use another volleyball player."

"Great. Well, we'll just mosey on outside and leave you two alone," Zip said and herded his date and her cousin through the breakfast room and out the patio door.

"I like seafood," Scott said, as he turned back to Kristi, one corner of his mouth lifted in that now familiar grin.

"What?"

"For the free dinner you owe me from our bet."

"Andrea's cousin," Kristi said, filling in the blanks of their conversation. "You were right."

"Do I know my men, or what?"

Kristi glanced outside at the group of people standing impatiently around the barbecue grill, as if watching the food would make it cook faster. "So I take it all of these guys are Blue Angels pilots, too."

"That's right. This is Alan and Chuck's last season. The Blues hold auditions every year, and the new squadron members will be announced this week, as well as who the commander will be."

"You mean, you might not be the commander after next week?" She was amazed at how relieved she felt at that news.

"There's a possibility, but I've already reapplied for the position and hope to be selected again."

"But if you're not selected as commander, would you still fly with the Angels?"

He gave her a gentle little half smile and said wryly, "Actually we'd prefer not to say that we fly with the Angels. We call ourselves the Blues. But, yes, even if I'm not selected as commander for another year, I'd fly with the squadron. It's in my blood. I love it and I can't give it up until it gives up on me."

"You're as hardheaded as my father," Kristi muttered. "There's no hope for people like you."

"No hope at all?" he asked, his look suddenly serious as he realized the subject was no longer solely his pilot status with the Blues.

Kristi's chest was painfully constricted as she replied with absolute conviction, "None at all."

Luckily Randy and his wife Donna had taken over the cooking and had kept a close watch on the grill. Before Scott and Kristi could leave the house, the others began filing in, circling the table, picking up their plates and cutlery, then helping themselves to the salads and vegetables before returning to the barbecue grill for a steak and baked potato.

Scott and Kristi walked silently to the end of the line and waited their turn. Kristi was sure he must now be sorry she had accepted his invitation. If she hadn't shown up, he could be having a good time with LouAnn, possibly all night long. And now he was stuck with a dud...a woman who, although she was both attracted and repelled by his status, was not ready to fall into his arms or his bed...or anyone else's, for that matter. Not even to herself was she willing to admit that the prospect had been just the teeniest bit tempting.

It would be rude if she were to leave too abruptly. She didn't want to arouse suspicion or cause Scott any discomfort, but she decided it would be a wise move to excuse herself as soon as possible after the meal, then disappear. Maybe no one, not even Scott, would even realize she had gone.

There was only one picnic table, so the adults let the kids eat at it while the pilots and their wives or dates clustered on the steps of the deck or sat in lounge chairs. Kristi and Scott joined one of the larger groups, which Kristi interpreted as a sign Scott didn't want to spend any more time alone with her than absolutely necessary.

"Would anyone like to comment on the oddity that all parts of the meal are ready at the same time?" Randy asked dryly while everyone dug into their food as if they were starving. "Thanks, of course, to Donna and myself, who absolutely saved the meal when our chef mysteriously disappeared."

"I was just thinking about the same thing," Scott replied, taking up the verbal challenge. "In fact, I was so impressed with your excellent management of time and skill with the grill that I am appointing you the official chef of the Blue Angels. Since this is no light honor, we will all meet at your house next Saturday to sample your culinary talents, initiate the new men into our group and say goodbye to the old."

Since Randy could take a joke as well as he could give one, he chuckled and knew when he had been beaten. "I guess I was asking for that one, wasn't I?"

"But your timing was perfect," Scott added with a wink.

Even though she was determined their friendship would end after today, already she felt a sadness. In spite of this, Kristi found she was enjoying herself. The members of this squadron were, without exception, extremely intelligent, witty, and lively conversationalists. She was soon lifted out of her gloomy mood, laughing at the corny jokes and adding bits and pieces of her own as the subjects changed from one moment to the next.

One of the men fashioned an unbelievably complex airplane out of the scrap of aluminum foil that had been wrapped around his potato and an impromptu contest began. Acting more like little boys than grown men who had been entrusted to fly twenty-million-dollar airplanes, the guys folded and modified their own foil, then stood at the rail of the deck and sailed their shiny creations through the air, trying to beat each other's distances and loft time. This game went on for several minutes, until most of the airplanes suffered irreparable damage or were hijacked by the kids.

When the last steak had been eaten and the last piece of pecan pie had vanished, everyone moved in a body to the volleyball court. Somehow Kristi let herself be carried along with the crowd. She knew that now would be the opportune moment to leave, but for the first time in months, she was having fun.

She wasn't certain if she was a people person because of her experience as a flight attendant, or if she had become a flight attendant because she enjoyed being around people. It was sort of like the riddle of the chicken and the egg, but whatever the sequence, after six months of being around very few people, all of whom had been as upset and depressed as herself, it was nice meeting and relating to a new group who didn't constantly remind her of the event she was trying so desperately to forget.

There was an informal choosing of teams, but after the first couple of games, the women retired to the sidelines to cheer on their favorite fella. The men were of course much more physical players, and the six of them, with three on each side of the net, carried on a very impressive game, covering as much ground as if they were full teams. And they obviously enjoyed playing to an audience.

Kristi sat on the sand next to Donna and Greg's wife, Lisa. It was inevitable that their conversation would turn to what it was like to be married to a Blue Angel pilot,

and Kristi discovered that both of the women shared her
fear for the men's safety, but they accepted it because
their husbands loved it and they loved their husbands.
Kristi accounted for their naiveté to the fact that neither
of them had ever lost a loved one in a plane crash; she
wished with all her heart that they might never have to
experience it.

They tried to reassure her that crashes were few and far
between. But to Kristi, the three Blues pilots who had
died in 1973 and the one who had been killed in 1978 were
four too many. It didn't matter to her that the ground
maintenance crew was hand-selected and the very best at
its job, or that the squadron practiced until the rolls and
turns were second nature. All she could think of was the
miniscule thirty-six inches that separated the wingtips of
one plane from the canopy of the next and the complete
wing overlap as they flew their maneuvers in tight formation. There was no margin for error.

The party began breaking up at sunset. During the day,
the clouds had gradually been building in the north and
it soon became evident by the wind that changed from a
warm southeasterly to a chill gust from the north that a
change of weather was brewing. The wives wandered
around the beach and deck looking for lost shoes and
abandoned shirts and toys, while the men struggled to get
the volleyball net down. Maverick added his assistance by
scouting for any food that had been dropped or forgotten and gobbling it down.

Kristi busied herself gathering up trash that hadn't
been thrown into the garbage bags, but the rising wind
cleared the area more quickly than she could, sending
napkins and foil airplanes tumbling down the beach.

She said her goodbyes to the other women, sorry she
would never have an opportunity to see them again. Af-

ter dropping the bag of garbage she had collected next to the basement garage, she waited until Scott was alone before approaching him to tell him she was leaving.

"I wanted to tell you I enjoyed the party," she said to him.

"You aren't leaving now, are you?" he asked.

"Why shouldn't I?"

"Because I'd like you to stay for a while longer. We need to talk."

"I think it's all already been said."

"But it hasn't been settled."

She shook her head and sighed. "It won't work. For one thing, I'm not ready and for another, I just can't go through it again."

She was aware he knew better than anyone else what she was talking about and how determined she was to avoid this relationship, but still he persisted. "There's a storm brewing, and you probably won't make it home before it breaks."

"All the more reason why I need to leave right now. Goodbye, Scott."

She felt his gaze still resting on her as she walked away.

"Kristi," he called, his voice almost snatched away by the wind.

She paused and turned back toward him.

"I'm really glad you came," he said.

Kristi's smile was wistful. She had no idea of what she might be throwing away. This could have been the beginning of something very special, yet she didn't dare find out. Instead of replying, she waved, then walked out of sight around the corner of the garage.

MAYBE IT WAS because of all the aeronautical conversation, the reminder of how very real and constant the danger was for pilots or the disruption of her friendship with Scott, but the nightmare was worse than ever that night. Each time she would reach a particularly painful part, she would wake up. But as soon as she fell back into a fitful sleep, the dream would pick up where it had left off, continuing until she could bear it no longer.

Feeling tired and drained of emotion, Kristi wrapped a warm fleece robe around her gown and walked to the patio door. It was almost time for sunrise, but she knew from the sound of rain on the roof that the sun wouldn't be able to break through the clouds this morning. She drew back the draperies and stared out at the gloomy, gray weather.

The beach looked so different when it was bathed in rain. The waves appeared rough and angry, the sand dirty and hard. The closest house was at least a hundred yards away, but the steady downpour cut off all visibility, so it was as if she were all alone in the world. Kristi shivered and pulled the robe tighter around her. She had heard on the television news last night that a cold front was pushing through the area, dropping temperatures and bringing a lot of rain, which depressed her even more.

At least the weather matched her mood, she thought wryly. She would have loved to go back to bed and spend the day catching up on her sleep, but didn't dare. Longingly she remembered how she used to enjoy crawling into bed for a nap or curling up on the couch with a good book on rainy days. She had finished the novel she had been reading late last night before she had gone to sleep. She supposed she could get dressed, throw on a raincoat and drive to the mall. Surely there would be a bookstore or someplace that sold magazines, where she could find some interesting and diverting reading material. Or she could go to the library, but since it was Sunday, she wasn't sure whether or not it would be open.

But no, she didn't really want to do any of those things. It was too much effort to try to shop in the rain, particularly in a strange city. She wandered listlessly into the kitchen, feeling both lazy and bored. If only she could think of something to pull her out of this mental slump. She wasn't normally such a dull person.

She had just poured herself a cup of coffee when the phone rang. Since she had given this number to very few people, she could assume it was either someone she knew from Worldwide, her mother, or a wrong number. At that moment it didn't matter, because she wanted to hear another human voice, never mind whose it was.

"Hello, Kristine. How are you feeling?" a voice inquired in answer to Kristi's greeting.

"Do you want honesty, Mother, or do you want me to tell you I feel terrific and this trip is doing me a world of good?"

"Of course I want you to tell me the truth. But I'll bet you've been holed up in that house the whole time you've been there. I told you if you got out and met some new people and made some new friends, you'd perk up."

"Is that what helped you get through Daddy's death? I seem to remember you went through a long grief period and a rocky readjustment."

"Sure, it was hard on me, but I had you, my mother and my friends at the church who were always there for me. I didn't try to go through it alone."

Kristi sighed at the simplicity of her mother's attitude. It wasn't as if Kristi didn't have a lot of friends. It was just that she had met all of those friends through Worldwide, and whenever she had tried to talk with them or socialize on even the most casual level, she had found it was uncomfortable for both of them. The crash loomed foremost in their thoughts, and being with Kristi, who had been most affected by having lost two extremely close friends and having narrowly avoided being a victim herself, served as a constant reminder that it could happen to them. And they reminded Kristi that they were the lucky ones, much luckier than Rick and Diane. Along with the pity, Kristi could see the distress in their eyes. It had gotten to such a point that she preferred to avoid her friends in order to save herself any more pain, so it came as no surprise that none of them had called since she left Denver a week ago. They all needed more time to let the dust settle and the memories fade.

"Well, Mom. Since you're so worried about my social life, you'll be delighted to know that just yesterday I went to a beach party and met a dozen or so new people."

"Any nice-looking, eligible young men?" her mother apparently couldn't resist asking.

"A couple, but you know it's too soon for me to even think about getting interested in someone."

"That's not true. Rick is the one who died. You're still alive. You're too young to swear off men."

"I haven't sworn off men," Kristi denied, then added, more cynically than optimistically, "I'm sure that in time I'll meet someone wonderful, fall instantly in love, get married, have two children, a boy and a girl of course, and live happily ever after."

"Just take it one step at a time, Kristine. And don't be too critical. That special man might be right under your nose, and you can't see him because you won't open your eyes. Rick was a nice boy, but I never did think he was someone you'd want to spend the rest of your life with. And I think, subconsciously at least you knew that, or you wouldn't have kept putting off the wedding for the last two years.''

"That's not true," she stated hotly. "I loved Rick, and we had pushed our wedding forward to the summer."

"Of which year?"

"Mother..." The low warning tone of Kristi's voice apparently made her mother realize she had crossed an invisible boundary line and that it was time to change the subject.

"So are you coming home for Thanksgiving?"

"Thanksgiving?"

"Yes... Pilgrims, Indians, turkey, dressing, cranberry sauce. It's only four days away. Don't tell me you've forgotten about it!"

"I've had a lot of other things on my mind and I guess it sort of sneaked up on me."

"I wish you would have waited until after the holidays to go on this sabbatical. Even when you were busy working all those extra trips, you still found a way to spend that time with your family."

Kristi didn't answer for a long moment. Should she explain that much as she loved those family gatherings, they had always succeeded in pushing her back light years into her childhood? She knew she would always be her mother's baby, and in her grandmother's eyes, she would always be a thin little girl with straight white-blond hair and gigantic blue eyes much too large for her face, who loved to hang around the kitchen and lick the batter bowls.

And then there were a couple of dozen cousins, aunts, uncles, spouses and children, some of whom she saw only once a year at these dinners and who usually spent all day catching up on the events of each other's lives. What would Kristi say when it was her turn? Her silence would be awkward, as would the self-imposed censorship of their own stories, so as not to make Kristi feel any worse than she already did.

As loving and supportive as her family might be, she knew they would still be tiptoeing around the subject of the crash—and that would, as it did with her friends, just make everyone feel uncomfortable. Kristi didn't think it would be fair of her to ruin the holidays for everyone.

"Please try not to get upset, Mom, but I'm going to have to miss it this year. I think everyone will feel more relaxed if I'm not there."

"That's ridiculous. It won't be the same without you."

"I'm sorry, but I just can't. Besides, Seattle is almost three thousand miles from here. I couldn't possibly make it, even if I left right this minute."

There was a brief silence at the other end of the line, then her mother, in a tone that clearly inferred the answer was obvious, suggested, "You don't have to drive. You could fly, you know. With your pass it wouldn't cost you a cent."

Kristi shook her head negatively, even though she knew her mother couldn't see her response. *No.* She definitely could not fly. Not yet . . . and maybe not ever.

"Mom, I love you and I'll miss seeing you, Grandma and all the others, but I simply cannot make it this year," she finally said aloud. She knew it would be difficult for her mother to accept, but Kristi had made her decision and was going to stand firm.

"What about Christmas? Will you be back in Denver by then? Denver's much closer to Seattle, you know, so you could drive up here. Maybe if you begin planning now . . ."

"We'll see," Kristi promised vaguely, picking up the response her mother had used so often when Kristi was younger and had asked a question her mother didn't really want to answer.

They spent a few more minutes talking about the weather and the latest family gossip. Kristi was surprised to learn that her mother was dating a widower from her church and, although she denied it was anything serious, Kristi could hear the excitement and almost girlish giddiness in her mother's voice as she spoke of him. If her mother could recover from the loss of the husband she had been happily married to for more than twenty-five years to speak of another man in such glowing and respectful terms, then perhaps there was hope for Kristi's own recuperation. She had to admit that it was more than a little disturbing to think of another man taking her father's place in her mother's life, yet this rebirth of her mother's happiness and romantic spirit was an encouraging sign that there was light at the end of the tunnel. She was glad her mother was having a good time and wished her well.

"I guess I'd better get off this phone before I have to take out a loan to pay the bill," her mother said with a laugh, then returned to the original subject of the call. "What will you do all by yourself on Thanksgiving? Are you going to cook or go out to eat?"

"I'm not sure. I doubt if many places will be open, but don't worry about me. It won't be as good as Grandma's cooking, but I'll find something special to eat."

"Well, take care of yourself. You can't afford to skip many meals. You're already as thin as a rail."

Kristi thought of the ten pounds she had lost in the last six months. That wasn't much in itself, except that Kristi had always kept her weight low because of her job, even though it was no longer a company policy. Now, however, even she admitted she was a few pounds lighter than she should be, but decided this was not something she ought to admit to her mother. "A person can't be too thin or too rich," she stated lightly.

"That's baloney," her mother retorted, repeating one of her favorite expressions of disbelief. "Just remember what I told you and be glad you're alive. You've got to accept that it wasn't your fault and there was nothing you could have done to stop it. You have a lot to give thanks for this season."

"I don't feel very thankful."

"Well, I do. My baby is strong and healthy and some-day soon will find happiness again. Let the past go, and the pain will gradually get smaller and smaller until it won't bother you anymore. Of course you can't forget completely, and you shouldn't. But you've got to sepa-rate the good memories from the bad ones. It's not easy at first, but it gets easier with time. And remember I'm always here for you."

"I know, Mom. Thanks. I love you very much." Kristi felt the tears rolling down her cheeks. "Have a nice Thanksgiving. Give Grandma a big kiss and eat a piece of pumpkin pie for me. And tell everyone I said hello." They exchanged goodbyes and Kristi wiped away the tears. As usual, her mother was right. Kristi had been complicating her own recovery by shutting off her feel-ings. She had been frightened and panicky when Scott had stirred up the emotions repressed within her. She still believed it was too soon to get seriously involved with someone. And she was even firmer in her conviction that that someone would definitely not be a pilot or in any flight-related field.

But there was no harm in continuing their friendship. Even though she had seen him yesterday, she had missed not being able to meet him at midnight for their nightly self-analysis session. And today had made her realize how very lonely she would be for the rest of her stay if Scott weren't around to tease and talk to. She had grown more accustomed to seeing him every day than she realized.

Suddenly anxious to hear his voice, she thought about calling him. She even went so far as to call Information and was disappointed to hear that his number was unlisted. She wasn't sure whether or not she would actually have dialed it, but she would have liked to have that option. The way the rain continued to pour down eliminated walking down the beach toward his house and casually stopping for a chat. And with the much colder temperatures and stiff wind from the north, she doubted they would be meeting tonight, even if the rain stopped.

It was aggravating that she would have to wait until tomorrow and hope for a nicer day. But at least now she had something to look forward to...even if it was only a temporary friendship.

Chapter Seven

Kristi awoke Monday morning feeling more energetic than she had in weeks. For a change she had gotten a good night's sleep after dozing off early in the evening while watching television. She had had several hours of peace before the dream had disturbed her, but as soon as she drank a cup of cocoa, turned off the TV and the lights and went to bed, she had quickly gone back to sleep and hadn't stirred again until well after daylight.

This was the day she was going to be more positive with her outlook and try to ease the unpleasant memories further into the past. But how was she supposed to be cheerful, when the heavy skies looked as though they were about to suffocate the world?

This would definitely further delay her peacemaking mission to Scott's house. She didn't want it to seem as if she had made a special trip to see him, in case he should think she was pushing the relationship. If only she could casually stroll by, hoping to bump into him somewhere between here and there, or even stop by his house to say "Hi," it would seem impulsive rather than premeditated. And it was important to her that he not misunderstand her intention.

But there would be no casual walks today unless this front decided to move on. According to the weatherman, when the cold air from Canada hit the warm, moist air off the Gulf, the front had screeched to a halt, stalled on top of northern Florida, and was showing no signs of wanting to leave. Combined with a gusty wind, the near freezing temperatures and rain chilled to the bone. This was the kind of weather not even ducks liked.

Determined not to let this reverse bring back the despondency that had taken over her days lately, Kristi dressed in a bright blue fleece jogging outfit that was both warm and comfortable. She pulled her blond hair into a ponytail, fastened it with a clip and added a light touch of makeup to her long, thick lashes and pale cheeks. Not really in the mood for the exuberance of game shows or drama of the soap operas, she decided to leave the television set off. Tuning a radio to an oldies channel, she turned it up loud enough to drown out the depressing patter of rain and hear the music as she tidied the house. As she pushed the vacuum cleaner over the beige carpet, she even felt moved to burst into song occasionally, whenever an old favorite was played.

With all the noise, she barely heard the doorbell, and even then she wasn't sure whether or not she had imagined it. Flipping the switch to Off, she listened to hear if there really was someone out there. She was reaching to switch the cleaner back on when the doorbell rang again, so she hurried to see who was there.

"Hi Kristi. You busy?" Scott asked as soon as she opened the door. The small porch at the front of the house was doing little to shield him or Maverick from the rain and both were getting drenched.

"I was just doing a little housework. Come on in." She held the door open, then hurried to turn down the volume on the radio and get a couple of towels from the bathroom. Returning to the living room, she handed one of them to Scott, then knelt to dry off the dog's sleek black coat. Unable to keep her gaze off Scott, she studied him covertly.

She had always been so wrapped up in herself and her problems that she hadn't really taken the time to look *at* him until now. *Oh sure,* she had noticed how tall and nicely proportioned his lean, muscular body was. And his neatly clipped, jet-black hair and midnight-blue eyes that seemed to be lighted with a perpetual twinkle had not escaped her notice. But today she looked beneath the handsome, slightly rugged features of his face, the sprinkling of dark hair that peeked out the opening above the buttons of his shirt, and the broad shoulders that seemed even more masculine covered by the old blue jean jacket he wore.

Today she saw the personality that lay below the surface, the character that had been formed through his childhood years in Texas, his tour of duty in Vietnam and the adaptation period after the war, as well as by his time in the limelight as a member of the world's best and most famous aeronautical stunt team. She sensed that for all his talk of living each day to the fullest, he was as lonely and unhappy as herself. He too had tragedies in his past that had been buried, left unresolved.

She watched as he rubbed the towel over his head, tousling his hair until it fell onto his forehead, making him look boyish and vulnerable. Something deep within her was touched, as if someone had stirred the coals of a fire, bringing them back from the seemingly dead to a red-hot glow. When he caught her eye and saw she was looking at him, one corner of his definitely sexy mouth lifted in that charmingly crooked grin she had begun to think of as his alone.

Kristi's heart did a little flip-flop in her chest, she quickly tore her gaze from his and returned her full attention to drying Maverick.

"So what brings the two of you out on a lovely day like this?" she asked with studied casualness.

"Actually I stopped by to ask you to do a huge favor for me."

Maverick reached around and plastered her face with a drippy lick, then trotted over to a heating vent. Lying down where the warm, dry air could blow on him, he rested his head on his paws and promptly fell asleep.

With the dog gone, the buffer between Kristi and Scott was removed and she was forced to look back at him. *This is silly,* she told herself. She had flown with movie stars and television personalities and had never felt unnerved by speaking to them. Yet here she was with a man who, although he had a certain form of celebrity status, was relatively ordinary and she was suddenly shy. But then, perhaps *ordinary* didn't really fit him at all.

"A favor?" she echoed, unable to think of anything intelligent to say.

"Yes, and I want you to be honest when I ask. You won't hurt my feelings if you say no."

"Okay, what is it?" She sat back on her heels as she waited for him to continue.

"First I need to find out what your plans are for this week. Are you going to spend the holiday with your mother?"

"Not this year. She had been staying with me in Denver, so it's been just a little over a week since I saw her. I talked to her yesterday, so I think she understands. Besides, I've barely begun to get settled here."

"But what are your plans for Thanksgiving Day? Do you have any friends in this area?"

Kristi shrugged and gave him a tentative smile. Here was her chance to mend some of the bridges she had tried to burn behind her on Saturday. But how subtle should she be? Deciding on a direct approach, she answered, "Only you and Maverick. What would you two guys think about joining me for a meal on Thursday? You know I'm not much of a cook, but even I can manage to warm up a smoked turkey and stick a frozen pumpkin pie into the oven."

He seemed oddly disturbed by her invitation, and she was immediately sorry she had spoken up at all. Maybe she had put him into a position too awkward for him to be able to decline gracefully. She had noticed right away he was a member of that rare, almost extinct breed—a true gentleman.

"But of course I understand that you might already have other plans. I'll be fine here alone," she rushed to add. "Or maybe I'll go out and let someone do all the work for me. Actually, I'll probably be a lot less likely to catch food poisoning if I stay out of the kitchen entirely."

"I survived on military mess for years and I can't believe your cooking could be as bad as that. I would love to be with you on Thanksgiving, but, unfortunately, I have a plane to catch in about two hours. And that brings me to the favor."

Kristi tried to ignore the surge of disappointment that dampened her spirits. What had she expected? She had made her feelings known to him at the party; now she was upset because he was honoring them?

"My mother still lives in Corpus Christi, and I was going to fly home for Thanksgiving," Scott stated almost apologetically. "There are two problems, one of which is that Mom lives in a small two-bedroom condominium that has the tiniest yard you've ever seen and no fence. The other problem is that I hate to put Maverick in one of those cages in the baggage compartment. I didn't have your phone number and I have no idea whose name it's listed under, so I came over to ask you if I could leave him here with you.

"Randy and Donna were going to take care of him for me," he continued, without giving her a chance to speak, "but their dog is a female and happens to be in a romantic mood this week. Since they weren't too excited about having their pedigreed Doberman Pinscher fall in love with my Lab, they regretfully declined. I thought it might be kind of cute to have little Labrador Pinschers running around. Or would they be called Doberman Retrievers?" he asked, pretending to ponder the question as if it were of earth-shattering importance, before letting a smile break through.

"Anyway, then I called Greg and Lisa, but her mother is sick and they were on their way out of town. None of the other guys have a place to keep him, so I was wondering if you would mind letting him stay here. The two of you seem to get along so well, and he's not very much trouble."

"No problem. I'd be glad to let Maverick stay here with me while you're gone," she answered graciously, hoping he wouldn't find out what she was really feeling. She had no idea what favor she had expected him to ask, but this wasn't it. She didn't mind taking care of the dog. She would in fact enjoy having the company, especially since it now looked as if she would be all alone for the next week.

"Great!" Scott exclaimed, the relief obvious in his voice. "I can't tell you what a load off my mind it is for me to know he'll be here with you. Not only will I not have to worry about him, but I won't have to worry about you."

"Worry about me? Why ever would you do that?"

His steady gaze locked with hers, not allowing her to look away. "I have no idea," he answered honestly. "But for some strange reason I do."

Kristi tried to swallow, but her throat didn't seem to be working properly. None of her other basic bodily activities were, either, because her breath had suddenly become irregular and her skin was tingling as if she had a bad case of goose bumps all over.

"I've always been a very independent person," she stated, her words filled with more assurance than her voice, which sounded shaky even to her own ears. "I can take care of myself."

"I don't doubt that for a second. But total independence can sometimes bring loneliness."

"It sounds like you're speaking from experience."

He furrowed his brow in thought. "Yes, I suppose I am. After Kahuna and I went down, I built a wall around myself, never allowing anyone to get as close to me as he had. I was afraid to make another friend because I might lose him, too, so I buddied around with everyone, but kept my distance emotionally. I tried to become Mr. Macho Jet Jockey, handling everything in as businesslike a way as possible. But I discovered that even if all I knew about a guy was his name and hometown, it still hurt when I watched them wrap his body in a bag and ship it home.

"It took me a while, but then I realized I was the one missing out," he continued. "The world was passing me by while I was freezing up inside. I was surviving, but I was miserable.''

"Is that what you think I'm doing?"

"I hope not. You've had a terrible experience, but you have a family and friends who can help you if you'll let them. Don't shut them out."

"Now you sound like my mother. We had a long conversation on the phone and she said much the same thing."

"So are you going to take her advice? And mine?"

"I'm trying," Kristi admitted honestly. "What you both have said makes a lot of sense, and I realize you both have been in similar situations, you with Kahuna and she with my father. I suppose it just takes time."

"Speaking of which," he said, glancing at his watch, "I've got to run. I'm flying commercial today and they don't hold the flights for anyone." He stood up and walked over to Maverick. Squatting next to the dog, he patted him and said, "Now you be a good boy while I'm gone. Don't track mud into the house, don't bring home any smelly dead things, and don't embarrass your master. And another thing," he added in a stage whisper, "take care of Kristi, whether she wants you to or not."

"Bullheaded," she said with an affirmative nod.

She walked with him to the door. In the small entry hall, she stopped with her hand on the knob and looked to see if Scott was following. He was, indeed, but he was much closer than she had expected and she found there were only inches separating them. Lifting her gaze, she was mesmerized by the warmth radiating from the depths of his dark eyes. As he lifted his hands to cup her face, she couldn't have moved even if she'd wanted to.

"The term bullheaded has such a negative connotation. I like to think of myself as persistent or tenacious.

But one thing I'm not—'' slowly he lowered his head until Kristi felt the gentle pressure of his mouth on hers ''—is patient,'' he murmured, capturing her lips in a slow, sensuous kiss.

Kristi's nerve endings had been shooting tiny sparks throughout her body since the moment Scott walked into the house. But now, suddenly the sparks became lightning bolts and her resolve disintegrated. Her hands crept up the front of his shirt until they twined around his neck, pulling him closer. Dimly she knew this shouldn't be happening. It would only complicate her life at a time when she needed simplicity.

But at that moment desire was more powerful than logic, and she responded with all the intensity of which she was capable. The feel of his body pressed against hers, the taste of his lips, his musky masculine fragrance all raced through her consciousness. The emptiness within her became almost unbearable. She hadn't realized how hungry she had been until his passion fed her. It wasn't so much physical fulfillment she needed so desperately as the emotional nurturing that she was now receiving from his caresses. This could be the beginning of a relationship that would have no ending. But there could be no true satisfaction.

Yet it was Scott who broke away first. There was a dazed look in his eyes that Kristi was certain must be reflected in her own. Apparently struggling to steady his breathing, he didn't speak for more than a minute.

''And I like to finish what I start,'' he was finally able to gasp. ''But I've got a plane to catch.''

''That's the problem,'' Kristi whispered. ''There will always be another plane for you.''

NOW THAT SHE HAD a guest for dinner, Kristi dismissed the option of eating her Thanksgiving meal at a restaurant. Instead, she spent the morning in the kitchen, baking a chicken, reading the directions on a box of Stove Top Stuffing and opening a can of cranberry sauce. She tried three times to make gravy, but it turned out so lumpy or gummy that she dumped it down the garbage disposal and gave up. The frozen pumpkin pie, although smaller and more orange than she was used to, looked normal enough, but a sample nibble confirmed her suspicions that it didn't taste as good as Grandma's.

"Okay, boy," she said to Maverick. "I think our dinner's ready. I want you to understand that there are no guarantees on whether or not it will taste better than your Kal Kan, but I've done the best I could."

As she tied a napkin around the dog's neck, he gave her an affectionate lick. Lifting one large black paw, he rested it on her arm as if trying to reassure her it would be fine. But his sad, chocolate-brown eyes surveyed the room, searching, as they had every few minutes of the last four days, for his master.

"No, Scott's not here, fella. It's just you and me, but we'll manage. We've done pretty good so far. Actually, you're better company than most people I know. Now jump up onto the chair and I'll bring our food from the kitchen."

Maverick obediently jumped onto the chair she indicated and sat down, calmly waiting for her to return.

"You know, my mother would have a heart attack if she saw me letting a dog sit at the dining-room table and eat off a plate," Kristi commented. "It does sound a little crazy now that I've mentioned it, and you have no idea how silly you look sitting there with that napkin around your neck. But then who am I to talk about silly, when I talk to you as if you could understand every word I say?''

Maverick thumped his tail on the wooden slats of the chair and stretched his mouth into a loose smile.

''You and your master have the two best grins I've ever seen on man or beast,'' she said, chuckling. ''I don't know which of you is handsomer. However, there's no contest when it comes to loyalty. But that's not fair. How could I expect him to choose to celebrate with a woman he barely knows over his own mother?''

Maverick whined and cocked his head, as if listening intently and agreeing with every word she said.

Kristi arranged the food on the table, trying to make it look more attractive than it did, then lit the candles. She had just sat down when Maverick's ears perked up as much as their floppy flaps allowed, he bounded off his chair and raced for the front door. His barks were so loud and excited, she could barely hear the doorbell over the ruckus.

''Hush, Maverick,'' she commanded as she joined him in the entry hall. Pushing the dog aside, Kristi peered through the peephole in the door and called, ''Who is it?''

''It's me, Scott. Is that turkey I smell?''

Kristi nervously wet her lips with the tip of her tongue and her hands automatically smoothed the sleek lines of her hair and straightened her blouse around the waistband of her white slacks. After clicking back the lock, she opened the door and stared at him as if she were seeing a ghost.

''What on earth are you doing here?'' she asked, her surprise evident.

''My mother's house was crawling with relatives, and I couldn't take another day of the noise and confusion.

Besides, I couldn't stop thinking about my two friends having such a good time without me. May I carve the turkey?''

"You'd better reduce your expectations. Maverick and I decided we'd have chicken since there were only the two of us. But you're welcome to carve it to your heart's content."

Scott looked from the table with its place setting for two to Maverick, who was still wearing his snowy-white bib, then back to Kristi. "It looks like I got here just in time. I think you both are on the edge of insanity," he commented wryly.

"Smart-alecky remarks will get you leftovers," Kristi called over her shoulder as she went into the kitchen to get another plate and flatware. "And the only thing worse than my cooking when it's fresh is my cooking when it's not."

With exaggeratedly meticulous care, Scott carved the small chicken and placed generous slices on everyone's plates.

"Looks a little dry, doesn't it?" Kristi remarked, testing it with her fork.

"Maybe a little," he agreed, but dismissed it with a shrug. "But some gravy will moisten it up a bit." He looked around the table, peering doubtfully into the bowls. "Where is it?"

"In the garbage disposal."

"Oh. Well, the stuffing looks good and the cranberry sauce is just like my mother's," he teased.

Before she could think of a snappy retort, Maverick jumped out of his chair once more and ran to the entry hall, just seconds before the doorbell rang again.

Kristi looked at Scott and shrugged, telling him more explicitly than with words that she wasn't expecting anyone and had no idea who it could be. She rose and with Scott following close behind her, walked to the front door and opened it.

"Jason!" she exclaimed as soon as she saw who it was. "Isn't this a little off your regular route?"

The man on the doorstep shifted a large box from one arm to the other and answered, "I had orders from someone who wouldn't take no for an answer."

Kristi could feel Scott peering over her shoulder, obviously wondering who this visitor was. Standing aside, she said, "Jason, this is Scott Sanders and his dog Maverick. They live in a house down the beach. Scott, this is Jason Williams. He's a pilot for Worldwide and a friend of mine." Thus completing the introductions, Kristi added hospitably, "Come on in. We were about to sit down to dinner. I'm sure there's enough for one more."

After shaking Scott's hand, Jason stepped inside, but as his gaze took in the assortment of food on the table, the large black dog who was wearing what appeared to be a bib, and the tall man who was watching him with an intensity that surpassed normal curiosity, he apparently decided he would rather complete his errand and leave. "No, I've got a flight to Dulles in a few hours, so I think I'll head on back to the airport as soon as I deliver this package to you."

"This is for me?" Kristi gave a more thorough inspection to the large rectangular box Jason had brought with him. "What's in it?"

"I'm not sure, but I was warned if I didn't get it here as soon as my plane landed, my name would be Captain Mud instead of Captain Williams."

Not having a clue as to what he was talking about, Kristi took a knife from the table and cut the wide strips of tape that were closing the lid. After folding back the flaps, she looked inside and was puzzled to see what looked like an ice chest. "Could you help me with this?" she asked and the men stepped closer, one on each side, reached into the box and lifted the chest out by its handles.

Like children opening a Christmas package, they all crowded around as she released the clasp and opened the lid. "It's from Grandma and my mother!" Kristi exclaimed as she surveyed the contents. On top was a letter that wished her a happy Thanksgiving and gave exact instructions on how to heat everything up, along with their hope that she would find someone wonderful to share the meal with. They told her they missed her and loved her very much, and that they were praying she would soon find peace so she could come home.

Kristi, Scott and Jason unpacked the chest, carrying the small smoked turkey to the oven, the homemade pumpkin and pecan pies to the refrigerator, and the Tupperware containers of gravy, corn bread stuffing, fruit salad, a loaf of French bread and candied yams to the appropriate places. For the next few minutes they all bustled around the kitchen, transferring the food into bowls and microwave dishes.

As the delicious smells filled the room, Jason changed his mind and decided to join them after all, so Kristi set another place at the table. Scott made a quick trip to his house and brought back a bottle of wine while Jason started a fire in the fireplace. While the three sat in the den, talking about Scott's experiences in the Navy and flying with the Blues and Jason's activities first as an Air Force pilot and now a commercial captain, Maverick dined on his slices of chicken and a generous portion of the stuffing Kristi had made.

Kristi's feelings weren't hurt in the least. She was the first to admit cooking wasn't her strong suit and was thrilled to have a good dinner to share with her friends. She occasionally joined in the conversation, but mostly she relaxed and listened to the two men. Scott and Jason appeared to be getting along famously now that the first awkward moments of introduction had passed ... or perhaps it had been Jason's reference to how sorry he was to be away from his wife and four kids, especially today. For whatever reason, Kristi was happier than she had been for a long time.

Of course, Jason's presence brought a reminder of Worldwide and it was a natural progression from there to think of Rick, Diane and the crash. But both men were careful to avoid mentioning it and Kristi found herself able to keep her thoughts focused on more pleasant things.

She and Jason had been friends since early in her flying days when she had accidentally spilled a glass of ice and cola into his lap while they were in flight and she was serving him and the first officer in the cockpit. He had quickly dispelled her embarrassment by laughing it off, and later they had enjoyed a pleasant dinner together. He had never made a pass at her, but always treated her with respect and friendship.

He and his wife had been a great comfort to her at Rick and Diane's funerals. Kristi's mother had apparently remembered this and accordingly enlisted his help in transporting the package to her today.

And Kristi had been deeply touched that Scott had returned home early, just so she wouldn't have to spend the holiday alone. It had been a very nice, generous, unselfish thing to do.

All these things combined to drive away her loneliness completely, at least for today. It served to remind her that she did indeed have a family who loved her and friends who cared; it gave her a lot to be thankful for.

The oven timer buzzed and Kristi hurried to finish the meal, closely following her grandmother's instructions. Everything had already been cooked, so the warming process was relatively quick and simple. Now that the mealtime was about an hour past schedule, everyone was very hungry and hurried to help her get it onto the table.

"My compliments to the chef, wherever she may be," Scott joked as he pushed away his empty dessert plate.

"I hate to leave good company, but I really do have to get back to the airport," Jason stated with a groan. "I only hope I can still button my uniform jacket. If I cause the plane to be overweight, it will be all your grandmother's fault."

"You can see now why I've given up on trying to learn to cook," Kristi commented. "I can never hope to equal Grandma. Actually it's a shame, because great home cooking seems to be disappearing with her generation. My mother is okay in the kitchen, but not spectacular, and I'm totally hopeless."

Jason waved them both back into their chairs when they started to rise to walk with him to the door. It wasn't until after the door had clicked shut behind him that Kristi worked up enough energy to get up from her chair and begin gathering the dessert dishes together.

"Let me help," Scott insisted, picking up the glasses and coffee cups and carrying them into the kitchen. He loaded the dishwasher, while Kristi put the tablecloth and napkins in the washing machine and finished putting away the food and wiping the crumbs and spills off the countertops.

As long as Jason had been here, the atmosphere had been light and fun. But now that there were only the two of them, it all changed. Kristi was aware of disturbing electrical pulses that were filling the small room. Even when her back was to him, she was aware of his every movement. She imagined the flexing of the muscles in his arm as he lifted a plate, rinsed it under the faucet, then bent to place it on the dishwasher rack.

Scott could hear her moving around the kitchen. Once when he twisted his head around to glance at her over his shoulder, she was trying to reach something on the top shelf of the cabinet. Her slender body was stretched to its full length, showing off her small waist, rounded derriere and long, shapely legs to their best advantage. The full curve of her breast thrust against her blouse, drawing his attention upward; and he forced himself to turn back to the dishes. He knew he should go to her and help her reach whatever it was she needed, but he dared not because he was certain if he was standing that close to her, his resistance would dissolve.

While he'd been away this week, he had kept reliving that goodbye kiss over and over in his mind. Even though he was sure it couldn't have been as wonderful as he remembered, the memory still burned hot in his mind...as well as in other parts of his anatomy.

But he had had a lot of time to think these last few days. He knew she was a special woman and this was a special situation. He wanted her so much, he ached, but any relationship that might develop between them shouldn't be reduced to a one-night affair.

"How about another cup of coffee?" Kristi asked as they were finishing up in the kitchen.

"Sure. I'll throw another log onto the fire while you pour." Scott raked his fingers through his short black hair as he left the room.

He knew he should leave now...go home before he began tempting fate. He was afraid that if he stayed, he would want to hold her in his arms and taste the sweetness of her lips again. But besides the obvious danger of that, he did not want to be alone this evening. He knew if he was alone, the nightmare of his crash would be there to haunt him. After visiting with Kahuna's family yesterday, Scott was certain he would have no peace. He hadn't last night, and the lack of sleep was beginning to catch up with him, but still he didn't want to go to bed until he was too exhausted to dream.

"Is something bothering you?" Kristi's voice surprised him. "Even though you talked and laughed all through dinner, you didn't seem quite the same as before."

After rebuilding the fire, he hadn't moved away, but had stood, staring into the flames. He took the cup of coffee she held out to him and started to deny that anything was wrong. But there was something in the way she was looking at him, trusting him with her own secrets and expecting him to be honest about his.

She sat on the couch, waiting for his response. Already he had told her more about his problems during the war than he'd told any other nonprofessional person, including his family and closest friends. Somehow, even from the beginning, he had felt she would understand.

"Was it the Blues?" she persisted gently, sensing he needed to talk but wasn't sure whether or not to share his problems with her. "Weren't they supposed to make the announcement this week?" Maybe he had been passed over and another commander had been selected. Or perhaps he was off the squad altogether. She knew it wasn't very nice of her, but Kristi felt an overwhelming relief at the prospect that Scott might not be airborne with the Blues next season.

"They're not naming the new squad until tomorrow." Scott had turned to face her, but now his eyes moved to stare out at the shadowy dusk that was quickly changing into night. "They found Kahuna," he stated flatly.

Chapter Eight

"They found him? Is he all right? Was he a POW?" Kristi bombarded him with questions. "Did you see him?"

"No, I didn't see him, and I'll never see him again. His bones were returned to the United States in a wooden box. His parents had just been notified by the Navy a few days ago. He should arrive in Corpus Christi sometime after the first of the year. First they have to process his paperwork in Hawaii, where they send all the POWs and MIAs."

"How awful for his family...and you," she breathed sympathetically.

"Not to mention Kahuna. The Vietcong's story was that they had come across his skeleton in the jungle and identified him by his dog tags." Scott sighed and added angrily, "He always wanted to go to Hawaii. He wanted to try his skill on its legendary waves and soak up the sun on its beaches. How rotten that when he finally made it there, it was in a box!"

Even though Kristi couldn't see his face because his back was toward her, she could tell by the slump of his shoulders and the droop of his head that he was totally torn apart by this. Rising from the couch, she crossed the room and, in a gesture totally from her heart, wrapped her arms around his waist, leaned against his back and gave him a comforting hug. She felt his big body shaking and even though he wasn't making a sound, she knew he was crying.

There was something about a man's tears that totally unnerved her. Kristi had no idea how to react and could think of nothing intelligent to say. Instead, she simply held him tightly, hoping he would know she shared his grief and didn't look upon his breakdown as being unmasculine. Nothing could have been further from the truth, since Scott was easily the strongest, most masculine man she had ever known.

A few moments later, Scott seemed to have regained most of his control. In a strained, husky voice he continued, "At least he must have died on impact and didn't have to suffer through the hell of prison. I wouldn't wish a minute in the Hanoi Hilton on anyone."

"Maybe it's good that now you know what happened to him," Kristi offered optimistically. "All the years of wondering if he is alive or dead are over."

"Yes, I suppose you're right. Maybe now I can close that chapter of my life. His parents are going to arrange a funeral for him as soon as . . . he comes home. It just seems so odd, after all the time I've spent wondering where he is or what he might be doing, to suddenly find out he was dead all along. I know it sounds crazy, but I *felt* he was still alive. I'd always thought we were so close, more like brothers than friends, that somehow I'd know if he was dead."

As they talked, Scott had swung around until they were now standing face-to-face, their bodies not touching, but their hands clasping each other's arms.

"I bumped into his old girlfriend while I was down there. She's married and has two kids and another on the way. I wasn't sure how she'd react when I told her about Kahuna, but she took it very well." He gave a bitter snort. "I wouldn't be surprised if she hadn't been involved with some guy even before Kahuna died."

Kristi frowned and tried to read his expression. He seemed extraordinarily upset about what he must view as some sort of betrayal of his friend. "Why would you say that? Was she a flirt?"

"She wasn't as bad as some of the women I knew. At least she waited to get married until after the crash."

"Were they engaged?"

"Yes, but a ring and a promise didn't count for much back then."

Something in his tone told Kristi this was far more personal than simply his best buddy's fickle girlfriend. "Were you engaged, too? Did someone hurt you?"

He lifted his head and focused a pensive look on one of the heavy wooden beams stretching across the vaulted ceiling. "Yes, I was engaged, and yes, it hurt like hell when she told me she had eloped with someone else. It was one of those times that is remembered with such clarity that every little detail is frozen in my memory. I had just gotten back to my ship after a bombing mission into Laos and the letter was there, waiting for me. I was so excited because even though we had fairly regular mail deliveries, we were so isolated from the real world that we couldn't get enough letters from home.

"Anyway, I didn't even take time to change out of my flight suit. I took the letter to my bunk, but there were a half dozen guys lounging around in the room and I wanted to read Barbara's letter in privacy. So I went back up on deck and walked around until I found a spot where

I could be alone." His expression changed to one of total disgust. "I remember ripping it open with great anticipation. Barbara and I had been dating since high school, tenth grade actually. She was pretty with short red hair and brown eyes. She was on the cheerleading squad and used to wear those miniskirts that turned all the guys on. Of course, at that age, almost anything was a turn-on, but all the guys were after Barbara. I thought I was the lucky one, because she agreed to date me. She was the only girl I had ever been interested in.

"We got engaged just before graduation, but she knew I wanted to be a pilot and we made our marriage plans for far enough in the future that my career would be established. I thought it was all settled and didn't worry about it for a minute when I left on my tour of duty, even though I knew we wouldn't see each other for over a year because I would be on the carrier for six months at a stretch."

He managed a humorless chuckle. "Actually, that was why I got the nickname Saint, because I was stupid enough to think a commitment meant I had to stay loyal and true. During that whole time I never once looked at another woman . . . well, I may have looked, but I didn't touch. And, fool that I was, I assumed Barbara was doing the same. So when I received that particular letter, I figured she would be telling me how much she missed me and was counting the days until I came back and we could be married.

"Instead, she told me she and someone she had met at the office where she was working had fallen madly in love and had eloped to Las Vegas. There I was, stuck out in the middle of the South China Sea, fighting for my country, when Barbara was fooling around with a draft dodger. It was as if she had punched me in the stomach.

Sure I enjoyed flying the planes, but there was so much about the war that was pure misery, and thinking about what I had waiting for me back home was the only thing that was getting me through, especially after my plane got shot out from under me. And with one very brief letter, Barbara had taken all that away from me.''

"And you've never forgiven her for that, have you?" Kristi asked perceptively. "Is that why you've never married?"

He shrugged. "I got over it. After all, I was just a kid. The marriage probably wouldn't have worked out, anyway. I heard from my mother that now Barbara is on husband number three. But I suppose it did make me cautious. If I made one mistake, I might be susceptible to making others, and falling out of love is no fun at all."

Kristi cocked her head to one side as she looked up at him. "For a guy who is living life to its fullest, as if each day might be your last, I can't believe you would be so extremely cautious about women."

He lowered his gaze and focused on her, and the twinkle that usually highlighted his dark blue eyes sparked back to life. "Maybe I just haven't met the right one yet," he drawled, giving her the full wattage of his slow, sensual grin, "or have I?"

"I wish you the best of luck," Kristi responded with all sincerity.

"I'm going to need it," he murmured, gently pulling her closer until he held her wrapped securely in his arms.

Kristi was pleased she had succeeded in cheering him up, but this was a little more than she had planned. For some reason, every time she was this close to him, her own thoughts about everything and everyone else seemed to vanish, and there was only him. As soon as his lips touched hers, the word "no" disappeared from her vocabulary.

But instead of kissing her, he buried his face in her hair and cuddled her body against his. "I think I'm falling in love with you," he whispered, his voice muffled, "and I don't know what to do about it."

Neither did Kristi. As much as she was attracted to this man, the last thing in the world she wanted was to fall in love with him. They would both end up being hurt, because she was very definite in her decision not to get permanently involved with another pilot. She was convinced his future was perilous and wasn't about to let herself risk more pain from the loss of a loved one.

And she didn't want him to love her. She didn't want it on her conscience. Already he had a low opinion of women in general. If he somehow thought she was leading him on, he would file her in the same category as Barbara and Kahuna's girlfriend, which wouldn't be fair. She had to let him know she wasn't interested in anything he had to offer, and she had to do it now.

But his arms felt so good around her. His warm breath ruffled her hair and she could feel the feather-light pressure of his lips against the top of her head. His body was hard and solid . . . and very much alive. Was she blowing her fears out of proportion? *No.* The danger in his life was very real, and her past experience with pilots had taught her they did not usually die of old age.

Kristi knew better than to let things progress any further with Scott. What she needed was a man who left for the office every morning at seven-thirty, sat behind a desk all day and returned home in time for dinner. Surely there was an engineer, a CPA or even a dentist out there somewhere who could make her feel safe and secure, and still cause her pulse rate to soar as it was doing at this moment.

Reluctantly, but knowing she had no choice, Kristi pushed herself away from Scott. "Don't," she cried softly. "I don't want you to love me. I can never return your love." Crossing her arms over her chest and hugging herself, she realized for the first time how cold it was whenever she stepped away from Scott's warmth.

He reached out and wrapped his long fingers around her forearm, halting her escape and urging her to turn back and face him. "You've got as many ghosts in your past as I do. But we can get rid of them together. It's almost as if you and I were predestined to meet and fall in love. We are a lot alike and have so much to give each other... if you would just give us a chance."

For several seconds she stared into his eyes. Part of her wanted to throw aside her reservations and let the relationship go where it would naturally. But the memories of losing Rick were still too fresh. And even though her mother seemed to have gotten over her father's death, Kristi still hadn't. She would be foolish to leave herself open for a repeat performance. And, too, there was the nagging thought that she must indeed be a little fickle if she could even consider getting involved with another man so soon after Rick. Surely she owed him a mourning period greater than a mere six and a half months.

"No," she said firmly, shaking her head in emphasis. "I can't. It won't work. I'm not going to be in Florida but another few weeks. You'll be traveling all over the U.S. with the Blues. We'll both be meeting new people, people who will love us as we need to be loved."

She could tell he didn't agree, but Maverick, as if sensing the tension in the room, picked that moment to walk to the patio door and bark to be let out. Scott released Kristi's arm and obligingly opened the door for the dog.

For a moment longer than necessary, Scott held the door open, allowing the moist Gulf breeze to cool his cheeks. It wasn't the same as a cold shower, but gradually it had the same effect, calming his overcharged libido and bringing back his sanity. This woman certainly had a dramatic effect on him. She could send him to the boiling point with a touch and drive away all semblance of logic with those wide sky-blue eyes of hers. Even though he knew it was all done unintentionally, she was driving him wild with longing.

And it wasn't simply a matter of wanting her in his bed, although he ached with desire for her. With Kristi, he wanted more. In fact, he wouldn't be satisfied until she was willing to give him everything, including her love. Having only known her a little over a week and a half, he knew it was much too soon to be feeling this way. But Kristi was different and right from the beginning his feelings for her had been different, too. The more time he spent with her, the more his first impression was confirmed ... she was an angel, hovering just beyond his reach; hopefully he could change that.

Her reactions tonight, however, even though he had felt her respond to him, had shown him she could not be rushed. If he only had to deal individually with her boyfriend's death or her father's accident, or the fact Scott was also a pilot, he could have handled any one of those problems with relative ease. Burdened down with all three as well as the bad case of guilt she had, for some unexplained reason, about the crash, Scott knew he was fighting an uphill battle.

The night air wrapped around his body and he shivered from the eerie chill. A heavy fog was hanging over the water and white fingers swirled around the beach house. Having finished his business quickly, Maverick came galloping across the deck, now eager to be back in the warm, dry house. Scott let the dog back in, then locked the door and pulled the draperies shut.

How quickly his moods were changing this evening. But that shouldn't come as any surprise, considering everything that had happened in the last two weeks. The Blues had flown their last show of the season, the nightmare had returned, Kristi had burst into his life—and now the news about Kahuna, along with his concerns about next year's squad—all tumbled together to make him feel uncharacteristically flustered.

When he held Kristi in his arms, all other thoughts but those of her were pushed from his mind. But when she wasn't distracting him, the distress about his friend dominated his consciousness, and probably his subconscious as well. He had gotten precious little sleep last night and had no hope of much more tonight.

Perhaps if he didn't pressure her, he could stall for time. Whether they spent the night talking or watching old movies on television, he didn't want to leave. The truth was, he didn't want to be alone.

"Why don't we make some popcorn and see what's on the late show?" he suggested hopefully.

Kristi was kneeling in front of the fireplace, adding another log to cut the chill that Scott had let in. She viewed him curiously. "You can't possibly still be hungry."

"There's always room for popcorn."

"Aren't you tired from your trip?" she asked, but he couldn't tell whether it was from genuine concern or if she was hinting it was time for him to leave.

"No, I feel fine," he lied. Hoping she would stop him, he added, "But I suppose Maverick and I should be heading home. We've taken advantage of your hospitality long enough."

A stricken expression crossed her face. "Maverick, too?" she murmured, then looked chagrined. "But of course you would take Maverick with you. I'll miss him a lot. We were great company for each other, although he never stopped looking for you. And if he's a little spoiled, I apologize. I'm afraid he got into the habit of sleeping on the bed with me."

"Lucky dog," Scott commented with a teasing grin.

As if the prospect of being alone didn't appeal to her any more than it had to him, her whole attitude changed. It didn't flatter him to think she was more disturbed because his dog was leaving than she was about his own departure, but he reminded himself that he would for once have to try to be patient if he hoped to break through her meticulously built wall of defenses.

"It's still early," she stated, going to the television set and pushing the On button. "You check out the channels and I'll fix the popcorn. And don't make any rude remarks about whether or not I can handle that, because even I can pop perfect popcorn in the microwave."

"Okay," he said with a laugh, "but call me if you need any help."

While she was in the kitchen, he turned out all the lights except a lamp at the back of the room and selected a channel that was showing a Hitchcock thriller, then settled on the couch. Maverick, thoroughly contented that both of his favorite people were in the same house with him, stretched out on the hearth and fell asleep.

Scott couldn't help but think how ironic it was that his big, rowdy dog might have been the first to open the way to Kristi's heart. Most women were impressed by Scott's celebrity status, his looks or his money, none of which he took too seriously. But Kristi was more attracted to his dog.

She soon returned with a large bowl of popcorn and two glasses of cola. Kristi joined Scott on the couch, but he noticed she carefully put the bowl between them, creating a physical barrier to reinforce her previously erected emotional one. But at least she wasn't shutting him out of her life completely. Usually that meager offering would not have been nearly enough to keep his interest. The difference was that he truly believed Kristi would be worth waiting for.

The delicious smell of butter penetrated Maverick's slumber and drew him to sit on the floor at their feet, where he begged shamelessly for handouts.

Scott chuckled as he watched the dog's head move from side to side as he waited for his next bite. "With both of us feeding him, he must be in canine heaven. Just look at that silly grin on his face."

"Silly grins must run in your family," Kristi remarked, not quite succeeding in keeping her expression serious.

He cast her a pained look and rolled his eyes, but the grin referred to twitched at the corners of his mouth. "Speaking of family, it was nice of your mother and grandmother to send dinner to you."

"Yes, it was. This is one of the first times I've missed spending Thanksgiving with them. Even though this is the busiest season of the year, I would arrange my schedule so I could at least eat lunch with all my relatives. It was sort of a tradition."

"Then why didn't you make an effort to be there this year?"

Kristi sighed wistfully. "Because this year was different. I didn't feel like spending the day trying to make small talk. Last year Rick went with me, so everyone had a chance to meet him, which would have made this year uncomfortable for everyone. Besides, I didn't want to spend a week driving there and back."

"Seattle has an airport, you know."

She didn't try to hide her shudder. "It's too soon," she stated simply.

"You know the old saying: if you fall off a horse, you should climb right back on."

"It's a lot shorter fall from the back of a horse than from thirty thousand feet in the air," she snorted.

"The principle is the same. How long are you going to wait?"

"I don't know. I just know I can't...not yet."

"I could help you," he offered, his voice filled with encouragement. "I could take you up with me in one of the demonstrator planes."

"Oh sure. There's nothing like a few vertical loops or upside-down passes over the trees to settle a person's nerves and give her back confidence about flying."

"You know what the Wright brothers said about that," Scott replied, his dark eyes twinkling knowingly.

His grin was irresistible, and Kristi found herself smiling in spite of her feelings about the subject matter. "No, I have no idea. But I bet you're going to tell me."

He waved off her response and continued. "They said that an airplane stays up because it doesn't have the time to fall. Besides, I would take it easy with you...at first, anyway. I have a feeling that once you get your air legs back, you'll like the speed and the maneuvers of a fighter jet. You've never felt acceleration until you're sitting at the controls of one of those sleek little F/A-18 Hornets the Blues are flying now.''

"Right now you couldn't get me in a huge 747 while it's sitting at the gate."

"You'll get over it. Flying's in your blood, just as it's in mine."

"And *was* in my father's and Rick's," she added solemnly.

Scott studied her, a worried frown momentarily pushing away his smile. He took a handful of popcorn, tossed some to Maverick and the rest into his own mouth, then tried to change the subject by getting Kristi interested in what was on television. "This is one of my all-time favorite movies. Cary Grant was a much better actor than anyone ever gave him credit for, don't you think? And that Grace Kelly! What a gorgeous lady she was."

They began a lively discussion of old movies and actors that continued until the movie's excitement began to build, capturing their full attention. As Kristi felt herself relax, the tension that had twisted inside her during their conversation about flying gradually faded away. She was glad she wasn't spending the evening by herself. She wasn't used to so much peace and quiet. It felt good having someone to talk to and even argue with. Since the accident, everyone, including her family and co-workers had treated her so carefully, she hadn't had a normal discussion until she had met Scott.

She knew he was trying to help her, and what could have been interpreted as pushing was simply his way of getting her through this rehabilitative period. His intentions were good and she appreciated his show of concern. But she could never let herself care about him as anything other than a dear friend.

The Cary Grant movie was followed by a Doris Day comedy, and still Scott and Maverick made no move to leave. That didn't bother Kristi, because she knew the longer she put off going to sleep, the less time she would have alone with her own memories. With the draperies drawn and the fire crackling in the fireplace, there was a cozy, comfortable feeling in the room that no one wanted to disrupt.

KRISTI SNUGGLED deeper into her pillow. She could tell by the light sneaking in through her closed eyelids that it was morning, but she was so warm and contented in her bed that she wasn't ready to get up yet. But the blanket was twisted around her so tightly, she could barely move, so reluctantly she forced her eyes open.

Instead of seeing the white walls of the bedroom, her gaze encountered the soft blue cotton of a man's shirt. Lifting her head slightly, she realized that what she had believed was a pillow was actually his chest and the blanket lying across her shoulders was his arm.

While her eyes had eased open before, now they snapped wide. For a split second nothing looked familiar. Her mind scrambled for any memory that would tell her where she was and why she was lying next to a man on what appeared to be the couch in the living room.

Don't panic, she cautioned herself and forced her body to relax. Immediately she became more rational and less frightened as she realized the man was Scott and they were both completely clothed. The sound of his heartbeat, steady and slow, beneath her ear told her he was still sleeping peacefully. She was grateful for that, because it gave her a few extra minutes to think.

They must have fallen asleep while watching the late movie. She remembered feeling very relaxed, even after

Scott's arm had somehow found its way around her shoulders and he had pulled her closer until she was leaning against his side. She knew he had been tired. He hadn't gotten much sleep the night before because of his distress about Kahuna, then he had gotten up early Thanksgiving morning and gone to the airport so he could be at her house in time for lunch.

Still, she found it difficult to believe that she had simply drifted off to sleep and had stayed asleep through the night. *Through the night!* she repeated to herself incredulously. It had been the first night since the crash that her sleep hadn't been disturbed by the nightmare.

In spite of their rather cramped positions, Kristi couldn't remember the last time she'd felt so rested. *Thank goodness,* the couch was one of those large modern ones with plump square cushions and well-padded, rolled arms. Otherwise, it wouldn't have comfortably accommodated her own body, much less Scott's tall, broad-shouldered one.

That thought generated a whole new perspective on the situation. Kristi became even more aware of the amount and quality of masculinity that was pressed against her. There was a hardness in the layers of muscle she could feel in the flatness of his abdomen and the bulge of his thighs. And yet his chest made a soft pillow for her head and his arm held her gently, but securely. His skin had a deliciously musky smell, as well as a lingering hint of his after-shave.

He shifted slightly and Kristi knew he was waking up. Her head was tucked under his chin, but even without seeing his face, she could tell he was registering the same surprise and disorientation she had earlier. Leaning back as far as she could, she looked up at him and with a wry arch of her brows, commented, "I think we missed the end of the movie."

"The end. I didn't make it nearly that far. The last things I remember were the opening credits," he said, his voice husky with sleep. His eyes were a soft liquid blue, as dark as a stormy blue sky, but as warm as the morning sun in summer. "This is certainly a pleasant surprise. I thought I was having one heck of a dream, but you really did spend the night in my arms."

"Speaking of dreams, mine never did put in an appearance," she said, anxious to switch to a safer subject this one was making her feel uncomfortably overheated "It's been so long since I haven't been awakened by it that I've forgotten what it was like to sleep all night long."

"Then maybe we'll have to do this every night," he suggested. "For medicinal purposes, of course."

"That's an original line."

"This is an original situation. I haven't slept with many women, but when I have, it's never been on the couch and we didn't just *sleep*."

"Are you bragging?" she asked, her tone unreasonably edgy.

"No, I'm complaining," he answered jokingly. "I can think of several things I'd rather do with you in my arms than sleep."

His meaning was perfectly clear, and Kristi didn't know whether she should lie there, waiting for him to make a move, or if she should leap to safety now while she was still able to reason coherently.

"I have this song running through my mind," he continued, one corner of his mouth lifting in his charmingly attractive grin. "Have you ever heard 'Kiss an Angel

Good Morning'? Well, this is one Angel who would like nothing more than for you to do just that.''

As he spoke, he pulled her up until their faces were on the same level, but so close she couldn't even focus her eyes on him. As his hands burrowed deeply into the tangled strands of her hair and his lips brushed across hers, she didn't need to see him to know what was going to happen next. Her eyelids fluttered closed and her lips opened to meet his.

For the first time in a long while she felt truly alive. As she answered his kiss with a passion she hadn't realized she possessed, parts of her body were aching with a need for him that had been building since the first time he had smiled at her. He hesitated, obviously surprised at her reaction, but he too was unable to hide the hunger and desire he was feeling. The evidence of his arousal was pressing hard and demandingly against her thigh, reminding her that this was a flesh and blood man, not a dream or a memory. Unlike the others, this man would have to be dealt with in the present—and the future.

Later she would blame it on that strange weakness that seeps into a person's limbs and brain while they are asleep, making them particularly vulnerable and responsive in the morning. Perhaps it was her joy over having an uninterrupted night's sleep. This gave her hope that she was overcoming the trauma once and for all. She felt as if a giant suffocating weight had been lifted from her, leaving her lighthearted and free of spirit.

For whatever reason, when Scott stood up, gathered her into his arms and carried her to her bedroom, she didn't stop him. Her own arms were wrapped tightly around his neck and her head rested comfortably on his shoulder. This might be something she would regret later, but at this moment, it was right. She was alive. Her body needed more than food and water to survive. It also needed love. She needed to feel desired and important, and this man made her feel all of that—and more.

By mutual but unspoken consent, they began to undress each other as soon as Scott placed her on the bed and sat down next to her. The same large fingers that deftly manipulated the controls of a twenty-million-dollar plane were now fumbling over the row of buttons down the front of Kristi's blouse. When the last one was opened and he gently pushed the material off her shoulders, it took him many long seconds to unfasten the clasp of her bra.

Kristi assisted him by pulling her arms out of the blouse and tossing it to the floor, then she helped him pull his shirt over his head.

He didn't speak, but the ragged breath he drew as he looked at her said more than words. Kristi's hands slid down the muscular convex curve of his chest, following the path of black curly hair that trickled down his abdomen and disappeared into his slacks. She could feel his skin tense beneath her fingertips as she reached his belt buckle and began to unfasten it. The sound of his zipper was abnormally loud in the silence of the room, but it was followed by a tormented groan as her fingers brushed against his swollen manhood. No longer able to take it so slowly, he helped her finish undressing him, then hurried to remove the remainder of her clothing.

Taking her into his arms once again, they lay back on the pillows, their mouths meeting in a hungry, impatient kiss. As if afraid to break the spell, neither spoke. Instead they let their hands and their lips do the talking... exploring, complimenting, asking and taking as they moved over each other.

When at last neither of them could stand it any longer, Scott positioned himself over Kristi and for an instant their gazes met. She could see the intensity and the passion boiling in the blue depths of his eyes, but there was something else there that caused her to turn her head away. She didn't want to see the love that softened his look or the genuine caring that caused him to hesitate long enough for her to call this whole thing to a halt before it was too late.

It was already too late.

Kristi tried not to think about the strength of her feelings for this man. She had never gone to bed with a man she hadn't been in love with...until now. But was that true? Was this attraction she felt for him merely physical, or did it go deeper, into her emotions...into her heart?

As he moved within her, slowly at first but more rapidly as the tension built, the pure primitive pleasure of their lovemaking temporarily drove all other thoughts from her mind. All she could focus on was the feel of his hands caressing her and his breath, hot and sensual against her cheek and neck. She could tell he was holding back, waiting for her. Selfishly she longed to linger on the edge of total satisfaction, savoring a passion that was so intense it was almost painful, but she knew how difficult it was for him.

She let the rhythm of his body sweep her higher and higher until together they punched a hole in the clouds. Kristi felt rather than heard the moan that was torn from her throat as she reached the top of the climb, then began floating weightlessly back to earth. Distantly she was aware that Scott had also peaked and was clutching her to him as he joined her on the exquisite trip down.

"And I thought flying a Hornet was great!" he gasped shakily, as he struggled to slow his breathing to a more normal rate. "I've been waiting for this...for you...all my life." He shifted his weight to one side and tenderly brushed the long, silvery-blond tendrils of hair away from her flushed face as he gazed down at her. "We're good for each other."

Chapter Nine

As much as she hated to admit it, there was a grain of truth in what he said. Never had it felt so good to be cuddled in a man's arms or to fall asleep sharing the warmth of his body. It was midafternoon before they woke again. Kristi had been vaguely aware of Scott getting up to let Maverick out, but he had returned quickly and after placing a lightweight blanket over them, he had pulled her close, wrapping her in the security of his presence. They must have gone back to sleep immediately.

Lying on her side, facing away from him, she couldn't tell if he was awake or not. Afraid to move and disturb him, she remained perfectly still. She didn't have to wait long. Apparently, he too, had awakened, but he was not so hesitant to bother her. She felt his hand slide over her rib cage, along the valley of her waist, then down to rest on the curve of her hip. Light, nibbling kisses on the back of her neck and across her shoulder blades bothered her very much, but only in the most exciting way.

When she moved and he became aware she was no longer asleep, he let his hand return to the firm roundness of her breast. For several seconds as his lips and teeth continued their gentle assault on her back, his thumb and forefinger massaged her nipple until it hardened beneath his intimate caress. The urgency began to curl within her, winding ever tighter as he rolled her over and his mouth replaced his fingers on the swollen tip of her breast. His tongue circled it, tasting her sweetness before his lips tightened in a suckling motion that drew a melting response from deep within her.

She stifled a moan of pleasure as his hand slipped down to find the warmth between her legs. The feelings generated by the combination of his mouth and his fingers were almost more than Kristi could bear. She longed for him to continue, yet she was rapidly reaching the point of wanting the satisfaction only he could give her.

Her fingers combed the thickness of his black hair and her body squirmed restlessly. He transferred his adoring attention to her other nipple, then reluctantly gave it one last lingering kiss before moving his body over her and lifting his lips to hers.

"Yes," she murmured, her voice swallowed up by his mouth. "Oh, yes," she repeated as he thrust into her and began the slow, sensual rhythm of love. They both tried to stretch the moment and hold on to the ecstasy, but it soon passed beyond their control.

"Oh, Kristi," Scott breathed huskily as he plunged deeper, faster. Her body arched against his, trying to draw even closer, although they would have had to meld together to bond any tighter. She felt herself rocketing recklessly through space until the stars seem to explode around her, their flashing lights blinding her, the rush of sensation leaving her weak.

With one last stroke, he filled her with his heated passion, then collapsed breathlessly on top of her, taking care not to allow his weight to overwhelm her.

For several moments they looked at each other with a new affection, their heads on the same pillow, until their heartbeats slowed and their breath steadied.

"Are you as good in the cockpit as you are in bed?" Kristi asked wryly, her eyes sparkling with humor and happiness.

"Better," he responded immodestly, his rakish grin flashing against the golden tan of his skin.

"If that's true, then maybe I have no reason to worry about your safety. You seem to be able to handle yourself very well," she teased.

"The only thing you have to worry about is my health," he laughed. "Because if I don't get some food soon, I'll be too weak to make love to you again...which would be tragic. Although I can't think of a better place to waste away than lying here with you in my arms."

"Just like a man. Always thinking of his stomach."

He pushed himself up until he was on his hands and knees above her, effectively fencing her in. "I think there were a couple of things besides my stomach I thought about today. Would you like me to point them out to you one more time?" As he spoke he leaned down and planted tender kisses on her breasts, roving up a crooked path along her neck, halting when his lips reached the fullness of her willing mouth.

Briefly their lips clung together, the spark within them leaping quickly back to life. But before it could burst into a full-blown flame, Kristi pushed him away.

"I thought you said you were too weak."

"I'm feeling stronger by the second," he said, playfully nuzzling her ear.

Kristi refused to let herself be tempted and sat up, pulling the blanket around her. "The one trait all career military men have in common is that they never know when to quit. I, for one, cannot live on love alone and I would like to register my vote for breakfast." She cast a curious glance at the clock radio next to the bed and amended, "Make that dinner."

"Good, because you owe me a dinner. Remember our bet?"

"Andrea's cousin," Kristi confirmed. "I'm sure she was glad to have you all to herself after I left the party last Saturday."

"She never *had* me for a minute," he explained. "You see, I've had this problem for the last week and a half. The only woman I've noticed or been able to think about is here in this room with me now."

His words buoyed Kristi's still fragile self-confidence. She had almost reached the bathroom door when she paused and added a final comment to him over her shoulder. "Poor LouAnn. If she knew what she was missing, she would be so very sorry." With a saucy toss of her head and a flirtatious smile, Kristi dropped the blanket to the floor and walked naked into the bathroom, firmly closing the door behind her.

They had to stop by Scott's house so he could change clothes and leave Maverick there. Scott unlocked the door and Maverick pushed his way in first, anxious to check out his territory to see if anything had been disturbed during his absence. Scott held the door open for Kristi, then followed her into the living room.

"Make yourself at home. It won't take me long," he said, then gave her one of his charming crooked grins. "Unless you'd like to come into my bedroom and help me."

She rolled her eyes and shooed him away. When she was alone, she circled the room, once again over-whelmed by the extensive collection of Blue Angels-related objects. The room itself was decorated with the touches of midnight-blue color of the planes. The walls were painted a pale dove gray, which provided a perfect backdrop for the navy-blue carpet, draperies, couch and recliner. A couple of other chairs were upholstered in a blue and gray stripe that tied it all together.

Everywhere there were not too subtle reminders that Scott's life was totally centered on the Navy and its demonstration squad of sleek, fast F/A-18 Hornets. On the mantle, the bookshelves, the television set and every end table stood aviation mementos.

Even his car, which she had seen for the first time a few minutes ago, was a high performance, sporty Porsche whose metallic paint exactly matched the Blues' team colors. It was proof more positive than words of just how deeply his devotion to flying with the Blue Angels went.

She suspected this was another reason why he had never married. He was totally in love with his career.

"I'm surprised your underwear isn't blue," she mused aloud.

"What?" he called from the bathroom where he had just stepped out of the shower.

"Nothing," she replied loudly. She noticed a blinking light on his answering machine and wandered over to investigate. "You've got several calls on your machine."

He walked into the room, dressed in tan slacks and a pale yellow dress shirt. He tossed his shoes and socks onto the couch and continued rubbing his wet hair with a fluffy towel, which was, of course, dark blue.

"Go ahead and punch the big button in the middle," he instructed as he dropped the towel and sat down so he could pull on his socks.

Kristi wasn't sure she wanted to hear the messages, especially if they were from a string of women, calling

Scott while he had been out of town and leaving personal remarks and pleas to get in touch with them soon. But she obeyed, her curiosity about his other acquaintances overcoming her reservations.

Sure enough, the first two were from women, but Scott didn't even look up, much less write down their phone numbers. The third was from Randy, but the only message he left was that he would call back. The next one was him again, but this time he said, "Hey man, where've you been? I tried to reach you at your mother's, but she said you left yesterday. Don't forget they're making the announcements about the new squad today at 1400 hours. The formal banquet is set for next Tuesday. And don't forget the party tomorrow afternoon. Yes for Kristi. No for Maverick. Sheila is still searching for a lover, and handsome as Maverick is, we'd rather not have to hose them down. But if you show up alone, you can count on a lot of flack. Everyone thought Kristi was much too good for you, but if she's desperate enough to date you, then you'd better not let her get away. Good luck on making commander again. Bye."

Scott glanced at his watch and exclaimed, "It's after seventeen hundred . . . er, five o'clock. I can't believe I forgot the announcement was today!" He looked up at Kristi and winked. "I can't imagine what distracted me so much that I wouldn't remember something so important."

Kristi was momentarily cheered, but as she heard the final message, her spirits fell. She hadn't realized how much she had been hoping, even counting on Scott's exclusion from the squad. Surely his age would not be an asset, as well as the fact he had been on the squad for the last four years, which was much longer than normal. Since he had been squad commander for the last two years, she had been convinced they would retire him, replacing him with someone younger and faster.

Perversely, part of her instantly rose to Scott's defense; she knew that although someone might have a few years on him, she was certain Scott was an excellent leader. Even though she had never seen him fly, she was also intuitively positive he was a top-notch pilot. He had the cocky, self-assured personality that seemed to go with the very best pilots. They, more than anyone in any other career, never had to have a second's doubt about their own ability, or it could prove fatal. It was, of course, this last possibility that scared the wits out of Kristi.

The next caller didn't identify himself, but Kristi could tell by the way Scott suddenly tensed, giving this message his undivided attention, that this was indeed his commanding officer. As the man named the two new pilots, then began listing the old squad members with their new team positions, Kristi realized she was holding her breath. The man could so easily announce someone else's name in the number one position. She could see how anxious Scott was and her heart was torn. He so obviously wanted to be commander that she knew his disappointment would be staggering. She wanted him to be happy, but she wanted him to stay alive.

"And as flight leader in plane number one, I'm pleased to tell you that for the third year in a row you've been selected by your fellow Blues and the base officers to serve as commander. You've done a fine job and we know you'll continue to provide solid leadership. We'll see you at the dinner Tuesday night."

A sigh of relief escaped from Scott's throat and Kristi realized she, too, had been holding her breath.

"Congratulations, Commander," she said with forced cheerfulness, hoping her own disappointment wasn't too evident.

He leaped up and lifted her into his arms, happily swinging her around. "Let's go celebrate," he said, his smile stretching all the way across his face. "This old dude isn't ready to hang up his wings yet."

The announcement put a definite pall on the evening as far as Kristi was concerned. But for Scott's sake, she put up enough of a front so as not to ruin the excitement for him.

The seafood restaurant he chose was located on a pier built out over the Gulf. Kristi and Scott were seated at a table near one of the large plate glass windows that provided a beautiful view. The food was excellent, but it was wasted on Kristi's depressed taste buds. Luckily, Scott was so pumped up he didn't seem to notice her withdrawal and carried most of the weight of the conversation alone. In a burst of goodwill, he even picked up the check in spite of the fact that she had fully intended to pay for their meal to settle her bet.

But Scott had noticed her sudden change of mood. He kept up a steady banter simply to fill the silence. He could see she was trying to make it through the evening without actually having to talk about his flying, but it was obviously weighing heavily on her mind. What worried Scott most was that the tenuous threads of affection that had begun to bind them together might snap under the pressure. But in this instance knowing the problem didn't help, because he didn't have the solution.

"How's your foot?" he asked later as they were leaving the restaurant.

She glanced down at it as if it were the furthest thing from her mind. "Oh, it's fine. Your mother was right.

You would have made a great doctor. It hasn't hurt since you fixed it."

"Good, then you won't have any excuse for not wanting to go dancing with me."

"Now? But I don't..."

"When was the last time you went dancing?" he interrupted, not wanting to give her a chance to end the evening on a downbeat. "It's good exercise, you know. Besides, I'll bet you and I would make quite a team on the dance floor. Come on. Let's show this town how to move."

They had walked across the parking lot and stopped at the car before she shrugged and said, "I haven't been dancing in years. I guess it would be fun."

Scott noted her lack of enthusiasm, but was encouraged that she had accepted. Apparently she wasn't writing off their budding relationship just yet.

They found a neat looking club whose sign promised that only the best oldies were being played. Inside in the semidarkness, Scott led Kristi to the dance floor and took her into his arms. For the next two hours they whirled through the fifties, rocked through the sixties and even tried to keep up with a Texas two-step. Scott had been right in his prediction; their bodies moved in perfect harmony, as if they had been dancing together forever. They went so far as to attempt a couple of dips and spins, dimly conscious of the fact they were gathering an audience. But first and foremost they were aware of each other.

The later it grew, the slower the music and the more sensuous the movements became. Kristi's head was resting on his shoulder, her arms were looped around his neck and his around her waist, eliminating any extra space between them as they danced to a song whose words were much more meaningful now than they had ever been in their youth. As the Vogues sang the last few stanzas of "You Are My Special Angel," Kristi looked up at Scott and whispered, "Let's go home."

"Your home or mine?"

"It doesn't matter. I just want to be with you tonight ... if that's okay with you."

Her voice was so vulnerable and held so much pain that he wouldn't have been able to turn her away even if he had wanted to, which he definitely did not. His arm tightened around her shoulder and he hugged her almost fiercely as they walked toward the door. "Are you kidding? I'd ask you to move in with me tomorrow if I thought you'd consider it."

She shook her head, sending a swirl of pale blond hair tumbling against her cheeks. "Let's take it one day at a time. I'm not sure how much of this I can handle." In the dim light of the dashboard and the street lamps, he could see she was studying him seriously, a determined frown crinkling her forehead. "I don't know why we're letting this go any further. Falling in love is absolutely out of the question. But you were right about us being good for each other. I need you right now, and I think you need me. But when it's time for me to go, I have to feel free to leave without any remorse. Do you understand what I mean?"

He understood, but didn't agree. Already he knew he would not be able to let her go quietly.

Later as she lay in his arms, he listened to the slow, steady cadence of her breathing as she slept and hoped she would be able to make it through the night, undisturbed by the nightmare. Somehow by concentrating on helping her overcome her problem, it was helping him with his own. Scott was certain that if Kristi hadn't come into his life when she did, he would have been even more devastated by the news about Kahuna. Without meaning to, she had provided enough of a diversion to cushion the blow, and, he suspected, his presence had done much the same thing for her.

Perhaps she was right and they would never have a permanent relationship with each other. Maybe he could not be objective about his feelings for her, because their situation was not ordinary. As time went on, and she worked through her problems and he overcame his, possibly he would be able to see there was nothing substantial between them on which to build a future. But right now, feeling the warmth of her body against his, with her fresh, feminine fragrance filling his nostrils and her soft blond hair fanned out over his shoulder, he couldn't believe he would ever be able to get this woman out of his heart.

Why did he have such rotten luck when it came to choosing women to fall in love with? First Barbara, and now Kristi. They were as different as night and day, but neither of them wanted him as a husband. Maybe he was just meant to be a bachelor. It could be an occupational hazard of sorts. On one hand, he had women throwing themselves at his feet, vying for his attention. But when it came to marriage, the women he was attracted to weren't the least bit interested.

Kristi stirred, snuggling even closer to him. Scott buried his face in the silken mass of her hair and sighed. She had the power to touch his emotions, to make him laugh—and cry. He wanted her to stay forever. But if all she would give him was a few weeks of her life, then, much as it would hurt later, he would take it. He wouldn't give up, however. As long as he was convinced he and

Kristi were perfect for each other, he would try to find a solution they both could live with.

THEY WERE THE LAST ONES to arrive at Randy and Donna's party the next day. Even though Kristi was still not comfortable with the situation between Scott and herself, she refused to feel guilty about not breaking it off right now. She was, after all, being totally honest with him about their future together...or lack of one. When their time was up, he would not be able to say she had led him on—assuming he even cared. There was also the possibility he would tire of her and be glad she was gone.

Kristi was greeted warmly by her hostess and introduced to the new squad members and their wives or dates, then taken on a tour of the property. Donna and Randy had a large sprawling ranch house surrounded by five fenced acres, on which they kept a couple of horses, some chickens and an adorable baby pig.

"His name is Marco Porko," Donna said as the two women bent down to pet the chubby little animal.

"I always thought pigs stank, but he doesn't smell bad at all," Kristi commented as she gingerly touched the almost hairless pink skin. Marco grunted his approval, closing his eyes in obvious delight when she scratched behind his ears.

"They don't smell any worse than any other animal, as long as their pen is kept clean. They like to lie in mud on a hot day to cool themselves off, and it's usually the mud that sours and stinks."

When they began walking away, Marco trotted along behind them, close at their heels, his little ears flapping up and down and his curly tail pointing straight up.

The men had set up a volleyball net, and the kids were batting the ball back and forth while their dads sat on the porch and talked. Kristi could well imagine the subject they were discussing, especially when one of them began demonstrating flight maneuvers, using his hand as an airplane. What was it about flying that made otherwise sane men so obsessed and single-minded? Whether they were career aviators or hobbyists, their enthusiasm raged strong and overpowering. But military pilots were the worst of the breed.

"Hey, don't look now," Scott called, jumping to his feet and striding toward Kristi as soon as he saw her, "but there's a strange-looking dog following you around." He turned to Randy and teased, "This isn't that full-blooded Doberman you guys are so protective of, is it? She leaves a lot to be desired in the beauty department. My dog wouldn't look twice at a porker like that, unless he was ready for lunch."

"Just one more insult and I'll let Sheila out of the garage and sic her on you," Donna threatened good-naturedly.

"Maybe this is our lunch," Zipper chimed in, bending down and hoisting the hefty pig into his arms. Immediately Marco set up such a loud squeal that everyone put their hands over their ears. "Quick, give me an apple and show me where the barbecue pit is."

Donna and Kristi rushed to the pig's defense and Zipper put him down again. The kids deserted their volleyball game for the much more interesting matter of playing with the little pig.

"With all those hands scratching him, he's in hog heaven," Donna commented. "I'd better finish the meal before the guys get any more crazy ideas and start chasing down the chickens."

"I'll help," Kristi offered, following Donna into the kitchen. "You'll have to tell me what you want me to do, and keep it simple. Scott will attest that cooking is not one of my accomplishments. Thank goodness these are not the good old days, when a woman's worth was measured by her culinary skills.''

''You and Scott seem to be getting along great.''

Although Donna's remark was casual, Kristi knew it was a subtle form of interrogation. Everyone here was like one big family, so it was just natural that they would try to protect each other and be interested in each other's lives.

''He's a very special man,'' Kristi agreed without volunteering any information.

''I've never seen him so crazy about a woman,'' Donna persisted, seemingly unaware of Kristi's reluctance to discuss their private situation. ''Do you think there's a chance you might stick around longer than you originally planned?''

''I don't know what I'm going to do. The airline gave me a six-month leave of absence, and I had another thirty days of vacation and sick leave accumulated. That means I have to decide whether or not I'm going to resume flying before the end of December. After that, I have to either accept an office job or change careers.''

''I'll bet Scott will come up with another solution.''

''Another solution for what?'' Scott's voice interrupted the conversation and both women jumped, startled by his unexpected presence.

Instantly Kristi's gaze met Donna's, silently asking her not to repeat her words. Donna looked puzzled, but apparently decided to abide by Kristi's wish and said, ''Another solution for helping the new guys learn the program for the show.''

''Yes, I've got to get back into the routine myself next week. I haven't sat in a cockpit since our last performance of the season, two weeks ago.'' He walked up behind Kristi and wrapped his arms around her waist. "I've been too busy with other things,'' he admitted, nuzzling her neck, oblivious to Donna's amusement.

Again Kristi and Donna exchanged looks, with Donna's arched eyebrows indicating "I told you so.'' Kristi, too, was puzzled because Scott implied he had given up his flying to spend time with her. She would never expect that of him. In fact, no matter how she truly felt about the danger, she would never dream of asking him to give up the Blues. Even if he would, which she didn't believe he would consider, there would always be that sacrifice hanging over them.

It was a no-win situation and she knew better than to ask him to choose. The simpler solution would be not to let their romance advance that far. Comforting each other and even enjoying themselves was one thing, but reaching the point where they felt they had to make a permanent decision was something to be avoided.

She should pack up tonight and drive back to Denver. Or if she wasn't feeling up to Denver, she could always head for Seattle. Her mother had a spare room and was sure to welcome home her daughter with open arms.

But the arms wrapped tightly around her now were holding her firmly in Florida. As much as she hated to admit it, she didn't want to leave him just yet. It was selfish, she knew. But he kept the dreams away and made her feel secure. The only fear she felt when he was around was for his safety. Surely it wouldn't hurt if she stayed a little longer? After Christmas they would both be leaving, he for winter training in El Centro, California, and she for Denver. If she couldn't force herself to fly again, Worldwide's corporate offices were in Denver and they had already offered her a position there.

"You're slowing down our progress," Donna chided Scott. "Either grab a knife and chop up some lettuce or go back outside so we can finish."

"Hurry," he whispered in Kristi's ear. "I miss you." Then with a jaunty wave in Donna's direction, he left the kitchen before they put him to work.

Donna thoughtfully didn't say anything more about Scott. Several of the other women entered the room and soon the meal was ready to be served. The party progressed much as the other one had, with everyone working off the meal on the volleyball court. Randy saddled the horses and the kids took turns riding around the pasture while Zipper and one of the new guys taught Marco how to shake hands, using the dinner scraps as a reward.

As Kristi and Scott drove home late that evening, she felt more like her old self than she had in months. In spite of all the things that were weighing heavily on her mind, she had thoroughly enjoyed herself at the party. The laughter and the comradery had lifted her spirits. Scott would not be the only person she would miss when she left Florida.

Over the next few days, she and Scott fell into a comfortable pattern. Sunday they drove into Pensacola and attended church services, then bought groceries. Each night they put together an evening meal or called out for pizza. And the evenings were wonderful, companionable times when they would play cards, watch television, read or talk. They did a lot of talking. Oddly enough, the more they said, the more they seemed to have left to say. They were like two old friends who had a lot of catching up to do.

The only time they were not together was in the morning, when Scott rose early and went to the base. Kristi didn't ask, but she knew he was back at the controls, streaking through the skies in a F/A-18 trainer jet. While he was away, she avoided going outside for fear she would see him. And every time she heard the roar of a jet's engines as it passed overhead, she shuddered.

Tuesday morning she escaped from the house, hoping to avoid the constant reminders that Scott was up there somewhere. She needed an extraspecial dress for the dinner that night, because she hadn't brought anything but casual clothes with her, so she drove to the mall. She spent several hours walking from store to store, trying on dress after dress until she found one she liked, then realized what she was really doing was everything possible to keep her mind off Scott. When she finally drove home with a beautiful new dress hanging from the hook in the back of the car, the thought occurred to her that if it was so painful now, when he was flying straight solo, how was she going to feel when he was doing dangerous stunts with five other planes flying in his pocket?

She wasn't expecting Scott to pick her up until six-thirty, so she took her time getting ready. After spending two weeks in shorts, slacks and sunsuits, it felt odd to pull on panty hose and step into high heels.

Kristi stood in front of a full-length mirror and studied her reflection critically. This might be the only time Scott would ever see her dressed to the nines, and she wanted to make a lasting impression. The cherry-red dress brought out the rosy color in her cheeks. When the weather had been nice during the first week of her stay, her skin had taken on a healthy lightly tanned glow. The full skirt swirled around her long, slender legs and the fitted bodice showed her figure to advantage. She had pinned up her blond hair in a loose, curly style and taken extra care with her makeup.

The doorbell rang and she hurried to answer it. As she reached for the knob she realized her palms were perspiring. She felt more nervous about this date than she could remember feeling since she was a teenager. Considering all she and Scott had already gone through together, that was really ridiculous.

Assuming she would calm down as soon as she saw Scott's familiar grin, she opened the door eagerly. But the sight of him standing there, wearing his full dress uniform, his hat tucked neatly under his arm, hit her like a brick in the stomach and left her quite breathless. Of course, she should have expected him to be dressed according to military regulations, but somehow seeing him like this made it all seem so real. When he had worn jeans or shorts, she had been able to set aside the fact that he was a career Navy man.

Her heart leaped into her throat. Never had he looked more handsome and appealing. There must be something in her hormones that made her feel this incredible attraction for a man in uniform. At this moment she had never wanted him more... or wanted him less.

Memories of her father flashed through her mind, followed quickly by Rick and other pilots she had flown with at Worldwide. To her the uniform stood on the one hand for strength and security and danger and death on the other. All her life she had been surrounded by men in uniform, many of whom had flown off to Vietnam and never come back. Those men hadn't asked for their fate, but had obeyed the laws of their country and their conscience. Scott, however, had chosen his path; he had already lived a dangerous life and survived. He was betting against the odds, and sooner or later it would catch up with him.

There was no doubt in Kristi's mind that his days were numbered. She would be crazy to stick around long enough to see him buried in this same uniform. Absolutely crazy.

Chapter Ten

"Aren't you going to invite me in? I realize I look a little different than when I'm wearing jogging shorts, but it's me, honestly." Scott looked down at himself, as if trying to see what had caused the stricken expression on her face. His tie was straight, his zipper zipped, and his buttons were buttoned properly.

"I—I'm sorry. Come on in," she sputtered, obviously rattled.

A knowing look softened his eyes as he realized what had shaken her. She was reacting as if she had seen a ghost, which was, in her case, almost true. Perhaps the uniform reminded her of Rick or her father, and that saddened him for two reasons. One, because he truly sympathized with her loss, particularly that of her father; Scott, too, had experienced the death of a parent. But the second reason hurt him more directly. The very fact that Kristi could still get so upset by a reminder of Rick made Scott feel both angry and helpless. What would it take to get that man out of her heart?

Scott had been certain that after the last few days she had come to care for him much more than she would admit, or perhaps even realized. And he had hoped her new happiness would permanently replace the unpleasant memories, gradually making him a more and more important part of her life.

But if the very sight of a uniform could set off such an emotional response, apparently Scott had not had much of an effect on her. Suddenly the evening lost a bit of the excitement that had built within him as he dressed. He had been looking forward to taking Kristi on a *real* date and showing her off to everyone at the base.

"It's the uniform, isn't it?" he heard himself asking, even though he already knew the answer.

"Yes," she admitted. "I know I should have been prepared, but it startled me. As soon as I saw you standing there, all the old fears came rushing back."

"I'm sorry."

"No, I'm the one who's sorry. It's just that you look so different. I've gotten used to seeing you dressed like a normal person."

"This is normal. Well, not exactly everyday normal, because we usually wear flight suits when we are flying, even at shows. But as an Air Force brat, you should be used to seeing uniforms."

"I am. But I had planned on avoiding them the rest of my life."

He followed her into the living room, where she had left her coat and purse. Laying his hat on the end table, he held her coat for her as she slipped her arms into the sleeves, then swung her around so that she was facing him.

"Fortunately, I have no adverse feelings for red dresses," he said, curling his index finger under her chin and lifting her face until their eyes met. "Kristi, you look absolutely fantastic tonight. I'll have to fight the other men off just so I'll get to sit next to you at dinner."

"You look pretty gorgeous yourself. I think you'll have more than your share of women drooling on all those bright brass buttons."

"I've said it before and I'll say it again. You and I make a great pair." He said it lightly, but he was dead serious. He kept reminding himself he had to be patient with her, give her as much space and time as she needed. But how it hurt to think she might never let him into her life!

Once at the mess hall where the dinner was being catered, the sea of navy-blue uniforms that surrounded her didn't bother her. It was then she realized that it wasn't all men in uniform that frightened her, or even uniforms in general. It was simply Scott who caused her heart to quake within her chest. And it wasn't a fear *of* him, but a fear *for* him.

After the meal the waiters wheeled in a huge cake that was iced with a picture of all six Blue Angels flying in a delta formation, with OVER THE TOP written above and the names of the departing members below. As commander of last year's squadron, Scott had the honor of cutting the cake. The waiter handed him a large knife, but before he could touch the blade to the creamy blue icing, Randy stepped forward.

"This is a military ceremony. Let's do it right!" he exclaimed, handing Scott a long, slender sword.

With all the pomp and skill of a seventeenth-century duelist, Scott brandished the saber and sliced through the entire width of the cake with one deft swipe while everyone cheered. By the time he had reduced the cake to small squares, things had gotten a little messy. But Scott retained his dignity through it all, even though he was obviously enjoying himself. As the waiters hurried in to lift the pieces onto dessert plates, Scott made a great show of wiping the blade clean with a towel.

"Now that I have succeeded with this most difficult of tasks, as a loyal knight of the realm, I seek another quest to challenge my mighty sword," he proclaimed with a courtly bow. "No deed is too great, no foe too fearsome. Has anyone a dragon that needs to be slain? A chalice to be rescued? A maiden to be kissed?"

"Stick it . . . back onto the table, Lancelot, before you cut yourself." Randy laughed. "Things are pretty slow this time of year, but you can rest assured. If any dragons should somehow get past the guard gate and onto the base, you will be the first person we call."

"Darn," Scott grumbled, pretending to be extremely disappointed. "And I was just getting warmed up to the role of quixotic defender of all that is good and pure. Actually, I think the military forces of the world should go back to fighting with swords. It's so much more civilized when you can face your opponent, rather than blast him all to hell with a missile shot from twenty miles out at sea."

"You can bring that up at the next strategy meeting," Zipper suggested. "I'm sure every branch of the armed forces will be thrilled with your idea."

"Just think of the money it would save taxpayers," Kristi added, getting into the spirit of the conversation. "Every man would be issued a $150 sword and we could scrap all the multimillion dollar planes and tanks."

"And if they shopped the Buyers Club on television, they could catch them on special for $99.95, if they could call in enough orders before the bell rings," Donna chimed in.

"Okay, I give up," Scott said, carefully laying the saber on the table. "You people have no romance in your souls."

"Look who's talking," Zipper exclaimed with good humor. "Mr. Lonely Heart has gone romantic. And we owe it all to this fair maiden." He indicated Kristi and everyone clapped. "We didn't think the old Saint had a heart until you came along."

Scott took all the ribbing in stride, flashing Kristi an apologetic smile and shrugging his broad shoulders as if to say he had no control over these crazy guys. But the fact that he didn't refute their statements said more than any words he could have spoken. Obviously there must be some truth in their claims, and Kristi felt as if she had been given an honor of some sort. The tender warmth in his eyes as he looked at her made her feel incredibly special, as if he had singled her out from all the women in the world.

Suddenly she realized it didn't matter if he was wearing a uniform with gold wings over his pocket or nothing at all. She had done the craziest, most ridiculous, stupid thing of her life. She had somehow managed to let her defenses drop just far enough to fall in love ... with a pilot ... even worse, with a military stunt pilot. How could she have been so careless? And what was she going to do about it?

The question dominated her thoughts for the rest of the evening. As usual, Scott seemed to have a sixth sense and noticed immediately how distracted she had become. But she couldn't tell him. This was something she would have to work out for herself before she let him know ... *if* she ever let him know. And at this point she didn't know what good could come of it.

She could admit to herself that it would hurt when she left. But it would hurt even more if she stayed, changed her whole life-style to be with him, only to see his plane explode from a midair collision or crash to the ground, nose first. Since there was little danger of that happening until January, when the training season would begin, she felt relatively safe. She might have let herself fall in love with him, but she wouldn't be foolish enough to stick around for his funeral. All the same, they could still have one more month together before she left. One more glorious, wonderful month of breakfast in bed and dinner in front of the fireplace, of walking on the beach and making love in the afternoon. During the next thirty days she would have to save up enough happy memories to last the rest of her life.

KRISTI DISCOVERED that December in Florida was not like December in Denver. One day it would be seventy-five degrees and the next, she would have to wear a coat to walk to the mailbox at the end of the driveway. The winds off the Gulf could be unseasonably warm, but when they switched and howled from the north, it would be bitter cold.

She talked to her mother a couple of times each week and was able to carry on normal conversations with several of her friends from work, something she hadn't been able to manage before Scott had brought her back to life. Scott's friends dropped in regularly or would invite him and Kristi over for dinner or an evening of enthusiastic games of Pictionary or bridge. It was a healthy, healing time for her and Scott made it all the more pleasant and easy by not pressing her for a commitment, even though she sensed he would like to discuss their future.

As the crash moved further and further into the background, she was even able to speak with Diane's sister on the phone without breaking down in tears. Oddly enough, it seemed her friend's family had been able to handle Diane's loss better than Kristi. But then, they didn't have to live with the guilt. Kristi wondered if they knew the truth, but she couldn't summon enough courage to broach the subject. What good would it do now? It was too late.

This had been the one subject she had never been able to discuss with Scott. What would he think of her if he knew? How would he react if he knew she was personally responsible for her best friend's death and—to a lesser extent—Rick's? Would she lose his respect? His love?

Not willing to lose his friendship and companionship just yet, she pushed those memories to the back of her mind, along with all the other things she would rather not deal with right now. She was so desperate not to let him find out that she went along with his plans for Christmas.

She hadn't planned to do anything to celebrate that holiday. All the Christmases in her past had been cheerful, wonderful days, filled with family and friends, good food, presents—and happiness. After the crash, she had believed it would be somehow disloyal to Rick and Diane to enjoy Christmas this year.

But Scott had convinced her that Christmas was a celebration for the living. After all, it was all about the birth of a very special child.

Kristi found Scott's enthusiasm contagious. She decided not to put up any decorations at the house where she was staying, especially since she was now spending most of her time at Scott's. On the first weekend in December, they had gone to a lot and picked out a tree. Kristi had wanted to wait another week, but Scott insisted all the good ones would be gone by then. Besides, he had pointed out, the tree would last longer if it was standing in a container of water rather than outdoors in the sun.

It had been logical, but Kristi could tell by the excited twinkle in his eyes that it was an adult excuse to give in to an almost childlike enthusiasm for the holiday. As they carried the sticky Scotch pine up the flight of stairs leading to his front door, she admitted that she, too, was having a wonderful time.

They spent an entire evening stringing multicolored lights around the tree's full body, placing a golden star on the top spike, and hanging ornaments on the dark green branches. With amusement and not too much surprise, Kristi noted there were several small airplanes among the ornaments. Some were whimsical in design, made of wire, hardened dough or papier-mâché; others were quite attractive, created out of porcelain or blown glass. After sprinkling the tree with icicles—and managing to get more on themselves and the floor than the tree—Kristi and Scott stood back and admired their handiwork.

Although a little too fat and a tiny bit crooked, in their eyes it was a beautiful tree, decorated with love and laughter. Maverick circled it, studying it with great interest, but a sharp reminder from his master made him remember his manners and return to his favorite sleeping spot in front of the hearth.

As Kristi and Scott sat on the floor, cuddled in each other's arms, sharing a bowl of popcorn and listening to carols on the stereo, Kristi knew this would be a Christmas she would never forget. Perhaps it was especially precious because she had expected it to be so awful. Or maybe it was because she was sharing it with a man like Scott. He had a way of making even the simplest things, such as sitting on the deck looking at the stars, or making grilled cheese sandwiches at midnight, interesting and fun.

"You hair looks like spun silver in this light," Scott commented to Kristi.

He had turned off the lamps, so that the only illumination was from the flickering fire in the fireplace and the tree lights that blinked their colors with merry abandon.

"That's probably because of all the icicles you threw in it." She laughed and automatically reached up to smooth back the stray strands that fell straight to her shoulders, then curled under in a modified pageboy.

Picking a long sparkling piece of tinsel from the top of her head, he replied, "Maybe if we add a few ornaments and a star, you'll create a new fad."

"You are not without decorations yourself," she countered, plucking a few icicles from his shoulder.

"You look better in them than I do. In fact, you look better in anything...or nothing." His voice had dropped to a lower octave, lending a tone of sensuality to his words. "I can't wait to see you in a bikini, although I'll probably go crazy if some other guy should look at you."

Kristi didn't want to point out to him that it wasn't likely she would be wearing a bikini anytime soon; she would be long gone by the time it was warm enough for swimming. It was a subject they both skirted, even though he had begun making casual references to what they could do together in the summer.

He had shown her his speedboat, its fiberglass hull a familiar metallic dark blue. He had shown her pictures of him and his friends para-sailing or skiing behind it, both of which looked extremely dangerous. Kristi knew how to ski on snow, but had never tried it on water, and certainly not on one ski or speeding off tall ramps. Before the crash had made her cautious, she would have been adventurous enough to try it. But since she had learned the value of life and the abrupt finality of death, she no longer thought a little pleasure was worth so great a risk.

Instead she said, "I'm too old for bikinis. No one would even glance at a thirty-two-year-old body when there are so many twenty-two-year-old ones bouncing around."

"Are we fishing for compliments?" he teased. "Haven't I told you over and over how absolutely gorgeous I think your body is? It may be thirty-two, but it's aged well, like fine wine or antique furniture." He dodged a playfully thrown pillow and added suggestively, "Maybe I could show you again how very nicely all the parts still work, in spite of their *advanced* age."

The room was filled with the heavy woodsy smell of the tree and the lights still twinkled, casting their red, blue and yellow colors on two thirty-plus-year-old bodies practicing the ageless art of love.

JUST AS SHE SETTLED into a comfortable routine, her peace was shattered. One morning as she puttered around the house, doing a little housework and catching up on her laundry, the doorbell rang.

Maverick had already run to the door and was waiting for Kristi to open it and see who the visitor was. She knew it couldn't be Scott. For one thing, he had a key to her house and for another, Maverick's bark would have had a tone of welcome rather than alarm.

Kristi's hands shook as she took the large envelope from the Federal Express delivery man. A glance at the sender's name and address told her this was what she had been waiting for with great anxiety. Although she desperately wanted to know what was inside, she couldn't work up enough courage to open it.

Scott found her sitting on the deck, moodily staring out to sea when he arrived several hours later. Maverick was lying at her feet, watching her with worried eyes as if he sensed something was wrong, but didn't know how to help her other than by lending his silent moral support.

It was windy and even though the temperature had hovered around sixty-five all day, it felt colder. She sat on a chaise lounge, her partially bare arms exposed to the elements. When she didn't appear to notice he had joined her, Scott reached out to touch her shoulder and was concerned at the chill he felt beneath his fingers.

Kristi jumped, obviously so deep in thought she hadn't heard him open the patio door. "Oh...hi," she said, looking up and giving him a distracted smile. "Is it that late already? I haven't even put anything out to thaw for dinner."

"That's okay," he reassured her and dropped a kiss onto her upturned lips. But her lack of response confirmed his suspicion that something was seriously wrong. "What's the matter, Kristi? Did something happen? Did your mother call? Did you get bad news?"

She sighed and handed him the envelope that had been lying on her lap, held down by her clenched fists. "Worldwide has released the preliminary report about the cause of the crash. A messenger brought my copy this morning."

"So what does it say? Are they blaming it on pilot error or did they find it was a mechanical problem?"

"I don't know. I haven't been able to open it. I've been expecting it for months, but once I actually held it in my hand, it scared me to death. The truth is very important to me, but I'm afraid I won't be able to accept it. And I'm sure there will be pictures, and details that might hurt too much to know," she cried, burying her face in her hands.

Scott felt his heart wrench at the sight of her tears. She had been growing stronger during the last few weeks, but obviously still had a long way to go. If she could spend an entire afternoon staring at a sealed envelope and not gather enough courage to check its contents, her emotional stability must still need a little more reinforcement. Perhaps the report *would* be as bad as she anticipated, though she would never know unless she faced her worst fears.

But not out on the deck in the cold. He leaned over, scooped her slender body into his arms and carried her into the living room. Setting her on the couch, he wiped the tears from her cheeks with his thumbs. "It's not going to do anyone any good if you die of pneumonia. Sit here while I get a blanket and something hot for you to drink. Then I'll read through the report and we can talk about it."

He brought a blanket from the bedroom and gently tucked it around her, then went into the kitchen. Not wanting to leave her long enough to make a pot of coffee, he heated water in the microwave and stirred in some instant cocoa mix. Returning to the living room, he handed her the mug and sat down on the couch beside her.

"Here, drink this," he said as he picked up the envelope, slipped his finger under the flap and ripped it open.

She nodded and obediently sipped the warm drink. Satisfied that she had recovered her composure, he began to inspect the papers inside. Several minutes passed as he turned the pages, reading the text and studying the diagrams and photographs while she watched him, trying to interpret his reactions from the expression on his face.

Finally he looked up and said, "This report is only the beginning. There's not enough here to establish an absolute cause, only a probable one. All the evidence has not been examined yet and something else may turn up, but at this point they have reason to believe that something went wrong with the hydraulic system."

"Then it wasn't pilot error?" she asked.

"It doesn't look like it. In fact, the N.T.S.B. made a comment in here that if it actually was the hydraulic system, the pilot and first officer did a masterful job of getting the plane onto the ground at all. It was pure rotten luck that they swerved off into that tank."

Kristi breathed a visible sigh of relief. "Really?"

"Really. If you would have read it earlier, you could have saved yourself hours of heartache."

"Uh-oh. I think I'm about to be scolded."

"You bet you are," he replied, gently but firmly. "Kristi, you've got to get over this. You're letting your fears control your life and, in this case, your imagination is your worst enemy. If you would stand up and face the truth, you might be surprised to find it's not as bad as you think. And even if it is, it will only hurt for a little while. It's like taking off a Band-Aid. If you pull it off a little bit at a time, it keeps on hurting, but if you just grab it and rip it off, it'll hurt for a second or two, then it'll be over."

Kristi wrinkled her nose at the choice of illustration, but didn't argue with him. "Okay, let me see it," she said, holding out her hand for the report. Taking it gingerly, she began flipping through the text and hesitantly looking at the photographs. "It looks pretty bad. How can they possibly determine a cause from this pile of rubble?''

"I'd say from the extent of the damage done to the plane itself by the explosion and fire, the inspectors had a difficult time sifting through that mess and identifying pieces. But they have the digital flight data recorder, which continuously tracks the plane's performance by computer, and, of course, there is the cockpit voice recorder, or black box as it is better known. From those two items alone they'll be able to compile a lot of important data.''

"You seem to know a lot about the technical aspect of crashes,'' she commented, looking at him curiously. "Surely this isn't something you learn with the Blues?''

"No, but I have learned it through the Navy. They've been encouraging me to train to be their official tin kicker.''

"Tin kicker?'' she echoed.

"That's someone who examines a crash site as soon as possible after the accident, sifts through the pieces and works up a preliminary report of probable cause. I've been on a few investigations, but I haven't decided if it's something I want to pursue. Right now I'm too busy with the Blues. It's challenging, sort of like trying to figure out a riddle, but it's not something I'd want to give up flying for.''

"But doesn't seeing all those planes destroyed and people killed make you think twice about your own time in the air? Haven't you ever felt you were pressing your luck and that sooner or later it'll be your plane lying in pieces on the ground?''

He shook his head. "I can't think about that. If a pilot has a negative attitude, he's in trouble. Being a pilot is the one thing I know how to do well and even if I say so myself, I'm damned good. But if all I'm thinking about is that I might die any minute, I'd be dangerous to myself and my men."

"But couldn't you be more cautious?"

"I don't take chances, but I don't worry about what could go wrong, either. Sure, there's tons of extenuating circumstances that can cause a plane to go down, but then there's tons of things that can happen to a person while he is walking down the street. My father was killed in a car accident. Should I never drive a car for fear I might have a wreck?"

Kristi had no answer. This was a subject about which they would only be able to agree to disagree. With a resigned shrug, she turned her attention back to the report.

"It says here that the FBI was called in to investigate the possibility of a bomb," she reported aloud. "That would certainly explain a lot of things."

"Yes, but if you'll read a little farther down the page, they haven't completely discounted the possibility, but they think it unlikely. For one thing, on the C.V.R., the pilots gave no indication of an explosion."

When she came to the part describing the probable scenario seconds after the explosion, a shudder shook her. "They think everyone survived the landing and was alive at the time of the explosion. I can't think of anything worse than being burned to death."

"Even though they didn't die from severe blunt-force trauma as most crash victims do, you know from your flight attendant training that within thirty seconds the toxic fumes of a burning plane are deadly. Most of them probably didn't suffer. It happened very quickly," Scott reminded her. He guessed that even though she already knew the facts, she needed to hear them from someone else to reaffirm her own conclusions on the matter.

"Death might have come quickly, but imagine how everyone felt. It was obvious the plane was flying erratically for several minutes, so everyone must have been terrified of crashing. Then when they actually touched down on the runway, they barely had time to breathe a sigh of relief that they had made it when the plane slipped off the runway and hit that fuel tank." Again a violent shudder shook her body and all the color drained out of her face at the mental image she had created of the last minutes of Flight 2302.

Scott reached over and pulled her into his lap, holding her tightly and burying his face in her hair. "It's over, Kristi, my love. It's over. Let it go. I know how awful it must be for you and for them. But thank God, you weren't on that flight."

"But I should have been," she whispered, her voice ragged with pain as she looked at a photograph of a row of yellow tarps at the site. The legend below the picture told her that they covered the bodies of the crew. "It should have been me. I've never told you this. In fact, I've never told anyone. But I killed my best friend and my fiancé."

Chapter Eleven

"There goes your imagination, running wild again."

"No, it's true," Kristi confirmed, absolutely convinced that she was guilty.

"But that's impossible," Scott cut in. "There's no way you could have been responsible for their deaths. Unless you knew something about the plane...?" His voice trailed off as he frowned doubtfully.

"No, of course not. If I had even suspected something was wrong with that plane, I would have done everything possible to keep it on the ground," she answered vehemently, then hesitated. She had told him too much, and now he expected her to explain. Her heart was pounding in her chest and her throat tightened. She knew she wouldn't be able to bluff her way out of telling him the truth. The time had come for her to admit her guilt and accept his disapproval—and possibly his disgust.

"Diane and Rick would never have been on that flight if it hadn't been for me," she admitted, her voice low and tortured. "Rick and I were planning on flying on to the Bahamas for a day at the beach. We had arranged our schedules weeks in advance, knowing May would be a perfect time to relax in the sun. We had both been working incredible schedules during the winter, because the airlines were having fare wars. We were booked solid for months and hadn't spent much time together.''

As she spoke, she made no move to leave the protection of Scott's lap and kept her head bowed onto his chest. She had not dared to share this part of her story with anyone else before now and could only hope he would understand. Although it had plagued her thoughts, actually speaking of it for the first time brought out more than she realized. Without meaning to do anything other than pass on the details, now that she had begun to talk, more was coming out than she had consciously known herself.

"Rick and I were engaged, but neither of us was in too much of a hurry to get married. Last year we had grown further apart than ever, simply because we had been so busy and our schedules had not meshed as much as usual. But we made the excuse we were working to build up our nest egg, and both of us kept up the hectic pace. But the truth is, we worked so much because we loved our jobs . . . more than we loved each other, I suppose. We didn't sit down and discuss it, but I think we both thought a couple of days in the Bahamas would bring back the romance to our relationship.

"Denver to Miami wasn't part of Rick's normal route. He went on it because of me. But two days before the flight I came down with the flu. I can't remember the last time I was sick, but this time it hit me hard. I felt really awful, with aches and chills. I kept hoping I would get better in time for the flight, but that morning when I was still running a high temperature, I knew I'd better not risk it. A friend of mine had to have an operation on her ears after flying with a fever and she's still partially deaf.

"Anyway, when I called Rick, he was disappointed, but of course there was no reason for him to change his schedule. We made plans to get together after he flew back into Denver. I'm not sure if he was still going to continue on to the Bahamas or not, but the way I felt right then, I didn't care."

"So you're saying that by making plans with Rick, it was your fault he was on that flight?" Scott interrupted.

"He wouldn't have been on it otherwise," she answered miserably. "And that's sort of the reason Diane was on it, too. She was in the middle of a long break, but when she saw how sick I was, she volunteered to take my place on the flight. She knew Worldwide was short-handed and might try to pressure me into flying in spite of my fever, especially since there were connecting flights. She wasn't a fanatic about work like I was, and usually took advantage of her days off to be with her boyfriend, who is a disc jockey in Denver. They were making wedding plans, too, but I think they would have beaten me and Rick to the altar."

"Which means Diane wouldn't have been on that flight either, if you hadn't been sick," Scott stated flatly.

Kristi nodded, vaguely aware of the softness of his shirt rubbing against her cheek. She had been able to read nothing in his tone and half expected him to thrust her away from him.

"Is that what's been bothering you so much?" he persisted.

Again she nodded. "It should have been me. If I hadn't been such a wimp, Diane would still be alive today and probably happily married to her DJ by now. In fact, they made the change so close to the flight time that my name was still on some of the crew rosters as senior flight attendant. They were on the verge of notifying my mother when someone realized the mistake.''

"What did your therapist say about all this?''

"Nothing," she admitted, "because I didn't tell him. I was so ashamed and felt so responsible that I didn't want anyone to know. Diane's and Rick's families would hate me almost as much as I hate myself.''

Instead of feeling his arms pushing her away, she felt them wrap more closely around her.

"You silly goose," he murmured sympathetically. "Why have you been holding all this inside you? This should have all come out in your rehabilitation therapy. Did they treat you with hypnosis? I've heard that's how they get people to overcome problems like yours.''

"They had trouble with my case," Kristi explained, almost apologetically. "If I had actually been in the crash and survived, they could have detraumatized the experience through a tried formula of therapy or experimented with hypnosis. But the doctor told me that because I wasn't really there, my imagination had created a series of events that might or might not be accurate. And because I didn't have a memory to explore, it was more difficult to help me; every time I got over one step, my imagination would kick in again and come up with something else.''

"That's what I was telling you earlier about things not being as bad as you imagine them. You should channel your creativity into more enjoyable activities than in driving yourself crazy about something that wasn't your fault. Rick and Diane were both adults and they made their decisions all on their own. You might have contributed to those decisions, but there's no way you were responsible for them.''

As much as she would have liked to believe him, she didn't pay much attention to his words. She knew he was just trying to make her feel better.

"You had no way of knowing that plane would crash," he continued. "Every time you went into the air you were taking a calculated risk, however small. Of course you wouldn't have let your friends die if you'd known, no more than you yourself would have gone up in that plane, knowing the outcome. But because they did and you didn't, Kristi, it truly wasn't your fault."

Kristi wasn't totally convinced, but his understanding was comforting. She had clung to the guilt for too long to let it go easily, but he had given her food for thought. She hadn't actually pushed either Diane or Rick onto that plane. However, she still couldn't resolve the fact that they had both been there directly because of her. If she had not wanted to have some quiet time with Rick in the Bahamas or if she hadn't been feverish, her two friends would still be alive.

She was afraid the nightmare would return that night, but once again the powerful refuge of Scott's presence kept her safe and she slept peacefully. Through the next days, she reviewed the report and reflected on Scott's comments. It still bothered her that the N.T.S.B. hadn't totally absolved her friends, but she felt as if a load had been lifted from her chest. If Scott believed in her, maybe things weren't as bad as she had imagined. Except for his rather too carefree view of life itself, she respected his intelligence and his opinions.

Scott met many of her needs. Physically, no one had ever given her more satisfaction or pleasure; mentally she felt they were equals, their conversations were stimulating and interesting; and emotionally, he had been the Rock of Gibraltar for her, a safe harbor in her time of storm. All of these things had caused her to view her relationship with Rick from a different point of view.

She had held on to Rick because it was convenient to do so and because, sharing her life-style as he did, he would have been an understanding spouse. But now that she had known Scott and been loved by him, she realized that she and Rick had never been more than close friends. They had never been truly in love, and deep down, both of them must have sensed that marriage would have ruined a perfectly good friendship. Why else would they have kept putting it off with lame excuses and open-ended promises?

But the fact that she had never felt for anyone else what she was feeling with Scott didn't alter her determination to avoid a permanent involvement with him. She wasn't strong enough to break it off now, but by the end of the month she would leave as planned. And from that point on, she would take care to avoid reading any articles or seeing any television reports about the Blue Angels, for fear Scott's name might be mentioned as a fatality. Somehow she would be able to close the door on the six weeks she'd spent with him, just as she was still trying to close her memory to the crash. She had to keep reminding herself that Scott was merely another part of her therapy.

Before the crash, Kristi had read several books by people who had survived disasters. She had even met a couple of flight attendants from other airlines who had been involved in accidents, none as serious as Flight 2302, but nevertheless very bad ones. She had learned that different people react in different ways. Some of them had turned to alcohol or drugs to dull the pain of reality. Others had had nervous breakdowns, spending weeks and even months in psychiatric hospitals. And still others had relied on the support of their friends and family, or on faith in God to get them through the rough spots.

It wasn't as if these people had consciously chosen to react the way they did, she learned, because at a time of stress a person usually responded automatically, drawing from inner sources that had been developed as far back as childhood.

But Kristi understood how easy it would have been to become addicted to something that would block out reality. Even she had been tempted. Right after the accident her doctor had given her a prescription for some very strong sleeping pills. She had hesitated to use them, because she had never approved of a dependence on drugs of any kind. But on the nights she took one of the small white pills, she had been able to sleep without the dream, though she had awakened more sluggish than rested. And after a few days of no dreams at all, she had started snapping everyone's heads off and being generally obnoxious. So she had chosen short periods of refreshing sleep over long stretches of unconsciousness—and had flushed the rest of the pills down the toilet.

Kristi's next response had been to get away from it all; escape to someplace that held no memories. She had been reluctant to share her grief with her mother, for fear it would bring back unpleasant reminders of her father's death. And she had not felt comfortable around her friends. Instead, Scott had become her break with reality. His kisses dulled her senses more intoxicatingly than alcohol, his sanity brought back her own, and his smile filled her with the warmth of a dozen friends.

She would be forever grateful to him. But she was wise enough to know that even though she might think herself in love with him now, her emotions were too raw and her judgment was too vulnerable for her to trust her own ability to make an intelligent decision.

So she kept putting it off, even as she counted the days to Christmas. At Scott's urging she had started a diary. In it she recorded all the facts of the crash as she knew them, and her feelings during the aftermath. At first she had had to force herself to write; it was painful to express the emotions she was experiencing. But gradually, as her responses became easier and more honest, she began to look forward to inscribing her innermost thoughts on the pages of a spiral-bound notebook. Having already filled two, she was currently working on her third. Self-consciously she didn't show anyone their contents, but kept them all carefully hidden in her overnight case.

After receiving the report and talking with Scott, the tone of her diary began to undergo a subtle change, Kristi noticed when she reread what she had written after that day. There was a lightness and optimism that hadn't been there before. Even her handwriting looked less cramped and stiff. It was as if by sharing her fear and self-incrimination with Scott, he had taken half her load.

She also saw that much more of each entry was devoted to Scott. She accepted the fact that he was bringing much happiness into her life, yet was unhappy because she wasn't contributing anything to his.

It wasn't for lack of trying. Her cooking had improved and his house stayed neater between the cleaning woman's weekly visits. Christmas would be her last chance to give him something special, but she couldn't think of anything he needed that he didn't already have. It was important that she come up with the perfect gift, because it would also serve as her going away present.

Kristi browsed at the mall, but found nothing that seemed suitable. She had even begun flipping through magazines and catalogs, hoping there would be some sort of specialty item about flying or the Blues in one of them that she could send for. Scanning the pages of the latest issue of *Newsweek* the mailman had just delivered, Kristi barely paused at each article, until one in particular caught her attention.

"Bones May Not Even Be Human." The headline drew her gaze and she continued reading, growing more excited by the second. She knew how very much Kahuna's death had upset Scott. Even though she was wrapped up in her own problems, she would have had to be totally insensitive to not see how melancholy Scott became whenever his old friend was mentioned or some reference to the war or POWs was made.

She knew it was a shot in the dark and honestly didn't know what would be accomplished if her suspicions proved true. Perhaps Kahuna's family wouldn't feel it was worth the added heartache of wishing and waiting even longer than the sixteen years they already had.

When Scott arrived home later that afternoon, Kristi met him at the door. She was trying to contain her enthusiasm, in case he should not be as excited about the prospect as she was. She waited impatiently until he had stripped off his flight suit and taken a shower. But when he walked out of the bathroom, a towel wrapped around his waist, she was sitting cross-legged in the middle of the bed, the article in front of her.

"Have you heard anything else about when Kahuna might be sent home?" she began cautiously.

She tried not to be distracted when Scott dropped the towel and stepped into a pair of Jockey shorts. "Sometime after the first of the year. Why?"

"Do you suppose they did some sort of chemical analysis on his bones to confirm his identity?"

She had his full attention now as he joined her on the bed. "I don't know," he admitted. "I understand the major source of identification was the dog tags returned with the body."

"I read something today you might be interested in. According to this article the Vietnamese are passing off bones as American when they are actually Vietnamese. A lady in Utah received a box of bones they said were her husband's. Apparently they passed through all the military channels without question, but before she had a funeral, she said she had a weird feeling they weren't her husband's and sent them to a university to have them tested. They called in some forensic experts who ran them through a series of tests and because of the size, structure and chemical content found out that not only weren't the bones American, but some of them weren't even human. It seems the Vietnamese had scooped up a boxful of bones, found some identification and claimed they had found an MIA."

She handed the magazine to him and he read through it quickly. She could tell by the guarded expression on his face he was considering the possibility and trying not to get his hopes up. But the light in his eyes revealed that the idea had caught his imagination.

"What do you think? Do you think it's possible it might not be Kahuna?" she asked hopefully.

"I don't know. I just don't know." He raked his fingers through his wet black hair, pushing it back from his forehead, but it stubbornly fell back as soon as he lifted his hand. "I don't know whether to hope it's possible," he admitted. "There was a lot of disappointment when they said he was found, because it destroyed all hope that he was still alive. On the other hand, there was a sort of relief that it was finally over; that we knew after all this time where he was, and that he could at last come home to rest in peace. I'm not sure how his parents will react . . . or what should be done if it's not him."

"Couldn't you make some inquiries before you contact them? If you were able to find out for sure or even that there was a chance that it wasn't him, then you would know whether or not you should tell them about the possibility."

"I could make some calls. I'm sure someone at the base would know whom to contact in Hawaii."

Kristi could see the thought growing and gaining credibility in his mind. She hoped she hadn't gotten his hopes up for nothing. And his concern about "What next?" was certainly valid, should the bones not be Kahuna's. Would it be more painful for his parents the second time they thought him dead? Kristi could imagine how devastated they must feel, but would Scott be doing them a favor by dragging out the grieving process even longer, especially since the bones might very likely *be* their son's?

Scott glanced at his watch. "Allowing for the time difference in Hawaii, it's still early there and someone should be at the naval headquarters to take my call. But we're supposed to meet Randy and Donna at the bowling alley in thirty minutes. . . ."

"I'll go to the bowling alley and you go to the base," Kristi suggested. "Randy and Donna will understand. We'll wait for you there."

He looked hesitant, as if he hated to upset their plans for the evening, but Kristi could see his thoughts were distracted. Now that he was considering taking action, he wouldn't truly be with them until he had set the plan in motion.

"Take all the time you need," she encouraged him. "We'll get in a few practice games and we can all go out to dinner later." Again she wondered if she had done the right thing by telling him about the article. But if she were in his shoes, she wouldn't be satisfied until she had explored every avenue and resolved all of her doubts. Her own experience with discovering the truth about the crash helped her understand his determination to see this through to the end.

He finally agreed to her plan and they set out. As Kristi expected, Randy and Donna didn't mind that Scott had taken a detour. They all had trouble concentrating on their bowling techniques and ended up taking a break in the coffee shop, which was where Scott found them when he arrived an hour later.

"Well? How did it go?" Kristi asked as soon as Scott joined them. "Did you get in touch with the pathology department? Have they administered any tests?"

"I had a heck of a time talking to someone who could give me any information," Scott admitted. "And even when I finally got the commanding officer on the phone, they were reluctant to discuss the case with me, since I'm not a member of the family."

"At which point you probably didn't mention that you were the commander of the Blue Angels, did you?" Randy teased his friend. "Rank does have its privileges sometimes."

"It did happen to work its way into the conversation," Scott admitted with a grin and an unapologetic shrug. "I figured Kahuna helped me, in a roundabout way, get to that position on the Blues, so I might as well use it to help him. They became much more cooperative after that, and I was able to find out no tests had been done. Apparently the Vietcong sent over a couple of dozen bodies they had 'found' and the medics at the base decided since there were enough dog tags to go around, there was no reason to question the identification. I suppose they thought most families would be so glad to finally have their sons back that they wouldn't care if all the pieces might not go to that particular person.''

"It all sounds gruesome," Donna said with a shiver. "And so impersonal."

"Let's hope they change that policy real soon," Kristi added. "It's not fair to the parents or the GIs, whether they are dead or alive."

"I think I got that point across to them. When they told me they couldn't possibly proceed with the tests without his parents' approval, I convinced them it would be in everyone's best interests if the tests were done quietly and quickly with the results relayed to me. If they prove the remains actually are Kahuna's, then nothing will be said and the funeral will go on as planned. But if they're not, the parents must be notified before they go through the painful and expensive process of burying a stranger."

"It's too bad you're having to put yourself through this," Donna commented. "I know this must be hard on you, too."

Scott gave Kristi an affectionate look. "It would be more difficult if I had to go through it alone."

It gave her a warm, happy feeling to know that she had at last done something *for* him. Now she could only pray that the results, whatever they might be, would satisfy Scott.

Actually Scott didn't know what to hope for. If the tests proved positive, then he would have to accept once and for all the fact his old friend was dead. And if they were negative, Scott would be back to square one, wondering if Kahuna was still alive and being held prisoner over there. It was tough trying to decide whether he should wish his friend were already dead—possibly proving Kahuna had not suffered long and had not been tortured in prison—or if he should wish his friend were still alive, waiting to be rescued or freed, possibly locked up somewhere in a tiny, dark cell, or spending his days working in a rice paddy and his nights fighting off rats.

Either way, he wanted to know the truth. If the Vietcong had substituted animal bones for Kahuna's and tossed his dog tags into the box for good measure, then Scott and Kahuna's family deserved an explanation.

Scott's gaze was still resting quite comfortably on Kristi. She had really blossomed in the last few weeks. She had put on a few well-placed pounds, her cheeks had a healthy rosy tint, and her soft blue eyes sparkled with good humor. He had noticed she enjoyed being around his friends and laughed more than she had when they first met. It was almost as if she had come back to life.

He had tossed undisguised hints at her about what they would do together in the upcoming months, but she had never taken the bait. She was always very careful to avoid making plans past the end of the year, and Scott was beginning to fear he wasn't going to be successful in changing her mind about leaving.

At first it hadn't worried him. Kristi had intrigued and attracted him, but she was certainly not the first woman who had done that. As he got to know her better, he'd also begun to admire her courage and intelligence, while at the same time feeling the urge to protect her and heal her hurt. It was a strange and original emotion for him as she filled many facets of his life with her lovely pres-

ence. Before that first night on the beach, he had begun
to wonder if he would ever meet a woman with whom he
wanted to spend the rest of his life. And now that he had
found Kristi, he had no idea what he would do without
her.

He sensed she cared for him, perhaps even loved him.
But her fear of his life-style was fueling her determination not to let him talk her into staying. While she had
never hidden her feelings about his flying, she had never
asked him to give it up. Actually, it would be easier for
him to get over her if she should demand he choose between her and the Blues. Then he would have an excuse
to get mad.

But she hadn't. He knew it was because she understood his love of flying and need for danger, but couldn't
bring herself to accept it. Without actually speaking the
words, she was forcing him to make a decision on his
own. For so long his career had been his life, and he
didn't see how he could give it up. But he was no longer
sure his career would be enough.

Of all the women in the world, why did he have to fall
in love with this one? There must be dozens, even
hundreds of women out there who would be thrilled to
follow him from air show to air show, basking in the
glory of his celebrity status. Unfortunately, none of them
mattered . . . no one except Kristi.

They bowled three games, with Scott and Randy going
pin for pin while Kristi and Donna cheered their men on
and tried to keep their own scores from being too em-
barrassing. Afterward they went to an Italian restaurant
and devoured two extralarge supreme pizzas, then went
to Scott's house and played card games until late. It was
after midnight before Scott and Kristi began getting ready
for bed.

Scott walked out of the bathroom and stopped, his attention captured by Kristi as she stood at the patio door, gazing out into the night while idly brushing her hair. The brush in her hand moved in long, slow strokes, following the rounded shape of her head, then pulling through the silky length to her shoulders. Irresistibly drawn to her, he crossed the room, stopping behind her. Lifting one hand to her hair, he buried his fingers in its thickness, then held up a section and let it trickle back into place like a sparkling waterfall.

"You have the most beautiful hair I've ever seen," he murmured, studying the strands as they fell soft and straight. "It's sort of gold and silver and copper, all mixed together. I'll bet in the summer if you spend much time in the sun, it gets even lighter, like corn silk." He pushed it aside and bent to place a kiss on her neck. *Will I be able to see it in the summer sun, Kristi, my love? Where will you be then?* he asked himself, not daring to voice the questions. He didn't want to hear the answers; she had already made them clear.

He let his lips trail down the smooth slope of her shoulder, gently nudging off one strap of her nightgown as he went. He slid his hands around her waist, pulling her slender body back against his until he could feel the heat of her skin through the silk of her gown. Slowly she pivoted in his arms until they were facing each other. Her other strap succumbed to his sensual onslaught and the gown slithered to the floor with an expectant sigh.

Kristi twined her arms around his neck as Scott bent and lifted her, then carried her to the bed. Their lovemaking was sweet and tender, almost wistful, as if they both realized their time together was running out, yet neither could make the ultimate sacrifice that would extend it.

"HOW SOON do you think they'll have the results?" Kristi asked as they sat at the breakfast table the next morning, each drinking a final cup of coffee before he left for the base.

"They didn't know. Since they have to test each bone separately until they find one that is definitely Kahuna's, it could take quite a while. But Kahuna's parents are expecting him to be shipped home soon, so unless the Navy brass want to make an awkward explanation, they'd better throw the throttle wide open."

"There's always the chance it truly is Kahuna, you know," Kristi reminded him gently.

"Yes, I know. And if I find out it is him, then I'll attend the funeral as planned. But if it isn't him, I'll make a quick trip to Corpus to tell his parents myself. The military isn't as subtle and compassionate as it could be in matters such as this." He paused as he swirled the last dregs of coffee in the bottom of his cup, staring down at the whirlpool pattern that was pulling him back through a time tunnel into the past.

He could almost see the lush vegetation of the jungles. He could almost hear the constant droning of the swarms of bugs and the screeches of the tropical birds that could never drown the distant boom of explosions or the staccato pulse of rifles. He could almost smell the damp, thick air and feel the heat and humidity prickle his skin.

Somewhere out there Kahuna was still alive. Even before the results were back, Scott felt it as strongly as if he were standing there, looking into the eyes of his friend.

"I've got to go back," he stated, forcing himself to return to the present. "All these years I've left it to fate to bring him back. And if those aren't his remains, then I'm going to go back to Vietnam and find him."

"But Scott! You're talking about a major undertaking. Those people aren't going to want to help you. They might not even let you into their country." Kristi's eyes were sympathetic, but also filled with a plea for him not to do anything rash. "They certainly don't want anyone to find any POWs after all the years they've sworn there were none left."

"I never have believed that lie. There have been too many reports of sightings of Americans to make me think there aren't still some left over there."

"It'll be dangerous, but that wouldn't stop you, would it?" she muttered with wry sarcasm.

"Someone needs to do something. Just think of what those guys have gone through for the last fifteen to twenty years . . . and are still going through."

"Maybe you're getting all worked up over nothing," Kristi said, visibly trying to calm him down. He suspected she was regretting ever bringing the article to his attention. "It could be Kahuna's bones in that box, and then it will be all over."

"How can it ever be over? Of all people, you know how difficult it is to let go. I feel responsible for him, just as you feel responsible for Rick and Diane. Probably neither of us should have carried that weight for as long as we have, but it's not easy to toss off."

Reluctantly she nodded her agreement.

"And I suspect neither of us will ever be able to feel free of the guilt until we face our memories and realize that nothing we could have done would have changed the outcome," he continued. "But just as you can't let it go, neither can I until I go back to where it all began. And someday soon you will have to get back on a plane and maybe even visit the crash site. I've learned from experience that you can't conquer your dragon until you've faced and killed him. It will come back to haunt you over and over until you do."

"You might be right, but—"

Before she could finish her sentence, the telephone interrupted. Scott had been so involved in the conversation that he had to steady his breathing before he answered it. For a few minutes he carried on a terse conversation, reaching for a scratch pad to write down some notes.

When he hung up the receiver, he turned back to Kristi, his expression dead serious as he asked, "Remember that dragon we were just talking about? Now's your chance to confront him. A Navy jet just crashed in New Mexico, and they want me to fly over there for the investigation."

He paused, studying her carefully as he added, "I think you should go with me."

Chapter Twelve

"No, I couldn't possibly go." Kristi quickly rejected his suggestion.

"Why not?"

Kristi's mind scrambled for a reason, knowing there must be a dozen or so that were excellent, but having trouble settling on just one. *A crash.* She didn't know how she would react to seeing the wreckage of a plane.

"Did it burn?" she asked, knowing it would be even more difficult if it had.

"Yes, there was an explosion and a fire."

"Then there's probably not much left, is there?"

"No, probably not," he confirmed, patiently waiting for her to resolve her dilemma.

"Were there any fatalities?" she forced herself to ask, barely able to speak around the lump of bile that had risen into her throat.

"One. It was a single-seater and the pilot was unable to eject in time."

Pieces of airplane strewn across the countryside. A man's body lying in the wreckage, probably burned beyond recognition. Horrible mental pictures flooded her imagination, pictures mingled with those of another crash. One more person claimed by the angel of death.

One more person who had taken one flight too many, and whose next and last flight would be to his home—in a wooden box.

Kristi lifted her hands to her face, her fingers digging into her forehead and her palms covering her eyes. But even with her eyelids squeezed tightly shut, she couldn't stop the images.

It could so easily have been Scott. He was up in a Navy jet of one kind or another almost every day. How long would it be before someone would call about him?

"I can't go," she sobbed, losing the last remnants of control. All her life she had prided herself on being able to handle any situation, no matter how strange or stressful. That was one of the reasons she had been such a good flight attendant. Crying babies and terrified old ladies hadn't fazed her. Puppies hidden in handbags or people who never took their heads out of their airsickness bags were all part of a busy day.

But since the crash of Flight 2302, her emotional strength seemed to have disappeared entirely. During the last few weeks, it had gradually begun to return and with it, her self-confidence and composure. Kristi had started to believe she was truly on the verge of complete recovery—until the very mention of a plane crash sent her right back to the beginning.

"I can't," she repeated, filled with disappointment and despair.

She felt his comforting arms around her and her face transferred from her hands to the front of his shirt. The steady beat of his heart and gentle touch of his fingers as he stroked her hair acted on her raw nerves, calming her immediately. She had become so dependent on him being there when she needed him, it was not difficult for her to understand how other trauma victims easily became hooked on alcohol or drugs. Scott was her addiction.

To get over her problem, she would have to get over him before he became just one more complication. Each time she had worked up enough nerve to face a fear, she had discovered it wasn't as she had imagined it. After she'd worried herself sick about the cause and effect of the actual crash, the report had almost been good news. And when she had finally told Scott about her feeling of responsibility for Rick and Diane, he hadn't been shocked or upset, but had defused her guilt. This trip, painful though it might be, would help her face yet another fear. Maybe then she would be able to let it go—and her reliance on Scott.

"I always seem to be getting your shirt wet," she sniffed, reaching for her napkin and using it to wipe the tears from her cheeks.

"I don't mind," he reassured her solemnly.

"I suppose we would have to fly to the site, wouldn't we?" she asked, trying, but not quite succeeding in keeping the tremor out of her voice.

"Yes, we would. But since this is official business, we can either go commercial or in a Navy jet."

Kristi took a deep, steadying breath. This would be her first flight since before the crash, and she wasn't sure she was ready for it. She knew she would never be cleared to fly after taking a medical leave of absence unless she went through recurrent training, which would include discussions and films of other crashes, some classroom work and, most important, yet frightening, an on-line check flight. Sooner or later she was going to have to walk up the ramp and step through the doorway onto a plane. She would have to steel herself not to see Rick's face on the first officer and Diane's on one of the flight attendants.

And the passengers on the plane would not be those doomed to die on Flight 2302.

Which would be easier? Should she put off her return flight as long as possible? Would she prefer sitting next to Scott on a commercial flight, taking a chance on having bad memories? Or would it be better to try something different, by flying with Scott while he piloted a Navy jet and she sat in the seat that was usually reserved for the news media during demonstration flights?

"I wouldn't ask you to go with me if I didn't think it would be good for you," he explained. "You know I would never do anything to hurt you."

Kristi forced herself to meet his gaze. Light blue, frightened eyes stared into dark, genuinely concerned ones. She didn't doubt his sincerity or the wisdom of his words. But she didn't know how much she would be able to take.

"I'm not sure if I'm ready, but I suppose I could give it a try," she said, her voice hesitant.

"You don't have to do more than you feel you should," Scott encouraged her. "But by attempting this, it isn't one small step, but a giant leap for you."

"Not exactly an original statement."

"But true." He flashed her a grin. "Now which will it be . . . the ordinary or the extraordinary?"

Because she simply couldn't face the rows and rows of passengers that would remind her of her own job responsibilities, Kristi chose the unknown. "I've trusted you with everything else, so I suppose I can trust you to get us to New Mexico and back safely. But you have to promise you won't do anything tricky or crazy. I'm not sure I'm ready for even a vanilla flight, much less anything fancy."

"No loops or rolls, I promise." His index finger drew
an X over his heart in a childhood symbol of sincerity.
"You have nothing to worry about. You've just accepted a ride with the best pilot in the world."

"You'd better be, or I'll be on the first Amtrak heading from New Mexico to Florida."

Several times during the next few hours, Kristi ques-
tioned her own sanity. She was shaking like a Chihua-
hua in January as she packed a few clothes and essentials
in a small bag, then rode to the base in Scott's blue sports
car. When she saw the sleek silver jets sitting on the tar-
mac, one of which they would soon be boarding, the
knots in her stomach tightened until she was afraid she
would become physically ill and embarrass herself in
front of everyone.

Scott was standing a few feet away, getting last-minute
details from an older man who had captain's bars on the
sleeve of his uniform. A maintenance crew was doing
last-minute checks on the plane directly in front of Kristi.
She could only hope they were doing their job well and
not overlooking some important details that would cause
the plane to malfunction while in flight.

"Ready?"

She hadn't known Scott had walked up to her until she
heard his voice. Her mouth was too dry for words to
form, so she stiffly nodded her head. They had both
slipped flight suits over their clothes and strapped on
parachutes. He handed her a helmet and tucked his own
under his arm.

"Let's go," he said and they crossed the paved area
until they stood at the base of a platform ladder that was
pushed against the plane. Scott turned to her and gave
her a calming, confident smile. His fingers tenderly
brushed across her cheeks and tucked her blowing hair

behind her ear. "Nothing bad's going to happen. I'll take care of you," he promised. "Trust me."

All the reasons why she shouldn't go on this trip that she hadn't been able to put her finger on earlier this morning suddenly became clear in her mind. Was she crazy? Why had she ever agreed to this excursion? Riding in the back seat of a fighter jet certainly did not fit into her new program of caution. Granted, the chances were slim to none that they would meet an enemy MiG between here and Gallup and become involved in an air-to-air combat. But that didn't mean the plane wouldn't crash. The evidence was in the fact that they were going to investigate an accident that had no known cause.

"Scott..." she managed to choke out.

She could tell by the understanding look in his eyes that he knew she was having second thoughts. "It's up to you, but maybe it's time to get back on that horse. The longer you put it off, the harder it will be."

"I feel sick," she admitted. "I've never thrown up on a plane before in my life, but... Are there any airsickness bags in there?"

"Probably. We carry a lot of reporters and politicians in this plane, and some of them are a strange shade of green by the time we land. But I think you'll surprise yourself. This baby flies as smoothly as an eagle. You won't feel as much motion as you would in a 727."

Kristi swallowed hard. The fear was so strong she could taste it ... smell it ... hear it pounding in her ears. If she didn't use the paper bag to be sick into, it would probably come in handy when she began hyperventilating. Boy, was she a basket case!

"It's up to you, Kristi. This is something you must do for yourself, but if you can't handle the stress right now, that's okay." He reached into his pocket, pulled out his car keys and held them toward her. "Here, you can take my car back to the house."

Something in his tone challenged her. His words were encouraging, but she sensed that if she couldn't force herself to face her dragon, he would be disappointed in her. If she took those keys, she was admitting defeat... failure... cowardice. Would it be any less frightening in a month? Two months? Six months? A year from now? She knew she couldn't go on with those feelings weighing heavily upon her. If she didn't do it now, with Scott along to offer his support and comfort, then perhaps she would never be able to.

Lifting her chin and squaring her shoulders, she spun around and raised her foot to the first step. The iron railing felt cold and hard as she wrapped her hand around it. But she continued upward, one step at a time until she had to swing her leg over the cockpit wall and settle into the narrow space. It felt odd to be sitting on a seat surrounded by dozens of gauges and a miniature radar screen. This was like no other flying experience she had ever had before. Even those times she had sat in the cockpit during a flight, there had been enough space for at least three other people and a perception of a much larger area.

Scott had followed her up the steps and stopped next to her long enough to check the tightness of her shoulder harness and help her put on her helmet, adjust it, and fasten the strap beneath her chin. Following the same procedure with his own, he gave her one more flash of his cocky, crooked grin and raised his hand in a positive, thumbs-up sign. Kristi managed a weak, shaky smile in return.

She watched as he settled into his seat and fastened his own harness. The mechanical hum of the canopy momentarily sent a wave of panic through her, and as it snapped shut, she knew there was no turning back. She was committed to seeing this through; the only thing she could hope for now was that Scott was as good a pilot as he had said.

The sound of the engines increased from a low whine to a screaming roar as the plane taxied down the runway and lifted off the ground. She didn't actually see the takeoff because her eyes were tightly shut, but she could feel her stomach sink as they defied the law of gravity and angled into the sky. Scott banked the plane into a right turn and headed west.

After a few minutes of steady, powerful climbing, the plane leveled off to its cruising altitude and Kristi could feel her tensed muscles slowly beginning to relax. Her eyes crept open and she was startled to find herself surrounded by blue sky. The clear canopy offered an unobstructed view on both sides and above. Since all of her flying experience had been in a passenger plane whose wide body and small windows had offered little chance to see more than an occasional wisp of cloud, this afforded her a whole new perspective.

It was as if she were suspended in the air almost like a bird, except that she was protected from the elements. Not even sitting in the cockpit of a jumbo jet had given her such a feeling of space and freedom.

"How are you doing back there?" Scott's voice crackled in her ear through the small radio set in her helmet.

"Fine," she admitted, surprised by her own relatively positive reaction. Tension still twisted in a tight ball inside her and she realized her fingernails were digging deeply into the interior side panels, but the nausea had subsided and her breathing had steadied to a more normal rhythm. "Much better than I had expected. It's really rather spectacular up here like this."

"And the pilot is doing a fine job, right?" he prompted and she could hear his chuckle rumble across the transmission lines.

"He's the best of the best," she answered solemnly, only partially referring to the way he was handling the plane.

Her view of the earth below was partially blocked by the sweep of the wings on each side, although from what she could see, she knew they were flying over the Gulf of Mexico, probably to keep out of busier airspace until absolutely necessary.

Around her was an almost three-hundred-sixty-degree view of the horizon. Directly in front of her the round back of Scott's dark blue helmet dominated her line of vision; in front of him she could see the long pointed nose of the plane as it streaked toward New Mexico. The entire time she could hear Scott's low-pitched, steadying voice in her ear, keeping up a light, easygoing conversation.

Although she knew it was over two hours, it seemed only moments had passed when they began their descent into Gallup. As she felt the plane lose altitude, Kristi's muscles tightened, making her realize just how much she had relaxed during the flight. Just as promised, with the grace of an eagle soaring on the wind, Scott turned the plane into a wide, easy circle until they were lined up with the runway beneath them.

Again the nightmare played in full detail before Kristi's eyes as if she were watching a movie, igniting her imagination. Even though the passengers' view must have been much different from her own right now, she could almost sense the relief they must have felt as they approached the runway. At that point they surely must have begun to believe they would make it. After the turbulence of the flight, when they all probably feared they would never be able to get down to earth in a safe landing, sighting the airport must have been the most beautiful thing they had ever experienced. As the plane touched down, ripping its belly apart on the concrete, their terror had probably returned, only to be calmed once more as the pilots wrestled with the aircraft, trying to keep control. The passengers had probably thought the worst was over—until the plane veered to the right, plowed through the field and into the fuel tank.

She grimaced as she felt the wheels of the Navy jet touch down. The engines' noise increased to an almost deafening level as Scott began the braking process. Kristi held her breath, waiting for a bounce, but the landing was as smooth as butter and she ventured to open her eyes as they taxied toward one of the larger hangars.

By the time the canopy had opened and the steps been pushed against the side of the plane, she had removed her helmet and shaken back some body into her hair. Scott bounded out of his seat and leaned over the side to peer at her.

"I see you stuck it out for the entire flight. Must not have been all bad," he teased, trying to test her spirits without coming right out and asking how she felt.

She stood up and let him help her step over the side of the plane, hoping her wobbly legs would hold her up once she reached the platform. When they did and she was able to face him without her knees buckling, she looked up at him and managed a shaky, but pleased smile. "Nothing to it. It was like a walk in the park," she responded with considerably more bravado than she felt.

It honestly hadn't been bad. Except for several nerve-racking moments when they had taken off and landed, she had almost been able to make herself forget her fear long enough to enjoy the beauty and excitement of being airborne. A hint of the pleasure she had always felt when she had flown before the crash had rushed through her, threatening to push aside her new resolve to live life more cautiously. It had felt good to be back in the air, especially with Scott at the controls.

If she could trust him with her life, why couldn't she trust him with his own safety? It was a question for which she still had no answer.

There was a car waiting for them, and Scott got directions to the crash site. It was too late to head out there that day, so Scott drove them to that appeared to be the nicest motel the city had to offer and they checked in.

"They aren't expecting me until tomorrow, so we might as well get a good night's sleep. I want to get up early," he said, unlocking the door to their room and letting them in.

Kristi was glad for the excuse to rest. She needed more time to gather her wits before she faced the destruction. Scott had asked her if she preferred her own private room, but after the weeks they had spent together, it would have seemed sort of hypocritical. Besides, she didn't want to be alone, especially when she was trying to get some sleep. For a woman who had never lived with a man and had had only two serious relationships, the depth of her dependency on Scott was growing a little alarming. But she knew she could deal with only so many problems at one time; since he was good for her and made her days and nights happier, she would deal with that dilemma later.

They found a restaurant and lingered over dinner, so that it was time for bed when they returned to the motel. They were both so preoccupied with what they would encounter tomorrow that they didn't make love, but spent the night cuddled in each other's arms in the unfamiliar double bed.

The next morning, they ate breakfast at the motel's coffee shop and Scott leveled a measuring look at Kristi.

"You don't have to go if you don't want to, you know," he said. "It's been a major step in your recovery to fly on that plane yesterday. You don't have to put yourself through anything else right now if you don't feel ready."

"It sounds like you're trying to talk me out of this. Is this the same man who was filled with encouragement and psychology yesterday morning?"

"I know I was tossing around free advice, but I've had second thoughts. Maybe you shouldn't rush into this. It might be better to take one thing at a time."

Buoyed by the success of her first flight since before the accident, Kristi refused to let him talk her out of it. She had slept well and woken up feeling refreshed and emotionally strong. "I've come this far. I might as well give it a try," she stated positively. "If I chicken out I'll wait for you in the car."

Scott still looked dubious, but didn't offer any further arguments.

He had told her last night the crash site was about thirty miles north of the city limits on the Navajo Indian reservation. She tried to concentrate on her surroundings in an attempt to stop herself from imagining the scene she would witness in a few more minutes. But there wasn't much in the rugged, mostly barren landscape, dotted occasionally with traditionally styled log and mud hogans or small, square modern houses to keep her attention. Idly she wondered how the shepherds managed to find enough food for their huge flocks of sheep, but that mild curiosity, too, didn't occupy her thoughts for long.

Kristi thought she was prepared for what she was about to see. All the pictures she had ever seen and the books she had read about crashes had been dredged up from her memory banks. During flight school she had been shown films and instructed with the help of examples on survival techniques in different types of accidents. And she had read and reread the preliminary report on Flight 2302, which had outlined in great detail what had been found when the inspectors arrived. She knew viewing this accident wouldn't be a picnic, considering the plane had disintegrated and the pilot been killed. But she felt prepared to see the worst, and hoped to be able to find some way to use it to help her accept that other crash.

The car stopped and Scott held the door open for her. Slowly she slid out of the seat and stood up, turning to survey the scene of destruction. It was even worse than she had anticipated. For once her expectations had been too positive.

A wide strip of earth was scorched and black, and whatever grass that had been growing was burned into short crispy clumps. Debris that didn't remotely resemble parts of an airplane lay scattered for dozens of yards in all directions. Only an engine and a chunk of fuselage remained intact; all the other pieces were battered or melted beyond recognition.

They had been the first to arrive today, but within minutes two other carloads of men parked and walked over to them. Scott cast her one last worried glance, then handed her the keys to the car.

"I'm going to be pretty busy for the next few hours, so if you want to leave early, go ahead," he told her. "I'll hitch a ride back with someone and meet you at the motel later."

She nodded and put the keys into the pocket of her slacks.

"If you need me, I won't be too busy," he added, lifting her chin with a bent finger and staring into her eyes, searching perhaps for any sign of panic. Apparently not quite satisfied with what he saw, he appeared hesitant to leave her and join the others.

"I'll be fine," she said, trying to reassure him. "Don't worry about me. Just concentrate on your job. If I get tired, I'll take you up on your offer." She patted the keys.

The other men commanded his attention and he was forced to turn away, but Kristi could tell he was distracted by his concern for her, which was touching. But she knew he was enough of a professional to be able to focus his full attention on the job at hand in spite of his worry.

Scott took a few items out of a small black leather bag he had brought with him. He hung a camera around his neck, stuck a pair of pliers into his rear pocket and carried a notebook with him as he walked toward the debris. For several minutes Kristi watched him move methodically in the area, writing notes, taking pictures, picking up pieces of twisted metal or broken gauges and placing them carefully in a cardboard box that had been placed on the perimeter.

Finally Kristi felt she had worked up enough nerve to examine the destruction at a closer range. It took every fiber of her being to walk among the wreckage. The second thing she had noticed when they arrived this morning was the stench, and now that she was so much closer, it was almost overpowering. After only a couple of minutes her nose stung from the combined odor of smoke, burned plastic, wet wool and jet fuel. It was a heavy, unpleasant smell that she was sure had been a hundred times worse at the Worldwide crash site. The pungent odor of burned human flesh and hair was not so evident here, but must have been extremely strong at the other crash.

Scott had told her the pilot had been immediately removed to the morgue, so she wasn't concerned about stumbling across anything that was totally morbid, although she knew from her training that when a planeload of passengers was involved, the inspectors would find all sorts of horrors as they sifted through the rubble.

Kristi rubbed one hand across her forehead, pushing her blond hair back from her face. There was a cool northerly breeze and she had worn a heavy sweater under her jacket. But in spite of the air temperature, the heat radiating from the wreckage made her feel flushed and hot. Several piles were still smoldering, even though the entire area had been doused with water and fire-retardant chemicals yesterday.

What had brought this plane down here in the middle of nowhere? What had caused the crash of Flight 2302? The questions, although not related, suddenly seemed to be entwined in her mind. Were there more crashes of both military and commercial aircraft now than ever before, or was she simply more sensitive to them?

Scott had told her this plane was an F-18, similar to the ones flown by the Blue Angels, although there was no resemblance now. The plane they had flown from Florida yesterday had also been an F-18, but it had been, like this one, silver instead of the royal blue of the F/A-18s the Blues flew. So what made the difference between a

plane that stayed up and soared like an eagle or one that
fell from the sky? Could an excellent pilot like Scott make
a difference? Were these crashes destined to happen? Or
was Scott truly tempting fate each and every time he
spent another hour at the controls?

Kristi knew that she was trying to reason with her own
logic that just because Scott was a pilot didn't necessarily mean he wouldn't live to a ripe old age. If she could
convince herself he wasn't constantly in a position of
danger, then perhaps she could overlook the risk and let
herself love him.

Somehow, looking at the crumpled remains of this
once-beautiful jet, Kristi didn't see how she could ever
manage to accept Scott's profession. This could as easily
have been his fate as that of a pilot whose name she didn't
even know. Somewhere there was a family grieving for
him; his parents, perhaps a wife and children who had
kissed him goodbye yesterday morning and been crying
for him by noon. Kristi had always prided herself on her
strength and capability, but she didn't think she would be
able to handle a situation like this, should it happen to
Scott.

It had been bad enough to lose her father and two
friends, Diane and Rick, even though she had realisti-
cally begun to think of Rick as more of a pal than a lover.
How much more difficult it would be to visit the crash site
of an F/A-18 with Cdr. Scott Sanders stenciled on its
side.

After the initial shock and feeling of nausea, she was
surprised at her ability to wander around the crash site
without breaking down. It made her sad as she thought
of the pilot and his family, and it depressed her that another young man had died needlessly. But she was able to
distance herself from the scene and view it dispassion-

ately. It was a vision she would never forget, yet it helped neutralize her feelings toward the Worldwide crash, whose location she had never seen.

The passenger jet had been larger, but the destruction had been so complete that there had not been much more debris than was left of this compact fighter plane. Obviously, everyone aboard had died as quickly and relatively painlessly as stated in the report. It was difficult to imagine anyone surviving this devastation for long. Her imagination would never again be able to elaborate on pictures she had seen or text she had read. She was at a maximum horror point; as she gradually let go of the details, relinquishing them to the past, her recovery should be able to progress smoothly.

Kristi looked at her watch and was startled to see it was after 2:00 p.m. The sights and smells surrounding her had driven away any thought of an appetite, so it didn't matter that they had missed lunch. Apparently the men had also been too busy to notice the passage of time. She glanced at Scott, who was squatting over a pile of rubble that had possibly been the cockpit; it was clear he wouldn't be leaving anytime soon.

In the distance she could see the tumbledown walls of an ancient adobe house. Since she did not want to drive back to Gallup and spend the rest of the afternoon alone in the motel room, she decided to take a little walk and investigate ruins of a different sort.

The air was somewhat fresher and the reddish dirt was a welcome sight after the black scars etched into the earth around the plane. It didn't take Kristi long to explore the small two-room house, so she climbed up onto a wide wall, whose remaining blocks formed a sort of stair step. Sitting on one block and resting her back against another, she watched a flock of several hundred sheep who were being kept in a loose group by a single shepherd and two hardworking dogs.

"KRISTI..."

She heard her name being called from a great distance and realized she must have dozed off. Carefully climbing down from the wall, she waved at Scott so he would see where she was. Apparently he was through for the day and was ready to leave, so she picked her way back across the rocky ground to where the car was parked.

"You're still here," he stated, but it sounded more like a question, since he was obviously surprised. "You made it through the flight, and now this."

"That's two in a row," she responded. "And I'm feeling pretty good, so your advice must have been what I needed. Maybe your mother was right. You should have been a doctor, a psychologist, or even a dragon slayer."

"Anything but a pilot, huh?" he asked perceptively.

"Anything but," she agreed, giving him a gently wistful smile.

Chapter Thirteen

"So what do you think caused it?"

Kristi and Scott were having dinner at Donna and Randy's house the evening after their return to Florida, when Randy broached the subject of the crash of the F-18.

"It's way too soon, but my guess would be the pilot pushed it too hard. He was young and had little experience in an F-18. I suspect he had that baby zipping across the desert and didn't realize he was subjecting himself to nine or ten times the force of gravity. It only takes about twelve seconds of that before the pilot loses consciousness, because there is no blood pressure to the brain under that strong a G force. When he came to, he was probably looking at the ground and couldn't react quickly enough," Scott answered. "If he hit the ground going the speed the gauges indicated, the plane simply disintegrated."

"Twelve *seconds*!" Kristi repeated incredulously.

"That's right. And while unconscious, the pilot is absolutely incapacitated. Then it takes him twelve more seconds to wake up and another two minutes or so before all of his responses return to normal," Scott explained. "In a dogfight situation it can be deadly."

"It sounds pretty deadly in any situation," Kristi commented.

"He should have been aware of the possibility and allowed for it," Randy commented casually.

So they were back to the good pilot-bad pilot defense, Kristi thought. But she found it difficult to believe that even the best of pilots wasn't tempted to go too fast or take one chance too many sometimes. Some made it and some didn't. Scott and Randy didn't think it was possible for bad things to happen to good pilots, but Kristi believed otherwise. Rick and Captain Mathison were excellent examples of good, but dead pilots.

"Of course, all the pieces will be shipped to a warehouse, where everything will be examined meticulously to make sure there were no defective parts or mechanical malfunctions," Scott continued. "And the pilot's blood will be tested for chemical substances that might have influenced his performance."

Kristi was becoming increasingly disturbed by the conversation and was relieved when the evening finally ended. All the talk of death and crashes and pilot errors made her so nervous that she had difficulty falling asleep later that night.

A glance at the luminous digits on the clock face told her that it was after two in the morning. Scott's steady breathing indicated he was not sharing her insomnia. Carefully she slipped out from under the weight of his arm and eased her legs away from his without disturbing him.

It had been weeks since she had taken a late-night walk on the beach and although the temperature was in the cool forties, the moon was beckoning her. She dressed warmly in jeans, a sweater, heavy socks inside her tennis shoes and a coat.

Maverick had been watching her actions with interest, and when she headed for the patio door in the living room, he jumped up and followed. As if sensing her distress, he stayed by her side instead of roaming ahead or lagging behind as she walked down to the water's edge. A large twisted log had washed up onto the shore and Kristi sat on a smooth, dry spot while Maverick settled at her feet.

The moon was almost full and would have been quite bright, had it not been for gloomy gray clouds scuttling across the night sky capturing, then releasing the light like the signal beacon on a ship flashing a message. In her melancholy mood Kristi could only assume it was God trying to tell her to be careful. Falling in love with a pilot would come to no good.

But it was too late. She had already fallen in love with a pilot, one named Scott Sanders whose nickname was the Saint and who, fittingly enough, flew with the Angels. Perhaps she had grown to depend on him too much. Maybe she was too close to see the situation in perspective. Their relationship had jumped from one of casual acquaintances, then tentative friends, to a peak as passionate lovers almost overnight. Possibly the love she felt for him was like what a student would feel for a teacher or a patient for a doctor. But she would never find that out until she put some distance between them.

It was time to go home . . . or at least what she considered to be home. It would be good to see her mother and her grandmother and spend a little time with them before Christmas. And now that she had summoned up enough courage to get back onto a plane, surely she would be able to handle a commercial flight. In fact, after she had swallowed her fears, she had actually understood the exhilaration Scott must feel whenever he pointed the nose of a Navy jet skyward. The power and speed must be addictive, especially to a man of action such as himself.

Kristi shook her head, trying to clear it. Why was it she could never have a thought into which Scott didn't somehow intrude? She had to get away for a while...maybe forever. Tomorrow Scott was scheduled to fly with the old squadron of Blues to the naval academy in Maryland for a special demonstration before the president and visiting dignitaries. Scott had explained that this was highly unusual, because the Blues' flight schedule usually ended in mid-November and didn't resume until mid-March—which normally allowed time for the pilots to relax and the planes to be repainted and reconditioned. But this was a special case, and because he was combining this trip with a follow-up investigation of the F-18 crash in Washington, D.C., he would be gone four or five days.

He had invited her to go along and she had been considering it, even though she had not been looking forward to seeing him go through the dangerous routine in the tight formation for which the Blue Angels were famous. But now Kristi knew she wouldn't be going. Instead she would be boarding a flight to Seattle...alone.

Scott stirred and automatically reached out for Kristi. Finding only a cool sheet where she should have been, he stretched, not necessarily alarmed by her absence. But several minutes later when she didn't return from the bathroom, where he'd assumed she was, he sat up. When he noticed there was no light on in the bathroom, he thought she must be in the kitchen. It wasn't like her to snack in the middle of the night, but he knew she had been upset.

Actually it had been building, beginning when she had forced herself to step onto the jet before their trip to New Mexico, then continuing through the visit to the crash site, and culminating in the discussion at Randy's house. On the way home she had been unusually quiet and hadn't seemed to be in the mood for any romantic overtures, so they had prepared for bed in almost total silence, then fallen asleep lying curled together on the bed.

Or rather he had fallen asleep. It appeared that she had not.

Scott got up and pulled on a pair of jeans. As he walked barefoot from the bedroom, he noticed Maverick was not in his usual place beside the bed. It was amazing how quickly that dog had adopted Kristi as his mistress. He obviously adored her, and Scott could certainly understand that, because he was completely crazy about her himself.

When he saw she was not in the living room or the kitchen, he began to get worried. The sight of her purse hanging on the back of a chair reassured him she had not disappeared altogether, but the fact that she had not decided to wake him caused him to crinkle his forehead into a worried frown.

The draperies had been left open and a shaft of moonlight oozed into the room as a cloud moved away from the moon. Suddenly he knew without a doubt where she was, and he crossed quickly to the patio door and stood staring out into the darkness. Another cloud had blotted out the light, and he had to wait for it to leave before he could see the beach clearly.

Just as he had expected, there she was, a coat wrapped tightly around her as protection against the chilling wind. For a second he was on the point of turning to get his shoes and a shirt so he could join her, but stopped. She obviously wanted to be alone. If she had wanted him to sit with her, she knew he would have been glad to, even if it meant waking him up in the early-morning hours. *No.* Apparently she needed the time and space to think something through.

He and Kristi had been together almost constantly since Thanksgiving. Until now they had both welcomed the companionship and hadn't wanted to spend much time alone. He knew it was silly, but he was a little bit hurt that she should feel any differently now.

He had helped her renew her feelings of independence and courage, but now he feared he had created a monster. When he had encouraged her to face her problems in order to overcome them, his intentions had been good. Somehow he had thought that by helping her get over the trauma caused by the Worldwide crash, she would be able to separate the past from the present and realize how much she needed him in her life. Now he was beginning to believe his plan had backfired.

When she had been able to handle the flight with relative ease, then had seen the crash site without breaking down, he felt they had gotten over a major hurdle together. But perhaps he had given her too much self-confidence, so that she didn't feel she needed him anymore—or anyone else. The thought had not occurred to him before, but what would she do once she had accepted Rick and Diane's death and was no longer hesitant about flying as a Worldwide employee again? Would she merely fly out of his life as abruptly as she had flown in?

He remained at the patio door, watching her and trying to figure out what he should do next. He felt as if he had pushed the first small rock that had started an avalanche and was now helpless to stop it. He either had to jump in and roll with it or get out of the way. This feeling of helplessness and indecision was very uncharacteristic for him, and he didn't know how to handle it.

She looked so forlorn out there on the empty stretch of beach, all alone with only a dog...his dog...at her feet to keep her company. But he had glimpsed a strength and determination within her that he had previously only guessed she possessed. When she had come to Florida a month ago, she had been a wounded bird, her wings clipped and her spirit broken so that she was unable to fly. He had taken her in, had doctored her spirit and protected her wings until the feathers could grow back. Unfortunately he had also fallen in love with her.

He searched his memory, running back through the conversations they had had and the kisses they had shared, but he couldn't recall ever hearing her voice her feelings for him. Not that he had ever come right out and admitted to her that he loved her. He had hinted at it, but she had always seemed to cut him off before he could actually voice the words. But she had never so much as hinted at what she felt.

The only encouragement he could take from their situation was that she seemed to enjoy their lovemaking as much as he did. And he knew, not only from what she had told him about her past but from his intuition about her, that she was not the type of woman to give herself too easily unless her emotions were involved. He truly believed she cared for him—but apparently not enough, and he didn't know what else he could do to capture her love.

When he saw her stand up and walk back toward the house, he watched until she had almost reached the steps, making certain she was okay before he sprinted back to the bedroom, stripped off his jeans and jumped under the covers. He heard the patio door open and close, then listened while she got a drink of water in the kitchen. A few minutes later she returned to the bedroom and stood beside the bed, staring down at him. Since he was pretending to be asleep, he couldn't actually see her, but he could feel the intensity of her gaze and it took all his willpower not to fling back the covers and confront her, admitting his love for her and asking her if she loved him, even a little.

But he remained still, struggling to keep his eyelids from twitching and his breathing slow and regular. Eventually she turned away, quietly stripped off her clothes and eased back into bed. Her body had brought with it the cold of the outdoors and though she cuddled against him, she felt stiff and tense. It was almost an hour before he felt her relax and eventually drift off to sleep. He knew he had to get a few more hours of sleep himself if he hoped to be ready to fly tomorrow, but an overwhelming sense of disaster kept him awake. It was not a premonition of trouble with his plane, but a painful suspicion he was losing Kristi . . . forever.

He was still wide-awake when the sun rose over the Gulf later that morning. Kristi had been restless and several times he suspected she was awake, but if she had been, she had chosen to remain silent and still until she eventually went back to sleep.

From the moment they met, Scott had felt an unusually easy communication with her. Because they had so much in common, they had been able to understand and almost anticipate each other's thoughts. But not now. She had shut him out completely, and he was confused and unhappy about it.

When she volunteered to cook breakfast, a task he knew wasn't her favorite, he suspected the worst. But as they sat down to perfectly fried eggs, crisp, but not over-cooked bacon, and unburned toast, he was dreading asking her about the trip to Maryland, because he suspected he already knew the answer. What was worse, he feared her rejection would go deeper and last longer than merely a week or so.

"Good eggs," he complimented sincerely, never taking his eyes off her face. Her gaze kept skittering away from his, never quite meeting and holding as if she, too, was not anxious for the conversation that seemed to be inevitable. "Your cooking is getting better and better."

"Thanks. But I'll admit there was a lot of room for improvement. I may have passed the danger-of-food-poisoning stage, but I know it's not something I want to do for a living." She seemed almost nervous as she combed her fingers through the silky strands of her hair, unconsciously letting it filter back to her shoulders where it obediently fell into place.

"So," he said, taking a deep breath as he drew patterns in the egg yolks with the tines of his fork. "Have you packed your clothes for Maryland? It might be a little nippy this time of year. I don't think they're predicting snow, but you never know."

"No, I don't think so."

"Maybe not, but you should pack some warm clothes just in case...."

"No, I meant I'm not going to Maryland." She stood up and carried her plate with its untouched food to the kitchen. Scott tossed his fork onto his plate and followed her.

"I've decided it's time to take the ultimate test," she continued as she scraped her food into the garbage disposal and turned on the faucet so she could wash her plate. "I'm going to fly to Seattle and visit my mother and grandmother."

"Will you be back for Christmas?" he asked.

"I don't think so." Kristi's full attention seemed to be focused on scrubbing every last speck off the plate.

Scott's voice leveled to a strained monotone. "Will you be back at all?"

"Of course I will," she answered lightly. "I have to come back and pick up my things, then drive my car back to Denver."

"Damn it," he said, tired of playing games. "You know what I mean."

She hesitated, then lifted her eyes, looking directly at him for the first time today. "No, Scott. I'm not coming back to stay. I've decided to try the rehabilitation training one more time. If it works, then I'll be back in the air. If it doesn't, then I'm going to apply for a ground job, maybe as an instructor or a reservationist. Worldwide's headquarters are in Denver, so it won't require that I relocate, which will be nice...."

"Why?"

"I have a great apartment there and—"

"Why are you doing this? If you don't want to go to Maryland, why can't you just wait here? I won't be gone but a few days and then we can talk some more." Already there was a hollowness in his chest, an emptiness he knew would only get worse if she left. "Kristi, I love you," he cried. "We're great together. I've never met anyone like you. I've been waiting all my life for you to drop into it, and now that you have, I can't let you go."

"I can't stay," she stated flatly, without any sign of emotion.

"We're two of a kind, you and me. We belong together. Whatever is bothering you, we can work it out.

Just as soon as I get back from the demonstration
we'll—''

The plate she had been holding shattered as it forcibly
struck the kitchen floor. "That's just it, don't you see?
Every weekend I'd be sitting here waiting for you to get
back from trying to commit suicide in front of thousands of spectators. Every day I'd be wondering if you'd
walk in that door or be carried to the morgue in pieces. I
know you very well. I've met your type in air bases all
over the world. They never know when to quit. It will always be one more flight, one more loop, one more knot
of speed. I can't take it. And I can't wait around for you
to kill yourself!'' By the time she had spoken the last
word, she was hysterical, practically screaming. Without
waiting for his reply, she brushed past him and ran across
the room, grabbed her purse and rushed out the front
door, slamming it shut behind her.

By the time he reached the door, she was in her car,
spinning the tires on the gravel as she backed out of the
driveway and took off down the road. He watched as she
passed her own house and headed toward the highway.

A quick inspection of his watch told Scott he didn't
have time to follow her. He was expected at the base in
less than an hour, when the crews were scheduled to meet
and run through their checklist before taking off for
Maryland. He was the leader and it was his responsibility to be there on time, and he had to allow a few extra
minutes to drop off Maverick with Donna, who had
agreed to dog-sit, should Kristi decide to go to Maryland. But still he was tempted. He was afraid that if he
didn't catch her now, he would never see her again.

On the other hand, how was he supposed to stop her
once he caught up with her? His Porsche might have her
Toyota beaten, but he couldn't very well force her off the

road or make her stop and talk with him. And in the mood she was in now, he could only assume she would stubbornly keep driving across Florida until she ran out of highway at the Atlantic coast.

"Damn!" he repeated and pushed the door shut with a bang. He tried to pull himself back into some semblance of control as he tossed some clothes, a toothbrush and shaving supplies into a duffel bag and zipped his dress uniform into a garment bag. A distracted pilot was a dangerous one, and he couldn't afford to think about this now. But as soon as he returned to Florida next week, he would concentrate all his energies on thinking of a way to get her back. He had only been shot down once in his life and had survived. Surely he could convince one beautiful, fascinating, woman that she couldn't live without him. But deep in his subconscious he knew it could be the toughest battle he had ever fought . . . and for the first time, his self-confidence wavered as he realized it might be the first battle he couldn't win.

HER MOTHER was delighted to see her. Even when Kristi arrived without any luggage and in obvious distress, her mother welcomed her with open arms and no questions, although she did give her many curious looks. Kristi was glad her mother didn't press her for an explanation; at this point she simply couldn't discuss it.

Kristi knew it had been silly of her not to go back to her house and pack her clothes. But she had been afraid Scott would be there waiting for her and she wanted, above all things, to avoid another confrontation with him. There was nothing left for them to discuss. It was over and she was relieved.

But she was also in pain. She accepted the fact that it would take a long time to get over Scott, if, indeed, she would ever get over him. Already she missed him desperately and she knew tonight, alone in the double bed in her mother's spare bedroom, it would seem even more final. But she felt stronger than ever and she would make it. During the last few months her endurance and sanity had been tested more than once. And even though it was a struggle, she had been able to get through it successfully.

The flight to Seattle had been a harrowing experience. If she had thought it difficult to climb the steps to the Navy jet she had flown in with Scott, it was a hundred times worse to have to walk up the ramp, cross the threshold and walk down the aisle of the first Worldwide commercial flight she had been on since the crash. She had resisted the urge to shut her eyes as her legs automatically carried her to seat 14D. With her seat belt tightened so much that she could hardly breathe, she kept her gaze focused on the back of the seat in front of her, rigidly avoiding the sight of the scenery flashing past her window as the plane gathered speed, then lifted off the runway.

Her jaws were clenched so firmly that they ached and her nerves were so tense, she felt herself shivering uncontrollably as if she were standing naked in a blizzard. Hearing the flight attendants repeat words that she herself had said hundreds of times to thousands of passengers of her own didn't help. Nor was it comforting that they were flying into a storm, a cold front rushing down from Canada. The plane pushed through the heavy clouds, finding blue skies at last, but the atmosphere above the storm was bumpy and rough. As they dipped through one air pocket after another, she had embarrassed herself after a particularly bad one by dropping her head to her lap and grabbing her ankles in the reflex action she had been taught as a crash position. She knew the passengers around her must think her completely insane as the tears tumbled down her cheeks. Her only consolation was that she wasn't personally acquainted with any of the crew on this flight, so this public humiliation wouldn't follow her in her career.

But she had made it. She had endured the lengthy flight, including an additional landing and takeoff in Denver, without using the airsickness bag or rushing to the bathroom. And she had been able to walk down the ramp in Seattle under her own power, however weak her knees might have been. Instinctively she knew the next flight would be easier, then the next and the next, until she could work her way back to ignoring the fact they were airborne as she pushed the beverage cart down the aisle or served meals.

Her mother, who made it a habit to buy things on sale and keep extras on hand, had risen to the occasion and given Kristi an unopened toothbrush and a nightgown she had planned to give her for Christmas.

The next day, Kristi drove to one of the local malls in her rental car and purchased the items she would need to tide her over for a few days or weeks, until she decided to return to Florida for the possessions she had left there.

The mall was beautifully decorated; somehow with the blustery cold outside, it felt more like Christmas here than it had in Florida. If Kristi had been happier, she could easily have slipped into a holiday mood in the bustling activity of the shoppers who packed every store.

It was only a few days until Christmas. Kristi realized with a start that she had left all her presents for the family in Florida. Since excuses would bring questions, she decided she would buy her mother and grandmother a little something to put under their trees, then ship the bulk of their gifts as soon as she returned to Florida. It didn't take long to pick out a dressy sweater for her mother and a new telephone for her grandmother. Kristi dropped them off at a wrapping booth rather than deal with the hassle of buying paper and ribbon or use her mother's supplies.

There were several gifts to be wrapped ahead of hers so, instead of waiting at the booth, Kristi continued her stroll down the mall. When she passed a men's store, she was immediately reminded that she hadn't gotten around to picking out something for Scott; now it was just as well that she hadn't. Anything she might have selected would have seemed either too personal or too impersonal, and even though she had wanted to give him something, she hadn't wanted him to get the wrong message.

She walked on, not stopping again until she reached a Christmas shop that specialized in everything anyone could possibly want to put on their Christmas tree. In the windows tiny mechanical elves moved about, appearing to be busy in Santa's workshop. One of them seemed to be hammering a wheel onto a wagon, while two others tested a seesaw and still another was painting the face on a doll.

In spite of her melancholy mood, Kristi couldn't resist investigating the store further and walked inside. There were dozens of trees, each one decorated with a certain theme. Some had different kinds of butterfly ornaments or were Victorian delights done up in old-fashioned toys, cranberry and popcorn ropes and twinkly lights that looked like candles. She didn't realize until she had circled the entire store that she had been searching each tree for an airplane ornament, but none of them had one, for which she was glad. If she had seen one Scott didn't already have, she would have been very tempted to buy it for him. *Good Lord!* she chastised herself. There she went again, not able to pass an hour without letting that man slip into her thoughts.

Suddenly angry with herself, she whirled and almost collided with a tall artificial spruce tree that was decorated all in blue and silver. Strings of silver-toned multi-faceted beads were draped from limb to limb, and feathered blue birds and tiny silver stars were attached to or hung from each branch. It was a lovely tree, although Kristi's personal taste ran to a less restricted design. She was used to her mother's trees, which were decorated with all kinds of ornaments in assorted sizes, shapes and colors, many of them older than Kristi herself. There had always been too many strings of lights and the branches had literally dripped with icicles. The trees of Kristi's childhood had always been gaudy, but in her opinion they had been absolutely beautiful.

She was about to maneuver around the tree when she lifted her gaze to its top. There, perched loftily on the tallest point was an angel. Its gauzy silver wings were raised in flight and the sweet, peaceful expression on its porcelain face was almost ethereal. But it was its gown that caught Kristi's attention. The royal-blue silk glittered in the artificial lighting as if it had been sprinkled by stardust.

Several minutes later Kristi left the Christmas store with the blue angel wrapped in many layers of tissue paper and resting snugly in a cardboard box. Kristi wasn't sure why she had bought it. She hadn't actually paused to think because as soon as she saw it, she knew she had to have it. It would be the first ornament she had ever purchased that would be placed on her own Christmas tree. Not that she had any idea when that would be, but this angel was the beginning of her own treasured collection.

When she returned to her mother's, she placed the gifts she had purchased under the tree and carried the bag from the Christmas store to her bedroom. She placed the angel, still in its box, in a dresser drawer, but for some reason it kept pulling her back. Finally, acting on the excuse that she didn't want the wings to get bent or the gown wrinkled, she took it out, unwrapped its layers of tissue, set it on the dresser, then stood back to admire it.

It wasn't until that moment that she realized what had attracted her to this particular ornament. To most people passing that tree in the Christmas shop, the angel was simply an ornament with beautiful delicate features and intricate detailing. But to Kristi it was her very own blue angel. Kristi sat on the bed, her gaze never leaving the sparkling, magical creation. She had bought it because, in a roundabout, subconscious way, it reminded her of Scott.

Scott. How had it happened? How had he become such an important part of her life? How had he become so deeply embedded in her heart that the mere thought of him caused it to skip a beat? And with every breath her very soul sighed his name.

Where was he now? She glanced at her watch. Would he be flying with the other Blues right now, getting in a little last-minute practice and becoming familiar with the airfield before the show, scheduled for the day after tomorrow? She hoped the weather would cooperate. She knew they wouldn't perform if the conditions weren't good, but what if it was stormy and they weren't able to get in enough practice? Or what if ice should form on the wings and no one noticed?

Kristi shook her head. She knew that fear was un-
grounded. With a maintenance and service crew that
numbered in the dozens, those planes were watched more
closely than most children. A more reasonable fear would
be that one of the pilots would slip up, make an error of
some sort and cause an accident. Flying in such close
formation, it wouldn't take much . . . a miscalculation, a
gust of wind, a fraction of a second. The Blues were the
first to admit that they never flew an absolutely perfect
show, even with all their practicing.

She jumped up and began pacing the room. To sit here
worrying about him, imagining the worst, couldn't possibly be worse than standing on the sidelines actually
watching the show, holding her breath until they were on
the ground safely, could it? At least then she would know
when it began and ended. And perhaps by being there,
the strength of her will would help protect him, because
she would be praying so hard that he would be okay.

Slumping back on the bed, she lay, staring at the ceiling. Instead of seeing the stippled white bumps, she was
visualizing a long strip of white beach and the foam of
the waves as they tumbled over each other and rushed in
to curl in pale green crescents on the sand. And she saw
a tall, well-muscled man jogging just above the waterline, the tanned skin of his bare chest glistening in the
sunlight.

As if her mind's eye had a zoom lens, she could suddenly observe his face close up. His eyes, laughing, tender, loving eyes, were looking at her, their corners
crinkling in friendly laugh lines. His mouth, so warm, so
delicious, so exciting, was curved into that now-familiar
crooked grin that had charmed her and so successfully
captured her heart. She remembered the magic those lips
had worked on her body and the words that had passed

them to heal her broken spirit. He had brought alive more than her emotions. He had made her feel good; better than she had ever felt before.

Why did she think about him almost every minute of every day? Why did she care desperately what happened to him? Why had she dropped her guard and fallen in love with him? Because he was a very special man. He had taken her when she was at the lowest point of her life and lifted her back onto her feet. He had given her moral support so she believed in herself again, and emotional support until she could stand to face another day. He made her feel important and capable and strong again—and she felt totally rotten without him.

She had to get back to Pensacola. She had to be there when he returned home on Christmas Eve—to tell him that she would worry and pray every time he was in the air, but that life with him was a million times better than life without him. She would have to trust in his ability as a pilot, because she could never ask him to give up something he loved so much. But with her by his side, perhaps he would value life a little more and take fewer risks, especially once they decided to begin a family.

Whoa, girl, Kristi cautioned herself. She was jumping ahead too quickly. He had said he loved her, but they had never discussed marriage. Now she knew exactly what she wanted for Christmas... her own special Angel.

Christmas! She had to get back. If she left tomorrow, she would have time to do a little more shopping and pick up some groceries. This Christmas would be special, like their relationship. She would have to stop by Grandma's and give her her gift... and pick up some recipes. Kristi's cooking had come a long way since fate had brought her to Florida. She was realistic enough to know that she would never be in her grandmother's category, but felt confident she could put together a passable holiday meal for Scott, and Maverick, of course.

Kristi leaped off the bed and hurried into the kitchen where her mother was frying chicken for dinner. Wrapping her arms around her mother's still-trim waist she said, "Mmm, it smells good. You always did make the best fried chicken in the whole world. Even better than Grandma's."

"Okay, what are you up to?" her mother asked, immediately made suspicious by the unexpected, profuse compliment.

Kristi started to deny that she was up to anything, but she knew her mother had always been able to see through her. "I really meant it about your chicken, but I do have something important to tell you. I'm leaving tomorrow."

Her mother dried her hands on a dish towel and whirled around. "So soon? But you just got here. I thought you were going to stay for Christmas."

"I thought I was, too. But I realized I shouldn't have left. You see, I've met this terrific guy and I've fallen in love with him."

"What?" The towel fluttered to the floor as mother stared at daughter. "I've talked with you on the phone every week and you've never mentioned anyone in particular. I thought you were still pining over Rick."

"I thought I was, too, but Scott, that's his name, just sort of fell into my life, Mom. And I'm sorry I didn't tell you sooner, but I didn't want to get your hopes up. You see, he has one huge flaw that it's taken me all this time to accept."

"Looks aren't everything, Kristine. You shouldn't be so critical."

"Oh, it's not his looks. He's incredibly handsome. His only flaw is that he's a pilot, a career Navy pilot, and he's the commander of the Blue Angels, no less."

"My, my," her mother said, clicking her tongue sarcastically. "He sounds absolutely dreadful."

"He's wonderful, but I wasn't sure that after my bad experiences I would be able to live with the constant risk. Today I realized that I'd rather be with him and worry than be away from him and worry. But I'm afraid I left sort of abruptly, so now I've got to go back and see if we can have a future together."

"Are you sure, sweetheart? I don't want you rushing into anything too soon. It's only been seven months, you know."

"I know, but what I feel for Scott is different from what I felt for Rick. Rick and I were great friends, but we weren't meant to be married to each other. I'm so sorry he's dead, but there's nothing I can do to bring him or Diane...or Daddy back. I've accepted that now and I'm ready to get on with my own life."

"But it's Christmas. You'll never be able to get a flight out."

"I'll go to the airport early tomorrow morning and sit there until there's space. I've already checked on the flights to Florida and there's quite a few. I don't care which airline I fly, even if I have to pay for my ticket or route through Alaska. If I go on standby at every counter, surely something will be available."

"Speaking of airlines...what about Worldwide? Are you going back to work with them?"

"I don't know yet," Kristi admitted. "That's something I need to decide soon, but I have to work on one thing at a time and at this point my emotional health is more important. Right now I've got to get back before

Scott does. He's so special to me. You'd like him very much."

"Well, I hope to get to meet him soon. At a wedding, maybe?" her mother hinted broadly. "I would love to have some grandchildren to spoil before I'm too old to enjoy them."

Kristi just smiled. "By the way, Mom, I liked your *young* man. I never realized before how lonely you must have been since Daddy died."

Her mother flushed almost girlishly. "I was hoping you'd like him. He'll never take your father's place, but he's a nice fellow. We've been talking about buying a camper and touring the United States. I've seen most of the States before, but never as a tourist."

"Why, Mother," Kristi said, pretending to be shocked. "I do hope you two are also talking marriage."

"Kristine Harrison! You know I would never..."

"Maybe we can make it a double wedding," Kristi suggested with a laugh. "Somehow I never imagined walking down the aisle with my mother, but it has a certain ring to it, don't you think?"

IT WAS LATE the next evening when Kristi arrived back at her beach house. So close to the holiday, the airport had been a madhouse, but she had finally obtained a flight out in the afternoon. Her mind had been so preoccupied with Scott and what the future might hold for them that her discomfort during the flight had been minimal. All she wanted to do was get back to him as quickly as possible.

With the time zone changes, just sitting around all day had been surprisingly exhausting, so even though her nerves were taunt with anticipation, she fell asleep almost as quickly as she crawled into bed.

She felt herself soaring like an eagle, gliding through the air and laughing from the pure pleasure of flying. She turned and saw that Scott was with her, flying alongside. Neither was in a plane, nor did they have to flap their wings like birds. Rather, with the absurdity of dreams, they were able to float weightlessly, dipping and swooping playfully through the clouds and looking down at the geometric patterns of the earth below them.

Then the scene changed; now she was inside a plane and was wearing her uniform. She was serving lunch to the first class passengers and could see through the open curtain that Diane was working in coach. Just then her friend looked up and their eyes met. Kristi wanted to cry out to Diane that she was sorry. She hadn't meant to be sick. She wanted to tell Diane how much she valued their friendship and how much she had missed her since the crash.

But there was too much space between them and too much work to do, so neither could leave her post. Instead Diane smiled, and as if she already knew what Kristi was thinking, without speaking formed the words, "Don't worry about me. I'm fine. Just be happy."

Tears welled in Kristi's eyes. "Goodbye, Diane." She had spoken softly, but even though Diane couldn't hear, Kristi could see she understood.

"Goodbye, my friend," Diane mouthed silently.

A man next to Kristi reached out and touched her arm. She glanced down at him for a second and when she lifted her gaze again, the aisle was empty. Diane was gone.

Kristi now had to serve the entire plane. She worked and worked, but couldn't seem to get everyone fed. It appeared to be impossible to make everyone happy. She was split too many ways. She knew she would have to concentrate on one section at a time. But before she could begin her new plan, a voice crackled over the loud-speaker.

"I'd like to welcome everyone to Worldwide Airlines Flight 2302. We will be reaching our destination in Maryland in approximately one hour and forty-five minutes, so sit back and relax."

Flight 2302! Maryland! Oh no! Kristi thought as panic twisted her stomach. What was she doing on this flight? And why were they going to Maryland? Flight 2302 had been heading for Miami. She had to warn the pilot. She had to tell him that the flight was doomed. She dropped the plate of food she had been holding back onto the cart and started to run down the aisle. She didn't remember it being so long. However fast as she ran, she didn't seem to be making any headway. Then suddenly it happened.

She felt the plane falter as one engine sputtered and stopped. Not overly concerned, because she knew from her training that the loss of one engine was not a major disaster, she continued to make her way to the cockpit. But when another engine choked and died, she knew she had to hurry. They had to be warned so they could avert a tragedy.

The plane began to shake and rapidly lose altitude. She could barely keep on her feet now as it dropped and shuddered violently. "Rick," she called. "You must watch out. Don't try to land on the runway next to the fuel tanks."

She was getting closer now. She was going to make it. Surely if they knew what was about to happen, they could change things and make it end differently.

"Rick," she repeated, trying to get his attention. "Did you hear me? I don't want to die. I've got to get home to Scott. We can make it if we're careful."

The curtain dividing the cockpit from the first class section stirred and a man's fingers curled around the edge of it before pulling it aside. He stepped through the doorway and stood calmly facing Kristi. "We're going to be fine. I'm a good pilot. I'll get us down safely. Just trust me."

Kristi's eyes widened in horror and her hand clutched frantically at her throat. It wasn't Rick as she had expected. And the man standing in front of her didn't appear to be at all concerned. His adorable crooked grin twisted up one corner of his mouth and his dark blue eyes twinkled confidently. *Oh Lord!* Kristi breathed. It was Scott! How did he get on Flight 2302? She had to make him leave or he, too, would be killed.

"Scott!" she screamed. "The plane's going to crash! We're all going to die!"

One broad shoulder lifted in a nonchalant shrug just before the plane's nose dipped earthward and they began to plummet like a stone.

"Scott," she cried hysterically. "Scott, I love you!"

Chapter Fourteen

The tears were streaming down her cheeks and her throat was hoarse from her cries. As she lay in bed, huddled into a miserable ball, her body was shaking uncontrollably.

It was a dream, she reminded herself, just a dream. She hadn't been on Flight 2302, and neither had Scott.

But he would be flying in the air show tomorrow. Was this some sort of premonition? Or had her own tension brought back the nightmare? It had been so many weeks since she had last suffered through it that she had hoped it would never return. When Scott was with her she felt safe and protected, and her sleep had been disturbed only by their passion for each other. But Scott wasn't here.

She was worried and she missed him very much. That must be the reason for the nightmare's return and its bizarre new twist. The only thing it meant was that she was anxious to get things resolved between Scott and herself. The flight must have exhausted her more than she'd imagined.

Gradually the trembling eased and Kristi's tensed muscles began to relax. She kept repeating to herself that it was just a dream and in only two more days Scott would be back. He would hold her in his arms and tell her he would never leave her again. She had nothing to fear because her nightmare was over and he would take care of her forever. She had survived, she was strong, and she was in love with the best pilot in the world.

In spite of her silent pep talk, she was still glad it was almost daylight and she wouldn't have to go back to sleep. Besides, she had a lot of things to do today.

As soon as the stores opened, she hit the mall with a vengeance, searching until she found the perfect gift for Scott. In an exclusive men's shop she discovered a good selection of leather bomber jackets. Even though they were most closely associated with the Air Force, she knew all aviators looked upon the jackets as a sort of badge of pride and patriotism. They had become popular during World War II and, although the Air Force had for some strange reason decided to replace them with nylon jackets, the leather ones were regaining popularity. Her hand stroked the supple seal-brown goatskin leather and she had no trouble picturing how handsome Scott would look in it. The fact that he looked terrific in everything didn't influence her decision and soon she had tucked the gift-wrapped box under her arm and was heading back to the parking lot.

The trip to the grocery store took longer than the one to the mall, probably because she felt less comfortable there. But eventually she was able to round up all the items on her grandmother's list, as well as a few staples and then pushed her cart to the checkout counter. Waiting her turn, she smiled as she recognized the piped-in music as "Kiss an Angel Good Morning" and her mind drifted back to the first time she and Scott had heard that song together. Kristi hummed along, mentally revising the words to fit her own special Angel.

Kiss an Angel good morning and let him know you
think about him when he's gone. Kiss an Angel good
morning and love him like the devil when he gets
back home.

Now that was prophetic!

Still humming after paying the total and letting the
sacker transfer her bags to the car, Kristi slid behind the
wheel and turned the key. The radio came on with the
engine, but she didn't pay attention to the announcer
until she heard the words, "...at the Blue Angels' air
show in Maryland. I repeat, there has been a crash and
at least one fatality has been confirmed. The details are
sketchy, but we will try to get more information before
our next newscast."

Her hand was shaking as she turned the dial, frantically searching for a news report on another station, but
all she heard was music and commercials. Dropping her
head until her forehead rested on the top of the steering
wheel, she sat for several minutes, her limbs too weak to
drive.

It was coming true. Her dream had been a warning; she
should have called him and stopped him from flying today. She had been given another chance to save a life and
blown it. But worst of all, it could be Scott that had been
killed today. When was it all going to stop? Why was her
life plagued with airplane disasters?

It had been hard to accept her father's unexpected
death, even though he was in the military and exposed to
danger. And it had been rough when Rick and Diane
died. But if she should lose Scott, especially in an airplane crash, she knew, without a doubt, this would be a
blow from which she would never recover. She felt bad

wishing the pain of a death on someone else, but all the way back to the beach she prayed it wouldn't be Scott.

She tried to keep reminding herself that Scott wasn't the only pilot at the air show. Just because *someone* had been killed didn't mean that someone was Scott. He was, as he had so often stated, an excellent pilot and he knew the routine well. He wasn't a green rookie at the controls of a plane he wasn't familiar with.

On the other hand, she remembered hearing about another flight demonstration team whose leader hadn't pulled up in time and had crashed, with three of the other pilots following him to their deaths. She knew the reason this had been able to happen was that when several planes were flying in a tight formation, the other three pilots did not watch where they were going, but focused on a single point on the leader's plane. If they always kept that spot in the same position in their sights, they would then maintain a uniform distance from the other planes as they flew their maneuvers. This, of course, required them to trust the leader with their lives implicitly, which was why the men usually were the ones who voted for their commander.

What if that was what happened today? What if Scott had, for some reason, made a mistake and had let the others down? Her dream had seemed so real. Had it been a forecast of the real event?

She drove straight to Scott's house and used the key he had given her, which she had forgotten to return, to let herself in. Even though she was scared to death, she tried to proceed as she normally would. It was easier to pretend he would be walking through the front door at any moment than to consider the alternative.

Automatically she unpacked the sacks and put away the groceries. It seemed a sensible way to keep herself from dwelling on the possibilities. But as she worked she was listening to a radio and keeping an eye on the television, hoping the station would break in with a bulletin, particularly because the Blues were hometown heroes. When nothing was said, she even called the television stations and the naval base, but neither had anything new to tell her. So she kept her hands busy and tried to think about what would happen *when* Scott returned.

Since her departure had been so awkward, she wasn't sure how he would react when he returned. He had told her he loved her and hopefully his feelings wouldn't have changed in less than a week. On the other hand, her own feelings were undergoing a real trial right now. For the next few hours she vacillated. One minute she was sorry she had left his side for even a minute. She was convinced that if she had been with him in Maryland, nothing bad would have happened.

Then she would become angry at herself for getting so involved with a pilot and putting herself in this position of panic. Was she some sort of masochist who enjoyed pain? The alarms had gone off almost the minute she met him. But he had been so helpful and understanding, it had simply crept up on her. If only she had been more careful. If only she had not had that awful nightmare and gone for a walk on the beach.

But if she hadn't, she would never have met Scott. And as upsetting as his career was, he had been the best thing to ever happen to her.

Stop it, Kristi, she scolded herself. *Stop thinking of him in the past tense, as if he were truly dead.* "He's alive," she said aloud with much more bravado than she felt. It would be the cruelest joke fate could possibly play. Scott had brought her back to life; and to lose him now would be the fatal blow.

Kristi puttered around the house, washing the dishes that had sat untouched in the sink since breakfast three days ago. She also swept up the shattered pieces of the plate she had broken and finished the job by mopping the floor. Somehow being here in his house, looking at his dirty dishes in the kitchen and his dirty socks on the bathroom floor, made it almost impossible to think that he might never come back. She stroked the sleeve of his uniform and breathed in the fragrance of the after-shave that clung to his robe. Here, in this house, she felt very close to him.

But she remembered when her father had been killed. Luckily she had been in Denver on a layover. When her mother's call had come to inform her of the bad news, Kristi had been able to hop onto a jet and fly to Seattle right away. It had been so difficult to accept, especially when she had walked into her parents' house and seen a pair of coveralls draped over the back of a chair and his house slippers on the floor next to the bed, ready for his feet to slide into them. It had been more upsetting to see everything just as he'd left it, so obviously waiting patiently for his return. Every time she opened the medicine cabinet and saw his razor or opened the kitchen cabinet and had to push aside his favorite coffee cup to reach one of her own, she had been reminded that a short time ago, he had been alive and well.

She also remembered hearing that of the pilots who stayed in the military service for twenty years, twenty-five percent of them would die in crashes—and that was not including combat, which increased the percentage considerably. One out of every four pilots! Obviously, a figure that high would include even the good ones. The fact that Scott had been in the Navy for only sixteen years didn't matter, because he had courted danger throughout his career—first in Vietnam and now as a stunt pilot with the Blue Angels.

The shrill ring of the telephone interrupted her thoughts and she hurried to answer it. Perhaps it was someone from the base calling with good...or bad... news. Or maybe it would be Scott, checking his messages to see if she had called. Quickly she snatched the receiver off the cradle and answered in a breathless gasp. "Hello."

"May I speak to Commander Sanders, please?" a polite young voice asked.

"He's not here right now," she said, feeling her throat constrict around the words, cutting off any further explanation she might have offered. "May I take a message?"

The man hesitated, obviously not knowing if he should leave a message or wait until he talked to Scott personally. "Is this Mrs. Sanders?" he asked tentatively.

Not yet, but I have high hopes, she wanted to say, but instead she responded with a more sedate, "No, but I'm a close friend."

"Oh." There was another long moment of silence, then the man continued, "When will he be back?"

Kristi wished she knew. "I'm not sure," was her painfully honest answer.

"Commander Sanders seemed to be in a big hurry to get this information, so I suppose I can tell you. If he has any questions, he can call me back."

"Okay," Kristi said, wishing this guy would hurry up and get to the point. He was tying up the phone lines.

"The results from Lieutenant Dayton's tests are in and I wanted to tell Commander Sanders as soon as possible."

For a few seconds Kristi couldn't assimilate what he was saying. Who was Lieutenant Dayton? Was he one of the new Blues? Had he somehow been involved in the accident in Maryland? *No.* It was too soon for results from that even with Scott putting a rush on them. The jet pilot who crashed in New Mexico perhaps? Kristi tried to remember his name, but couldn't. Maybe his drug and alcohol tests were ready.

Lieutenant Dayton! Suddenly the name rang a bell. Billy Dayton, Kahuna, Scott's RIO officer who had gone down in North Vietnam and whose bones were in Hawaii.

"Is that Lieutenant *William* Dayton?" she asked.

"Yes." She could almost hear the man take a deep breath, as if he wasn't looking forward to whatever he was about to say. "It seems there's been a mistake of some sort. The bones that were identified as Lieutenant Dayton's were in fact someone else's. We're not sure whose yet, but they're definitely not his. We tested all the other remains that were sent in the same release, but none of them were his, either. Uh... would you tell the commander I'm terribly sorry about the mix-up, but with the ID that was sent with the bones, we didn't question it."

"So Kahuna might still be alive," Kristi mused, not missing the irony of the situation. On the very day Scott might have been killed, it was discovered that his best friend, whom everyone had thought was dead, might not be.

"I couldn't tell you that, ma'am. He might have come through in an earlier shipment and been misidentified. All I know is that he's not here now."

An earlier shipment, Kristi repeated to herself. For all the compassion in his voice, he might just as well be talking about a load of cow manure. But the military had a way of dehumanizing its people, whether they were dead or alive.

"...the plane stalled just as it reached the top of its climb and the pilot was unable to restart it before it hit the ground. Thirty thousand spectators looked on, horrified as the plane exploded upon impact. No one could get near it to help the pilot until it was too late. They are withholding his name until the next of kin are notified. Luckily, none of the other planes were involved and those pilots, although badly shaken, were able to land their aircraft safely. And in other news..."

The receiver fell from Kristi's hand and clattered to the floor. Once more she had gotten in on the very end of the announcement, and if they had transmitted a picture, she had missed it. She ran to the television set and switched channels, hoping they would be showing a video of the accident and she would somehow be able to identify the plane. A quick glance at her watch told her this was the evening news and if she didn't see it now, she would likely have to wait until later.

It had been more than seven hours now since the air show began and her nerves were almost shattered. For a moment she considered calling Scott's mother in Texas to see if she had heard anything, but the thought of alarming her, perhaps needlessly, kept her from trying. For the same reason, she resisted calling some of the other pilots' wives. Most would not be home, having traveled to Maryland for the show, but those that were might not have heard the news. Besides, the base had promised they would call her as soon as they knew for sure.

The other pilots. That phrase kept repeating itself in her mind as she frantically flipped through reports on the Middle East and a blizzard in Montana. That meant there had been several of them in the sky at once. She wasn't familiar with their air show, but how many squadrons or teams could there be flying at the same show?

Kristi's gaze was drawn to the top of the tree. She had had a hard time reaching it, but by standing on the television set and leaning way over, she had been able to pluck off the golden star and settle the beautiful blue angel on the uppermost point. It looked very different when surrounded by the variety of airplane ornaments than it had on the formally decorated tree at the shop. But on no other tree would it look so perfect.

A tickle of icy fingers raced up her spine as she looked around the room. She had sensed it before, but now the feeling was stronger than ever. It was almost as if she was in a shrine, a sort of memorial to Scott's aviation history.... As she looked at the pictures of his buddies from Vietnam on the walls, she wondered how many were still alive. And which of the Blues' various formations that were captured in enlarged colored photographs had been his last?

Suddenly it was all too much for her. She couldn't stay in this house a minute longer. Not even Maverick was here to comfort her or make her wait more tolerable.

Face your dragon. She heard the words as clearly as if he had been in the room and spoken them aloud. *It might not be as bad as you think. Your imagination can be your worst enemy. Confront your fears.*

He had been right so far; she had to trust him now. It was time she stopped whimpering and worrying without knowing any of the facts. She had to find out the name of the pilot and she had to know now. First she would drive to the base and see if she couldn't browbeat the name out of someone, but if they couldn't or wouldn't give it to her, she would head for the airport and board the next plane to Baltimore. Of all the things Scott had given her, the ones that were most important to her now were her courage and her ability to handle the situation without falling apart. If she collapsed now, she knew he would be disappointed in her after they had come so far together.

She brushed the tears off her cheeks, grabbed her coat and purse, and walked to the door. Her hand had just closed around the knob, when it turned in her hand and the door opened . . . from the outside. Automatically she stepped back, not knowing whether to run or scream as she looked up into the intruder's startled face.

Instead she did neither, but launched herself off the ground and into his arms.

"Scott, it's you. It's really you!" she cried, covering his face with kisses and wrapping her arms around his neck. For a split second, he seemed too surprised to react.

"Of course it's me," he answered, a little bewildered. "But what are you doing here? I thought you had left."

"I couldn't stay away. I love you, Scott. I realized life wasn't worth living without you. So I came back to see if we could work things out. Then the nightmare came back, except it was you I was trying to reach instead of Rick, and I was so afraid I'd die before you knew I loved you. When I heard about the accident in Maryland and the reporters wouldn't give out the name of the pilot, I was so afraid it was you." She knew she was babbling like an idiot, but she was so thrilled to see him and touch him and feel his arms holding her securely that she couldn't seem to stop.

He grabbed her in a bear hug and swung her around the room. Maverick, joining in with the celebratory mood ran around them in circles, barking his approval. He was obviously thrilled that his two favorite people were happy... and together.

"You love me?" Scott echoed. "I thought I'd never hear you say that. You have no idea how depressed I've been for the last few days. That was one of the reasons I came back early. I had to find some way to get you back, even if it meant giving up the Blues."

"I'm not asking you to give up anything, except maybe your bachelor status, which should please your friends and their wives, and will make me the luckiest, happiest woman on earth. Everything else we can learn to deal with, just as you've made me accept the past." She looked up into his dear face and repeated, "It's going to be hard because you mean so much to me. I didn't know how I'd be able to stand it if it had been you in that crash."

"It wasn't me," he answered with a reassuring shake of his dark head. "The Blues hadn't even flown yet. In fact, we canceled the rest of the show after the crash and decided to come on home. The man who was killed was a civilian pilot who belonged to a vintage airplane club. He and his friends were flying World War I biplanes in a simulated dogfight when his plane developed engine trouble and went down. It was one of the few remaining original warplanes from that era and although the pilot had done extensive work on it, those planes weren't built as good as the ones today and are always a little risky."

"Risky? Did I hear *you* say *risky*?" she asked incredulously. "I didn't realize that word was in your vocabulary."

"It wasn't...until lately," he admitted, flashing her his devastating crooked grin. "A certain lovely lady has taught me that each day is a treasure and that I shouldn't take anything for granted. Especially when she walked out on me and I didn't think she would be coming back, which made me realize just how much I had risked...and lost."

Kristi smiled up at him and hugged him tighter. "She's back...forever. She realized that once she'd been loved by an Angel, she couldn't hope to be happy with a mere mortal."

Epilogue

"Good Lord, is he going to use the saber again?"

"This is the last cake I'll cut while I'm still the commander of the Blues, so I want to do it in style." Scott chuckled as he held the long, shiny sword poised over the cake for a few seconds before slashing it downward and severing an entire section. After he had made a great show of subdividing the remainder of the cake, he picked up two plates on which someone had already placed generous pieces and carried them across the room to where Kristi was waiting.

"Well, Mrs. Sanders," he said as soon as he sat down next to her. "It's almost over. How does it feel to be the wife of an almost ex-commander of the Blue Angels?"

Kristi searched the dark depths of his eyes for any signs of regret or sadness, but found none. "It's been the best year of my life," she answered honestly. "I've enjoyed traveling around the States with you and the Blues and their wives, and I even got to the point where I could watch you fly in the shows without having an anxiety attack. But I must say that I'm glad you won't be doing any more delta vertical breaks, dirty rolls or diamond formations."

"I'll miss it," he admitted. "It's been an important part of my life for a long time. But I think I'll like being the squadron's narrator and PR man. We'll still get to travel and be a part of the organization. And it's not like I'm giving up flying altogether. My experience as an instructor and a tin kicker will keep me plenty busy in the off-seasons."

"Are you sure you're not sorry?"

"Are you kidding? It's time for this *old* man to settle down and start a family of his own."

"Funny you should mention that," she said casually, her eyes twinkling secretively. "How would you like a new recruit to join our family in about seven months?"

"Really? Are you sure?"

She nodded and waited, holding her breath for his response. They had not been taking precautions the last few months, so it was not exactly unexpected. But she knew this would be the strongest tie of all. If he had any regrets, he would feel them now.

The delight in his expression was so genuine, the last of Kristi's fears flew away. Finally she knew that the past year had been as special for him as for herself and that their love would survive. It was only the strength of her love for him that had helped her overcome the terror of seeing him leading the formation through their routine at one show after another. But he was a good pilot, as he had told her, and he had proven to be a good husband. Now he would have a chance to be a good father, a duty at which she was certain he would excel.

"I heard the two of you are going to be spending a little time overseas," Randy commented as he and Donna sat down at the table with Kristi and Scott.

"Vietnam, to be exact," Scott confirmed. "But I've just heard I'm going to become a daddy soon and I'm not sure if we'll be able to make the trip."

"Of course we will," Kristi declared positively. "This baby had better get used to traveling, because he or she will be doing a lot of it. Besides, you made a promise to a friend and we're going to keep it. I just wish we could have gone sooner, but your schedule was so full." Turning to Randy and Donna she said, "Now that Scott isn't tied so tightly to the Blues, we can do a little traveling of our own."

"Funny you should mention that. I just happen to know of a terrific travel agency," Donna suggested with wide-eyed innocence.

"Can they get us some good discounts?" Kristi asked, pretending curiosity.

"I can guarantee it," Donna answered with a teasing smile. "They probably will even agree to babysitting with that big black pony you claim is a dog, if you'd like them to."

"Are you referring to the Horizons Travel Agency in Pensacola? Isn't that the one that even though it has been open only eight months already has hundreds of happy, satisfied customers and that claims they can give the best service in Florida? I understand the two owners are not only shrewd businesswomen, but incredibly attractive, too. Maybe I'll tag along with you and see what kind of special service they give their customers," Randy chimed in, earning himself a swat on the arm from Donna.

Kristi just laughed. Since she and Donna were co-owners of Horizons, she didn't mind hearing the compliments, especially since she knew they had earned them. Randy was right about the agency's success. It had exceeded their wildest expectations, so much so that they had had to hire four employees and a part-time manager to work while the two women were following the Blues on the road. For a former flight attendant who still loved to travel, the business had been a natural progression after she turned in her resignation at Worldwide. What made it even better was that she had not quit because of her fears, but because she wanted to spend as much time as possible with Scott, especially after their Christmas Day wedding last year. The travel agency gave her something to do while he was at the base and bolstered her sense of personal achievement.

"I can't believe the Saint has finally had his wings clipped," Zipper declared good-naturedly as he joined the group. "I must admit if I had someone like Kristi to go home to, I might not be as gung ho to spend all my time in the air, either."

"I have a friend from Denver who's coming for a visit in a few weeks. I'll bet you and she would hit it off great," Kristi said thoughtfully. "Maybe we'll have a barbecue...."

Scott was barely suppressing a chuckle as he leaned over and whispered in her ear. "Watch out. You're becoming a regular military wife; always trying to set up the single guys with dates."

"But I want everyone to be as happy as I am," she defended, "and as lucky." She smiled at him with pride and love sparkling in her eyes. "A person's life will never be the same once they've been kissed by an Angel."

Harlequin American Romance

COMING NEXT MONTH

#285 HOME IS THE SAILOR by Kathryn Blair

Sarah Mitchell was a strong believer in the power of love to heal. It was behind her every move at Puppy Power. Her dogs had brought a lot of happiness into people's lives, but they were not enough to fill the emptiness of her own—until she placed a puppy with her new neighbor, and the elderly woman's merchant marine officer son came into her life to challenge her convictions and her heart.

#286 TIES THAT BIND by Marisa Carroll

When Kevin Sauder came to Lisa Emery's quiet world on the wooded shores of a Michigan lake, he was looking for a sanctuary. But the young conservation officer and her little family, consisting of a teenage brother and sister, opened their lives to him—and Lisa opened her heart. And soon Kevin realized he may have found more than the courage to face life—he may have found love.

#287 FEATHERS IN THE WIND by Pamela Browning

Her face had been her fortune, but Caro Nicholson couldn't rely on her beauty anymore. She wanted to run, to forget what had happened. Mike Herrick was a man determined to make her feel alive again . . . alive in ways she thought long buried. But was he a man willing to wait for the woman he loved?

#288 PASSAGES OF GOLD by Ginger Chambers

Linda Conway knew there was only one way to save her family legacy. . . and Amador Springs, California, held the key. Gold, shiny and yellow, was there, and Linda had the fever. She would be strong and unafraid. That is, until Tate Winslow entered her heart and made her reveal her deepest fears. . . .

CHRISTMAS IS FOR KIDS

AMERICAN ROMANCE PHOTO CONTEST

At Harlequin American Romance® we believe Christmas is for kids—a special time, a magical time. And we've put together a unique project to celebrate the American Child. Our annual holiday romances will feature children—just like yours—who have their Christmas wishes come true.

A reddish, golden-haired boy. Or a curious, ponytailed girl with glasses. A kid sister. A dark, shy, small boy. A mischievous, freckle-nosed lad. A girl with ash blond braided hair. Or a bright-eyed little girl always head of the class.

Send us a color photo of your child, along with a paragraph describing his or her excitement and anticipation of Christmas morning. If your entry wins, your child will appear on one of the covers of our December 1989 CHRISTMAS IS FOR KIDS special series. Read the Official Rules carefully before you enter.

OFFICIAL RULES

1. Eligibility: Male and female children ages 4 through 12 who are residents of the U.S.A., or Canada, except children of employees of Harlequin Enterprises Ltd., its affiliates, retailers, distributors, agencies, professional photographers and Smiley Promotion, Inc.

2. How to enter: Mail a color slide or photo, not larger than 8½ × 11", taken no longer than six months ago along with proof of purchase from facing page to:

> American Romance Photo Contest
> Harlequin Books
> 300 East 42nd Street
> 6th Floor
> New York, NY
> 10017.

Professional photographs are not eligible. Only one entry per child allowed. All photos remain the sole property of Harlequin Enterprises Ltd. and will not be returned. A paragraph of not more than 50 words must accompany the photo expressing your child's joy and anticipation of Christmas morning. All entries must be received by March 31, 1989.

3. Judging: Photos will be judged equally on the child's expression, pose, neatness and photo clarity. The written paragraph will be judged on sincerity and relationship to the subject. Judging will be completed within 45 days of contest closing date and winners will be notified in writing and must return an Affidavit of Eligibility and Release within 21 days or an alternate winner will be selected.

4. Prizes: Nine Prizes will be awarded, with each winner's likeness appearing on a cover of our December 1989 CHRISTMAS IS FOR KIDS special series. Winners will also receive an artists signed print of the cover. There is no cash substitution for prizes. Harlequin Enterprises Ltd. reserves the right to use the winner's name and likeness for promotional purposes without any compensation. Any Canadian resident winner or their parent or guardian must correctly answer an arithmetical skill-testing question within a specified time.

5. When submitting an entry, entrants must agree to these rules and the decisions of the judges, under the supervision of Smiley Promotion, Inc., an independent judging organization whose decisions are final. Sponsor reserves the right to substitute prizes of like substance. Contest is subject to all federal, provincial, state and local laws. Void where prohibited, restricted or taxed. For a winner's list, send a stamped self-addressed envelope to American Romance Photo Contest Winners, P.O. Box 554, Bowling Green Station, New York, N.Y. 10274 for receipt by March 31, 1989.

Photo-2

Have You Ever Wondered If You Could Write A Harlequin Novel?

Here's great news—Harlequin is offering a series of cassette tapes to help you do just that. Written by Harlequin editors, these tapes give practical advice on how to make your characters—and your story—come alive. There's a tape for each contemporary romance series Harlequin publishes.

Mail order only

All sales final
